Annette Vendryes Leach

SONG *of the* SHAMAN

MINDPRESS MEDIA

NEW YORK

First Mindpress Media Edition, August 2013

Published in the United States by MindPress Media
32 Fort Greene Place, Brooklyn, New York 11217

This is a work of fiction. Names, characters, places, and incidents either are the product of the author's imagination or are used fictitiously. Any resemblance to actual persons, living or dead, events, or locales is entirely coincidental.

Grateful acknowledgement is made to:
National Museum of the American Indian
CEDIA: Center for the Documentation and Investigation of the Arts
Professor Ron Mills de Pinyas and Jorge Luis Acevedo

ISBN 978-0-9894912-0-4 (pbk)
ISBN 978-0-9894912-1-1 (ebook)

Library of Congress Control Number: 2013909996

Book design by Elizabeth Kim
Cover design by Laura Duffy

www.mindpressmedia.com
Printed in the United States of America

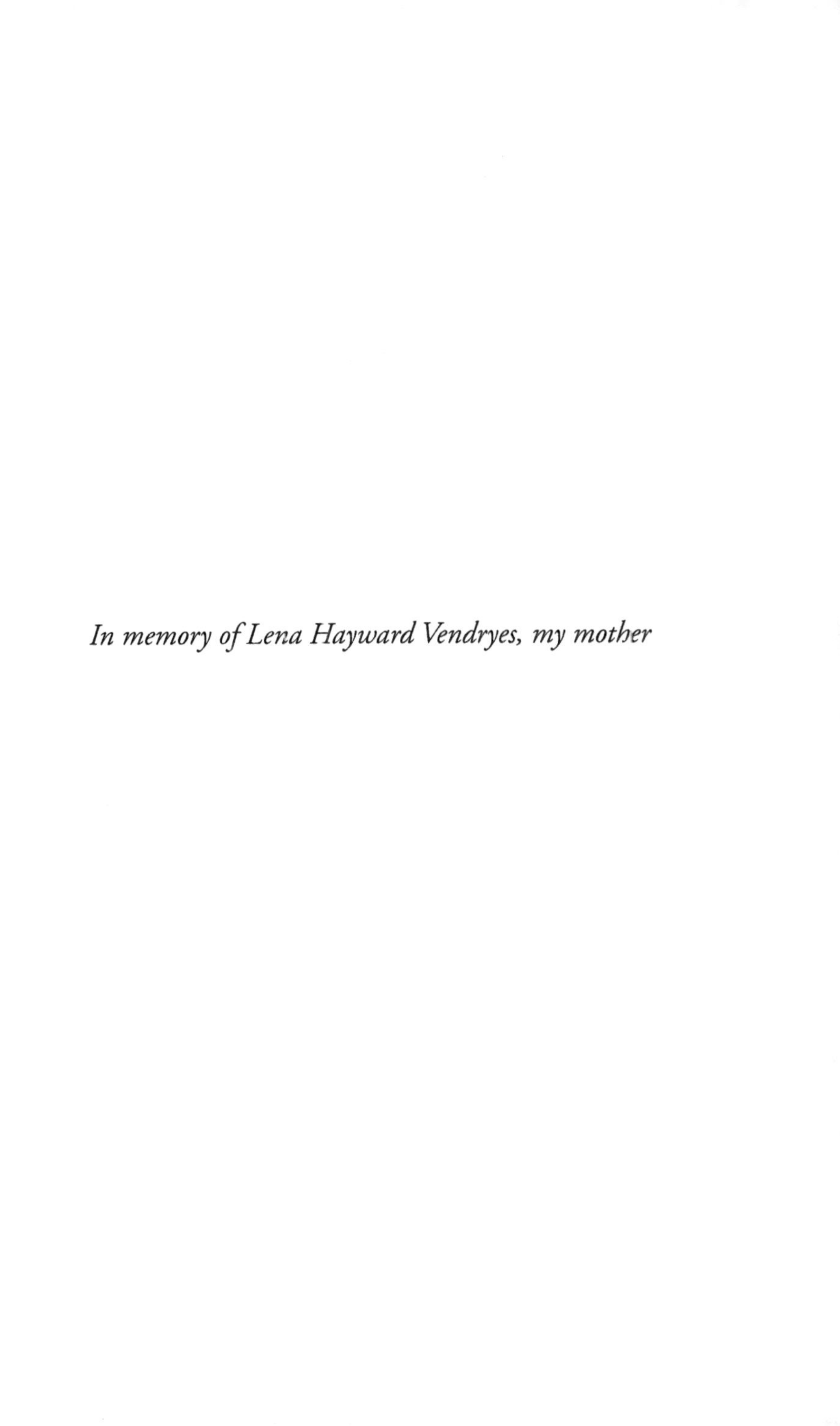

In memory of Lena Hayward Vendryes, my mother

1996

Brooklyn, New York

ZIG WAS BORN ON THE BROOKLYN BRIDGE in the backseat of a yellow taxicab. Sheri pushed him from her womb onto the slick vinyl seat, with century-old steel cables, limestone, and a cab driver as her sole witnesses. The small of Sheri's back bucked against the ashtray of one door; her shoeless left foot dug into the floor of the cab. Her right leg, up on the seat and bent at the knee, banged against the backrest. Blood pooled inside her thighs. The cabbie's frightened eyes flashed at her in the rearview mirror. She glanced at his ID; the name was long and crammed with consonants.

"Aye, Miss! Please, Miss!" He cussed himself and ran a hand through clumps of oily hair. Sheri's senses left her, jumping somewhere off the edge of the bridge. She screamed.

The August night air was hot and foul. Around her the city boiled: horns blared, trucks roared, and street hustlers shouted while the cabbie weaved through traffic. The faint lilt of Middle Eastern music wafted to Sheri's ears. Nothing had prepared her for this moment, not the monotonous Lamaze classes, What to Expect books, or birthing DVDs. All directives from her midwife were forgotten like yesterday's lunch. Tufts of white fiber hung from a gouge her fingernails had torn in the backseat. Her costly new maternity dress was hiked up under her breasts. The dappled street light revealed a prunelike face and wispy hair pasted to a round head. She quickly cleared his gummy mouth; thread-thin fingers then stretched as Zig wailed. Eyes squeezed shut to the world, tiny arms quivering, he let out a newborn howl that plunged the depths of the East River. It was as intense and unwavering as a tribal call.

A queer feeling of déjà vu came over her. This scene had happened before. Hadn't she, too, ripped her mother's insides open in birth, saving herself yet killing her mother? Long-buried nightmares flooded her mind. Born again were all the horrors she had concocted as a child about her mother's death, images that in no way resembled anything her adoptive parents had ever told her.

The cab raced toward Beth Israel Medical Center. Sheri held Zig's little trembling body to hers. Blood was everywhere. Jabbing pains crashed inside her, as relentless as a prize fighter. She looked down at the ropey umbilical cord that led from her vagina to Zig's navel, the precious lifeline that connected them, and wondered what she had passed on to him. *Would he live or die?* Sheri lowered her son onto her lap, wrapped him in the damp hem of her dress. She wiped his face, feeling the curious, pulsating warmth of a new life in her hands. The earthquake in her body subsided. She wasn't afraid anymore. All her life she had felt like half a person, the other half shrouded in anonymity. Zig was lithe and small boned, like Sheri. She looked at him and she saw herself.

"Shhh...don't cry, Zig. Mommy's here...I'm right here."

At the sound of her voice, he closed his mouth and opened his eyes. Her toes slid in her lone Stuart Weitzman sandal as the cab lurched onto the hospital's sidewalk.

"Miss, lady, lady, look—emergency entrance!" The panicked driver stuck his neck out the window and yelled. *"Help! Somebody help!"*

He leaped from the cab, gesturing wildly to a man and woman in blue uniforms. They rushed over. The man swung open the cab door and reached inside for Sheri. Blood trickled down on his sneakers.

"She's hemorrhaging," he said.

The woman turned and ran toward a wheelchair. The man spit some words into a two-way radio. City lights swam in Sheri's eyes, then went black.

"SHERI…CAN YOU HEAR ME?"

Sheri lifted her eyelids. She saw the hills of her feet at the end of the bed. Her stomach was flat. Confusion gripped her. Through a murky haze, images of a crying baby crossed her mind. *Where was he?* Her tongue felt like wood. She rubbed it against the roof of her mouth. A hand came into view and put a paper cup to her lips.

"Take a sip."

The woman had short red hair…stooped shoulders…

Cool water slid down her throat. Sheri dug her elbows into the mattress, struggling with the weight of her arms.

"Easy now. You want to sit up?"

She nodded. The woman pressed a button. The bed hummed; it raised her back as if she were a stiff, inflexible plastic doll. *Joanne. That's her name.* Joanne Bergen, her midwife.

"Everything's fine," Joanne said, sensing Sheri's anxiety. "Your son's fine—he's asleep in the nursery."

Joanne's voice was reassuring but also loud and direct. She took Sheri's blood pressure, read the monitors behind her head. Sheri's tongue became a little more pliant, and she finally spoke.

"Where am I?"

"That's more like it!" But the corners of Joanne's mouth quickly bent into a frown. "You're in Beth Israel's Mother-Baby Unit. You also spent some time in the ICU. How do you feel?"

She was weak. The smallest movement was exhausting.

"Like hell. What happened?"

"The report says your water broke and you went right into labor," Joanne boomed, shuffling through paperwork on a clipboard. She looked worn, and something else, regretful, like she had failed her in some way. "That boy was in a serious hurry—a whole three weeks ahead of schedule." Joanne checked the tube attached to the IV drip. "You lost a lot of blood, Sheri."

Sheri looked up at the plastic bag of fluid. So she didn't die. *Childbirth had not killed her. Both she and Zig were alive.* She let her eyes wander around the dingy room she shared with another mother, separated by a thin hospital curtain.

"How long have I been here?"

"Three days. That's normal, given your circumstances. What do you remember?" Joanne sat down on a stool near the bed. Sheri laid her arm across her forehead and looked out the window. The flat gray sky was as dull as her memory.

"I went into the kitchen to scrape Chinese food into the garbage. I felt a gush on my legs. I thought I spilled something." She licked her lips. Joanne studied her. "Somehow I left the apartment and got into a cab. The contractions were coming faster and faster. I tried to lie back…the pain was blinding. Then I heard him crying." Sheri paused. "Where is Zig?"

"Zig?"

"That's his name."

"Oh! How cute! He's in the nursery. Is that a family name?"

"No. It's not associated with anything. No boyfriends, uncles, Hollywood stuntmen…"

Joanne smiled. She glanced at her watch.

"Let me see if *Zig* is awake."

She pulled the curtain aside and marched out into the hall. Sheri caught a glimpse of the mother in the bed across from her, a beaming, chubby-cheeked woman surrounded by bouquets of roses and what looked like her mother, two sisters, and a shell-shocked man—probably the father. Silvery blue balloons with *It's a Boy!* printed on them bobbed around the ceiling vents. Sheri had little choice but to listen to their joyful banter while she lay spent and weary.

She turned her face away from the curtain. She thought about Rene and his broad, teasing smile, how it squeezed his wandering eyes into slits, a smile full of late-night sex and devoid of commitment. A pleasure-seeker and sought-after percussionist, Rene wanted little from life off center stage. This came as no surprise to her. She had built up a steely resistance to disappointments in love. But despite this Rene was different. With him, Sheri felt a great sense of freedom. She felt alive.

Rene made her laugh and taught her how to waste time, and she dated him on and off when he wasn't touring outside the country. There would be no divorce or custody battle. No teary scenes. No delinquent child-support payments. Nine months ago, on her thirty-fifth birthday, she got drunk and slept with him, hoping to become pregnant. By the time she knew for sure, he was on tour somewhere in South America with a world music band. It didn't matter if or when he would ever return. Rene was already married. Music was his first and only love. The night she saw him perform a solo, she knew. The pounding rhythm wrapped its feverish arms around him, swept him away like a sweet, hypnotic lover. She understood, too. She had once felt that way when she took up a paintbrush or charcoal pencil—the thrilling sense of creation, of the unknown making itself known through your own hands. Still, that was in her youth, and unlike Rene, she gave up her first love when she grew older.

Behind the hospital curtain the grinning new father looked proud but also frightened, as if he had just lost something terribly valuable. Sheri couldn't bear to see that expression on Rene's face. Why should she be the one to put an end to his happy childhood?

Conceiving alone was a running joke, passed around like salt among soured, unattached girlfriends at lunch. No one would admit the underlying truth—the wish to have a child by any means necessary. For Sheri, it was tangled and deep rooted, a yearning that threw a harsh light on the greatest source of sadness in her life: her adoption.

She had met Rene at a jingle recording session. He wore a black fedora with a long, brilliant green feather in the band, and when he smiled at her it was intimate, as if they were alone in the crowded studio. Months later, in a rare moment outside of music and sex, she heard him say, "I got my chops from my Panamanian grandmother...I love my *abuela*!" Right then she knew what she wanted.

Her birth story began at JFK airport when a cheerless middle-class couple brought her back from an orphanage in Panama. People said she was lucky. There's nothing lucky about being abandoned. She started her journey alone. Her son would not. She would hold Zig and imagine what it might have been like for her birth mother to hold her; she would kiss him and feel her mother's lips on her cheeks. She longed to validate her childhood through a child of her own. Little splinters of dazzling sunlight, of azure water glistened in Rene's DNA, and she imagined joining them to the unknown threads of her heritage. He was the right choice. A small house of love for her birthright, a child who was tied to her genetically—this was all she hoped for.

On the hospital wall near the door was a large white calendar marked with cryptic nursing notes. Was it Monday or Tuesday?

The agency crept into her mind; she had missed an important pre-production meeting. Other than Joanne, no one knew she was in the hospital. Then again, there wasn't anyone she wanted to call or see. Both her parents were dead. For a moment she pictured their remains, combined like a giant ashtray in a blue and white china urn and stored in the back of her coat closet. The grandmother across the room rattled off exhaustive tips to a daughter who only had ears for her fussy baby. Something about the grandmother's voice reminded Sheri of the chattering aides who had cared for her mother at the nursing home when she was dying. Their simple powder-room conversations drifted around the vacant eyes and silent lips of the woman who, at the end of her life, didn't recognize Sheri from a stranger on the street.

She reached for the paper cup on the bed tray and took another drink of water. A plastic ID bracelet dangled from her wrist. She turned her hand over to read the scribbled writing:

LAMBERT, SHERI. BABY BOY. 6 LBS., 4 OZ. 21" LONG. BORN AUGUST 21, 1996. *Veintiuno de agosto...*

One night she was coming home from work, around seven, and although it was late the subway was packed. Sheri leaned heavily on the metal straps. Books and newspapers covered the closed faces of seated passengers. No one stood up for her. She resisted the urge to rub the spot where a little foot pressed into her side. In a couple of weeks she'd be on maternity leave. Just when the pressure in her stomach got uncomfortable, the train doors opened at Eastern Parkway. Among the commuters who pushed past her to get out was a large, elderly woman in a dirty gray smock. Sheri had not noticed her on the train. Scraps of thin hair pulled tight into a bun matched the color of her dress. The woman's bloated feet were bursting out of cracked sneakers. When Sheri stepped off the train and walked toward the platform stairs, she felt a heavy hand grip her forearm. She jerked around to see the woman pointing a grimy finger at her belly, whispering in hoarse English and Spanish.

"El veintiuno de agosto you will have a boy. He will save you! Dios lo bendice! God bless you!"

The subway platform quickly emptied out. Deep inside her the baby kicked, sending a parade of tiny flutters to her side. Sheri snatched her arm away and rushed up the cement steps, the stench of urine filling her nostrils. There was a tightening below her navel—Braxton-Hicks cramps—a false alarm. But her heart pounded in her ears. *Pregnant women are not public property,* she fumed, climbing the steep stairs. *People reach out to squeeze your belly like a ripened fruit, gauging its proper time to fall to earth. Construction workers shout genders from sandwich-stuffed mouths based on the size of your girth or nose. Now this, strange predictions from a bag lady.* The heat from the woman's sticky palm lingered on Sheri's arm. At the top of the steps, she turned to look back at the platform. A crumpled paper bag skipped down the steps. The woman was gone.

"GUESS WHO'S AWAKE AND READY TO BE FED!"

Joanne came back carrying a blanketed bundle and placed it in Sheri's arms. Zig's football-shaped body was snugly swaddled in flannel. Below a pale blue knit cap, steady brown eyes pierced her to the core. Sheri took off the cap and pressed her lips to his little forehead. A mottled hand appeared from beneath the blanket and touched her chin. The image of the homeless woman faded away. Joanne presented Sheri with a small, warm bottle of formula. The nurses had been giving Zig formula for several days, she said. It might be hard for her to breast-feed now. Latching on could be painful. She was weak… still recovering…on the IV. The midwife's strong principles gave way. It was excusable, recommended even, for Sheri to opt out of her first important duty. Sheri looked at Zig's tiny waiting mouth. She never drank from her own mother's breast. Long ago in some place where all the babies were motherless she fed on the charity of strangers. She glanced at the manufactured liquid and the rubber nipple, then slowly opened one side of her hospital gown. Joanne caught the IV needle before it slipped out the vein in the back of her hand. Sheri brought Zig to her breast. He immediately latched on and suckled as if he had done it a hundred times before.

Four days later, Sheri left the hospital and headed home alone with her newborn son. It was one in a string of blazing hot afternoons. She took another yellow cab back over the Brooklyn Bridge, this time with Zig strapped to her chest in a navy blue Swedish baby carrier. Seeing the cab's interior— her crude birthing room—made her instantly nauseated, so she kept her eyes on the world outside the window. A muscle still ached where the ashtray had rammed into her back. Perspiration dripped from her temples down between her swollen breasts. She tried in vain to shield Zig from the city buses belching their gritty exhaust. Zig slept through the ride, limp and burrowing into her armpit. She held his cheek to steady his head, gazing at his sweet face. In the space of a few days, her life had been irreversibly changed. Her body felt ravaged, but excitement pulsed through her veins. It was as if she had transformed into crisp white drawing paper or a taut canvas on a frame, and was about to illustrate her life with new blood and bones. Funny thing was, she couldn't remember the last time she had touched real drawing paper or a canvas.

She had stumbled into advertising out of art school, wet behind the ears, eager to make a decent salary, and she'd quickly adapted to the culture of consumerism. Success as senior art director at Aeon Worldwide was like a glamorous lover with an infectious disease: the sex was bound to kill you, but not just yet. Not while you could shoot award-winning television commercials in exotic locales, sleep in five-star hotels, and dine in restaurants where celebrities were regular customers. The highs were like a cocaine hit that sent you flying along a moonlit skyline. The lows were more frequent and gutter level. Ball-breaking clients. Caustic executives who amused themselves by manipulating the staff. Long, life-draining hours. Ad agencies were laden with talented addicts stumbling down a gaily lit ditch. Before she knew it she had become one of them.

Gradually she awakened. The glitzy showcase of personalities and possessions could no longer distract her from the utter barrenness she felt inside. Love languished in the back of her mind, on tomorrow's wish list, and then it was too late. At thirty-three she woke up to find the above-average Joe either already married with kids or recently divorced and not interested in another serious relationship. But she wasn't the only one in a rut. Some of her most savvy and sophisticated friends were wait-listed and turned desperate: married for marriage's sake, then soon after divorced—many even before they had a chance to get pregnant. She no longer wanted to be a part of those endless, disheartening conversations. Over time she distanced herself from her girlfriends, migrated to Brooklyn, and took the road less traveled to forge her own happiness. Becoming a single mother was the most frightening, sobering decision Sheri had ever made. She did not regret a minute of it.

The glaring metal street signs seemed to yell out directions. Men and women of myriad colors were like a box of crayons slowly melting down Flatbush Avenue. Prospect Park's tree limbs hung low to the ground, its leaves curled and pale. At the sight of her building on Eastern Parkway, Sheri breathed a sigh of relief.

Raised in a soulless neighborhood of roller-coaster high-rises and rent-controlled walk-ups on the Upper East Side, she had chosen Brooklyn with its wide vistas as her new home. Here she could start fresh, carve out a new identity or disappear into the woodwork without the cold, condescending looks of Manhattanites. In her seventh-floor apartment her living room windows boasted picturesque green views of the Brooklyn Botanic Gardens and Brooklyn Museum, while her bedroom windows overlooked sparkly stretches of the New York harbor. These were the only things that greeted her daily since moving here six months ago. She knew no one in Brooklyn. That suited her just fine. Once she became pregnant all her old girlfriends slunk away anyhow, the suffering they once shared dried up now that she had left the pack. Even Reyna, her manic, beloved yoga teacher, disappeared. Reyna, who was so fascinated with Sheri's gestation, who carefully spotted Sheri's Tree posture and her wide belly in the Cat-Cow pose, Reyna who had had her ovaries taken out when she was thirty. All the same, instant messaging took the place of Sheri's face time socializing. Virtual became real and vice versa.

Sheri hauled herself and Zig out of the cab and into the lobby. Juan, the doorman and local ballyhooer, looked up from his newspaper. On the front desk a battery-operated fan whirled next to a mountain of balled-up deli napkins.

"Is that you, *mami?* You had the baby!" Juan cried, throwing aside the *Daily News* and dashing to her side. "Awww, look at his little face…*qué lindo!* He looks like you, *mami!* He's gonna be so lucky!"

Sheri thanked him for the compliments, knowing there was some dirt to come. Alarming residents with the drama of the day was a job Juan took very seriously. He carried her overnight bag to the elevator bank, adding in a low voice, "You didn't miss nothing—central air is out in the whole building. Three days now! I coulda fixed it but they won't pay me. *Pendejos.* They better fix it soon. It's hot as shit!"

She rolled her eyes. Back to reality, but she was glad to be home. "Thanks for the heads-up, Juan."

He snorted and put the bag at her feet. When the elevator came, she pressed the button for the seventh floor. The doors opened to thick, humid air and the scent of fried garlic. Someone's toy dog yapped and a telephone rang on and on. As she neared her door, she heard a recorded voice coming from the apartment. *Damn! That's my phone!* She groped for her keys and opened the door.

The apartment was stifling. The living room windows were sealed shut. Her jade plant had dropped half of its leaves on the coffee table. Two boxes of Chinese food, now rancid and pungent, were also on the table. Liane, the Machiavellian media director, was leaving a message on Sheri's answering machine. She picked up the phone midsentence.

"Sheri Lambert," she said, forgetting where she was.

"Sheri? Thank God you're there! Are you okay? Everyone was worried when you missed the pre-pro meeting!"

"I'm fine, Liane."

Liane paused.

"Did you have the baby?"

"Yes, he's right here with me." Zig started to squirm.

"Well, congratulations! Aren't you early? How did everything go?"

Sheri looked around for a place to lay Zig down. The maple wood crib was packed flat in the box by the front door. The bassinet was halfway put together, sheets still in their plastic sleeves. She fumbled with the lock on the baby carrier—*how did the darn thing open?*

"Good. I had natural childbirth."

"Really? I didn't think anyone these days bothered with natural—"

Zig started to holler. She tried to pull him out of the carrier.

"Uh-oh, I better go. You've got your hands full."

"No, it's okay. I can talk. Any word from JetSet?"

"They absolutely loved the television. I'm pretty sure it's a go with—hold on a sec."

Their conversation was interrupted by hip-hop Muzak dotted with a sugary announcer plugging the agency's awards. By now everyone was over the shock of her being a single mother. Lots of successful women were doing it—even Madonna. Madonna was a gap-toothed woman just like Sheri. Sheri liked to believe she was as cool and self-ruling as the superstar, too.

She flipped the central air switch in the hallway, half hoping the A/C would start up. It didn't. She was still struggling with the baby carrier when Liane clicked back.

"That was Roland—our three o'clock was moved up. Gotta run, sweetie. Don't worry, we'll handle everything till you get back in December."

"November twenty-second." *Bitch.* Zig was turning four-alarm-fire red.

"Anyway, Roland's aiming to have the JetSet commercials shot and in the can by early November. Take care, Sheri. Motherhood—"

Zig's shrieks drowned out Liane's last words. *Shit!* Sheri slammed the phone on the kitchen counter. *They better not shoot my spots before I get back.* She pried her arms out of the carrier, wrestling Zig and the whole contraption over her head. Where could she put him? The leather sofa held a sea of teetering toys, baby bottles, bibs, and onesies. Shoving them to the floor, she placed him on the seat. A penetrating, terrifying cry surged from his tiny body. Sheri sat on the edge of the sofa and whipped off her shirt. Her bra was dripping wet—was that milk? Sweat? She pulled the straps down to an alarming sight. Her breasts were stiff and misshapen; her nipples taut and hard. They didn't look like that in the hospital. Zig's screams got louder. A stream of milk sprayed out of one breast and across his little face. Sheri scooped up her son, brought his mouth to her leaking nipple. He could barely latch on before milk flooded his nose, mouth, and chin. Zig gagged and coughed, and soon his crying stopped. The silence that followed was almost as deafening as the screaming. Sheri took deep breaths. She was shaking. The clumps in her life softened and dissolved as Zig drank long draughts from her.

DURING THE EARLY WEEKS of Zig's life there were many days when they saw no one but each other. Ironically, she felt her solitude more acutely now that she had a baby. Bombarded with meetings and phone calls at the office, she had eagerly looked forward to quality time at home. Now that it was here, she felt cut off. The phone seldom rang. At first she tried to keep up with IM's, e-mail, and phone calls, but every time she turned on her computer or picked up the phone Zig would start crying. Sheri spent hours pacing the floor with him cradled in her arms until all the loud demands of the world slowly died out, like the tin-can clatter of a circus miles and miles away. Their bonding had a soothing, hypnotic effect. One thought remained constant in her mind: *He will always know his mother.*

No one claimed Sheri after her mother had died during her birth, so she was sent to *Cuidad del Niño*, a local orphanage in Guabito, a farming town on the border between Panama and Costa Rica. In the summer when she turned three, through a surreptitious adoption, a Jewish couple traveled to the orphanage and brought Sheri back to New York. Well into their fifties, the Lamberts ran a small stock brokerage firm that kept them bickering and drinking when they weren't buying and selling. If Wall Street had a good year she went to private school. When it was bad she went to public school. In private school she noticed that the handful of honey-colored girls had parents that looked like Sheri's. In public school there were many more girls that looked like her and they had parents that matched.

Obvious signs of her Latin descent became more apparent in the sixth grade. Her eyes were the shade and shape of warm almonds, unlike her father's, which were heavy lidded and the color of murky water. Her hair was dark and thick with loopy curls, not flat and golden like her mother's. Sheri's nose was slightly round, her lips fleshy even when stretched with a smile. And by the end of the summer her olive skin turned the color of sandalwood, while her parents turned blotchy and red.

Her mother and father told her the truth a few days after her eleventh birthday party, mechanically, like it was part of some kind of benchmark guideline in a parenting book. She heard the words halfway through a slice of leftover chocolate birthday cake. She was adopted.

Sheri felt as if she had been thrown off a moving carousel. She knew there was no Santa Claus or Easter Bunny or tooth fairy. That was nonsense. Anyone could figure that out. But her mother and father were not real? *This is what happens when you grow up, lucky girl. Truth is given to you like a birthday gift. It's the gift that takes your speech and breath away. Takes your known life away. You cry every night and even when you stop, the tears rain down inside but the gift givers never see. They never know your tears have no end.*

How stupid she had been! The boys and girls she laughed with as they chased her around at her party—they knew all along. Just like Anna and Leah, the best friends who stared at her and whispered in each other's ears on Parents' Visiting Day. The teachers. The neighbors. Everyone knew. Sheri locked herself in the bathroom and vomited, the sweet chocolate cake turning to bitter slime in her mouth. She heaved until her guts were squeezed dry, until her organs pushed against her throat as if she were trying to spit out her heart. Paramedics took her to Lenox Hill Hospital where doctors made her swallow some nasty liquid. She remembered the numbness that came over her legs. It swept up her back to her ears and forced her eyes shut, a deadening that lingered inside for years and had begun to recede only with the birth of her son.

ONE MORNING BEFORE DAWN while Sheri was nursing Zig, she thought she heard a voice. A word was spoken just once.

Tukitima.

She glanced around her cluttered bedroom. A torn box of Pampers sat on the floor next to the bassinet. Booties, blankets, and hooded towels were heaped on the end of the changing table. What caught her off guard was Zig. In the ashen stillness his unblinking eyes were locked on hers. *That's weird.* She thought about it for a moment, then shrugged it off. Zig exhaled, his tummy full and contented. Sheri lay down in bed with him curled up on her chest and fell asleep.

1899

Guabito, Panama

THEY REACHED THE BORDER AT GUABITO exactly twenty-one blasted minutes late, according to Father, who snapped his pocket watch shut for the hundredth time. So it was past noon! Louise, half asleep and slumped against the carriage door, kept a brown paper parcel from sliding off her lap. Maud also slept, her pale sweaty cheek pressed into Louise's shoulder. For days they had traveled over dust-clouded roads in the heat from Panama City, stopping only to lodge in shabby taverns along the way. Louise tilted her head to gaze through the open window. Watching endless walls of banana groves spotted with workers chopping off large bunches—*racimos*—made her all the more drowsy. Across from her sat their father, Charles, a soggy handkerchief tight in his fist.

With his spectacles, red-rimmed eyes, and pasty skin he looked like a nervous clergyman and not the chief financial officer at the Canal Commission. The way his white linen suit clung to his paunchy middle made her frown. She wondered, if he ate one less *cocadita* a day he might find comfort in other things. He might even see her.

Louise glanced at Maud. She brushed stringy blond wisps off her younger sister's temple, listened to her clogged nose sip the hot, humid air. Maud was fair and fragile, but not as naïve as Father made her out to be. She was almost sixteen, four years younger than Louise; still, he doted on Maud, spoiled her from the day Mother died. Maud took full advantage, playing the precious little daughter, ever pouting and preening for his loving eyes, and when he wasn't looking she took her privileges even further. Why not, the two of them looked just alike. Together they struck a lovely family portrait. Louise rolled her tongue against the small gap between her front teeth. With her dark eyes and ruddy complexion she favored her mother, whereas Maud and Father had eyes the color of sea foam and thin skin that burned in the midday sun. Louise was glad she took after her mother—what she could remember of her.

The Sixaola River stretched before her like a soothing balm, linking Panama with Costa Rica. Its jade green water, still as glass, mirrored an array of glittering trees and shrubs, a welcome sight from the monotonous banana plantations. Maud raised her head an inch from Louise's shoulder to let out a rattling cough. Charles sprang up, his back stiff. For months Maud's health had not improved. Doctors from Panama City to Colón proved useless as her asthma grew more and more chronic. Soon Father dismissed the doctors and took matters into his own hands, the way he did with most everything. An engineer at the Canal had told him about Don Pedro, a famous shaman, or "awa," as the Nrvai Indians call them, who lived in the Talamanca Mountains of Costa Rica on the other side of the river. Benjamin, the awa's grandson, was to meet them at the river with a canoe and escort them to his grandfather's house. Maud whined about being away from home. The thought of seeing a medicine man frightened her. But for Louise, travel meant escape; a chance to break free from the narrow-minded upper crust of San Felipe; a chance to reinvent herself as someone other than the eldest, unmarried daughter of a Canal Commission officer.

Louise stretched her cramped arm, careful not to wake Maud, and took note of her father's grave expression, which he put on daily like his hair tonic. After Mother's death he had relied heavily on Louise to be a role model for Maud. *Mind all you say and do, Louise* was his never-ending drill. She leaned against the rattling carriage and shut her eyes. Sparks of a dark, stifling night rolled in her head.

"Louise!"

Mother had cried out for her from behind the bedroom door. Like a wildcat Louise had fought Father's clutches, scratching, screaming. But his iron grip held her tight.

"Let me go! Mama! Mama!"

Louise grabbed fists full of air. Midwives took Mother and a stillborn baby away in blood-soaked sheets, leaving Louise behind to forever make sense out of life.

The coach stopped abruptly and they were all jostled about. Charles snapped at the driver. Maud stifled a cough, draping a eucalyptus-laced hankie over her nose. Louise, a bit disoriented, gathered her fallen parcel—a gift of chocolate and tobacco for the shaman. Outside a tall, slim young man stood on the side of the road. In the bright sunlight his amber eyes seemed colorless. They lingered on hers politely, then an instant longer than politeness allowed. She looked away. In that brief instance it was as if he saw what had happened to her and her mother, like he peered into the window of her most private thoughts.

The driver hastened around to open the coach door, but Charles had already let himself out.

"Come come, girls! We're late and must be back by sunset!" Charles grumbled. He was helping Maud down when the tall young man appeared before them.

"Señor Lindo."

Charles looked up. Holding Maud like an injured dove, he seemed momentarily surprised at the young man's graceful demeanor.

"I'm Benjamin Xyrmach—Don Pedro's grandson."

"Aha! Right on schedule. Charles Lindo." Charles passed Maud to the driver and gave Benjamin's hand a hard shake. "These are my daughters—Miss Louise and Miss Maud." Charles reached for Louise's arm to help her off the carriage. Her heels sank into the soft soil and she lost her footing for a moment. Benjamin caught her by the elbow.

"Pardon me!" Louise said, flushed with embarrassment.

"The swells are to blame." The young man apologized for the river, his eyes settling on hers again. Loose waves on his head tossed easily in the hot breeze. His skin reminded her of café con leche, and stood in contrast to his plain linen shirt. Maud's cough started again with a sequence of hacks. Father and Benjamin rushed to her side to assist her to the canoe. Louise trekked behind them, still feeling the pressure of the handsome stranger's hand.

Benjamin rowed them across the river while Louise, fascinated with the excursion, had many questions to ask. How many kilometers to the other side? What species of fish were there? Are there truly red monkeys, tapirs, and jaguars in the Talamanca Mountains? Benjamin answered casually. Did he welcome her interest? Then Charles, filled with hot air, had to remind everyone of his rank and great intelligence.

"In Panama City we have an abundance of the same flora and fauna and then some, Louise, as we are practically neighbors." Yet his presumptuous tone did not match his nervous tapping feet and darting eyes. The fact that he had to seek help from these simple people troubled him.

Like other prosperous men in Panama, Charles viewed the Indian population as one would coconut trees or sugarcane:

indigenous and almost invisible. He never took into account how his own Sephardic traditions, as inconsistent as they tended to be, kept him somewhat distanced from the country's culture. Louise tossed a leaf into the rushing water. *That's the irony of arrogance.*

She set the package on the floor of the canoe to open a parasol over her and Maud's head, and found herself daydreaming about a river outing she had made with her parents when she was little. How happy Mother had been that day, splashing water on Father and ruffling him in his new suit. She remembered Mother's laugh most of all, a rhythmic, gutsy laugh that rose from her hips. If she were here, she might have asked Benjamin about his grandfather, how he became a shaman, and what sort of lessons he learned from him. Louise stared at the radiating circles on the surface of the river. *Perhaps a shaman could have saved Mother.* At last Father stopped talking; he slid closer to Maud to pat her limp hand. Louise twirled the parasol, sending a welcome draft of air to her neck, and watched the young man push the oars through the deep water.

The canoe landed with ease on the Costa Rica side, and as there were no horses or carriages, they began their journey by foot, following Benjamin up the steep and isolated Talamanca hills. The quiet beauty of the countryside moved her; the still cedars and laurels lounged peacefully against the turquoise sky. Maud took several needed rest stops along the way. Father reeled at the slightest crackle in the bush; Louise half expected him to brandish his pistol.

"Is it much further to your village?" Charles asked, winded, glancing over his shoulder and swatting at flies.

"It's just past the next clearing." Benjamin helped Maud cross a knobby cluster of stones. Insects were not attracted to him like they were to Father.

"Your grandfather has the reputation of being a celebrated shaman." Louise said, eager to change the subject.

"Don Pedro is well known for his songs and medicines." Benjamin broke off a branch that hung in the path and tossed it into the bush. "We have few visitors from outside our way of life. Grandfather knows by your effort you are worthy of seeing him."

Louise glanced at her father's tight face and braced herself for a tart reply, but he remained silent. For now.

Charles had arrived in Panama from New York City full of vigor for the canal and its potential. He hailed from a long line of bankers in the United States and Central America with vested interests in financing the project. Twenty-two years ago, at an extravagant dinner party held to celebrate the newly built mansion of French engineer Monsieur de Lesseps, he met Ethel Louise, a raven-haired young woman whose beauty was the talk of the town. Charles, fiercely competitive in matters of business and pleasure, saw courtship as just another blood sport, with Ethel Louise as the grand prize. Immediately he barricaded her with his prowess. No man could match his wit. Eventually his persistence and confidence won her over. Born and raised in Panama, Ethel Louise was the daughter of a wealthy linen export merchant. She had never met anyone like Charles.

WHEN THEY NEARED THE CLEARING they came upon an enormous circular dwelling. Thickly thatched with palm leaves, it rose from the ground to a sharp point at least forty or fifty feet in the air. Its peak appeared to be covered with a sort of bowl or jar. There was a large square doorway with an awning over it. Benjamin strode to the opening. A brood of feeding hens clucked and scurried. Maud clutched Charles's arm as they entered the unusual home.

"Grandfather! Your visitors are here!" Benjamin called out. Inside the abode was dark and cool, and there was a smell of burned wood. Louise adjusted her eyes to the dimness. Monkeys chattered from above but where she could not tell. Carrying bags and baskets of various sizes dangled from beams in the ceiling. Bows, arrows, and long poles were stuck in the thatched walls. Wooden drums swung from a rafter on one side, along with striking bird plumes and animal skins. Opposite the entrance was a hearth where three hammocks hung—one occupied by a man who lay sleeping, his arm dangling over the side. Benjamin quietly approached the hammock and gave the man's arm a gentle tug. The man stirred. He groped for Benjamin's hand and then pulled himself up in the hammock. He was small and wiry with sparse hair, sharp cheekbones, and leathery skin several hues deeper than Benjamin's. He rubbed his face with his palms while Benjamin introduced him.

"Señor Lindo, this is Don Pedro, the man you and your daughters have come to see."

Benjamin whispered something to Don Pedro. Don Pedro turned and studied the three visitors. He motioned for Maud to come forth, gesturing for her to sit in the empty hammock next to him. Holding tight to each other, Father and Maud walked deeper into the dark room. Don Pedro shook his head with rigor. He pointed at Maud. Charles, somewhat apprehensively, let go of his daughter's arm. She inched over to Don Pedro and sat on the edge of the rough-hewn hammock. At that moment a butterfly descended on her lap; its yellow, blue, and black wings beat against her hand as she frantically waved it away. Don Pedro leaped from his hammock and followed the butterfly's flight, staring for some time. He spoke with excitement in his native language, nodding after the beautiful insect.

"Grandfather says the butterfly represents a deceased soul. He wants to know who in your family has died," Benjamin said, interpreting his grandfather's words. Maud shot a confused look at Charles.

"My mother died when I was eight." She twisted a ring on her finger and glanced back and forth between Don Pedro and

Benjamin. Don Pedro spoke again, his broken Spanish rapid and emphatic.

"The butterfly is a sign that her spirit is here."

Chickens darted into the room. Louise put her hand on her father's rigid arm. How tense he was! Don Pedro continued asking Maud questions about Mother, whether her asthma started before or after her death. Though no one addressed him, Charles butt in.

"I can't see how my daughter's mother's passing has anything to do with her illness. Maud has been congested and short of breath for weeks. The wasted hospital stays. Useless physicians. Obviously what she needs is an alternative medicine—a more effective tonic or poultice!"

Louise lowered her head. *Must he embarrass her like this?* Don Pedro went back to his hammock and fell silent for a long while. Benjamin brought stools over, inviting Louise and Charles to sit. He then stood next to his grandfather and waited. Maud wiped her nose repeatedly. Father grew restless. Just when Louise thought the awa had fallen asleep he jumped up, turned to Benjamin, and rattled off a list of words, counting on the fingers of one hand. Benjamin explained the plan to Charles.

"Don Pedro needs certain plants, flowers, and roots for the curing ceremony. I'll go out now to gather them." He unhooked a coarse sack that hung from the ceiling and slung it over his arm. "You and your daughters can rest here until I return."

Louise blinked. She longed for a break from her father and sister.

"Can I be of any help?" Louise's question was for Benjamin, but she looked at her father instead. He seemed preoccupied, lost in a reverie.

"You're welcome to come if you like," Benjamin said. He pulled a machete from the thatched walls. "What grandfather needs is on the grounds nearby."

Louise started to take her father's hand but thought better of it.

"May I go?"

Charles pushed his hands into his pockets and looked past her absently. "You must be in plain sight." He walked with them to the front of the dwelling. Benjamin pointed to an area ten meters away. Charles glanced back at Maud and Don Pedro.

"Perhaps that will move things along more quickly," he said, frowning at Benjamin's machete. "Be sure to hurry."

Relieved, Louise went with Benjamin to the field, feeling her father's eyes on her back. They came upon a charming ravine bordered by egg-shaped stones and lush shrubs.

"My, how beautiful it is here! I wish I had brought my drawing pad."

His direct glance caught her off guard. She swept aside ringlets that drooped into her eyes.

"You're an artist."

It was more a statement than a question. An artist? Her ears burned. She didn't consider herself one. Though she loved sketching and painting, her art was more of a hobby; none of it warranted serious attention. Still, what should she say? Mother had always praised her work, but Father never seemed to be impressed. *I do believe that's a tree,* he'd uttered recently upon viewing one of her sketches. He handed her the paper and went back to whatever was on his desk or his mind.

"I studied art in school."

Benjamin squinted at her, the overhead sun accentuating the hollows of his face.

"Art is a gift from Sibo, the Great Spirit. You can't learn it."

She paused, feeling both flattered and conflicted. He surveyed the grounds before him.

"Where in Panama do you live?" He parted a bush and pulled thick vines together to chop at its roots. Louise picked up the sack, holding it open for him.

"In the city. My father works for the Canal Commission." She watched him shove a bunch of tangled vines into the bag.

"Many Costa Ricans went to work on the canal. It's either that or the coffee plantations."

"What about you?" Louise shook the bag to settle the vines.

"Grandfather is training me to become an awa. I spend hours at his side learning the songs and rituals." He inspected a thorny twig cutting before wrapping it in a banana leaf.

"How interesting! What kind of songs?"

"Mostly healing songs. There are hundreds of them." They traveled a bit further, stopping in front of a sprawling hedge with hanging red blossoms. "I have to learn them all from memory." He began plucking flower buds from the tree.

"Do you know the healing song for my sister? I'd love to hear it."

Benjamin cradled an armful of blossoms like a newborn baby.

"The songs are sacred. They're meant only for the person who is sick."

"Of course! Stupid of me to ask," Louise added quickly, feeling her cheeks redden. *What was she thinking?* Benjamin studied her for a moment. He casually picked a few more flowers. She opened the sack to catch the waterfall of crimson that spilled from his arms into the bag, wondering if it matched the color of her face. He then reached into this shirt pocket and pulled out what appeared to be a small white whistle. There were half a dozen holes drilled into it, and one end was plugged with wax. He blew slowly through the larger opening. Several soft, shrill notes floated into the air. All was still; even the insects and birds seemed to hold their breath. Louise took a step toward Benjamin, captivated by the sound.

"That was lovely…like a bird's call. What is that?"

He held out the whistle in the palm of his hand.

"It's a kind of flute made from the bone of a pelican's breast," he said, turning the smooth, curved instrument over with his thumb. "The tune was meant to call the quetzal. I sometimes see them here in the aguacatillo tree." He looked up, peering through the branches of the fruit-laden tree. "They love to eat wild avocado."

"Oh, I hope we see one! Their green tail feathers are so long and stunning. My mother used to read us stories about the quetzal."

Side by side they searched the rain forest trees for a glimpse of the resplendent bird. Benjamin described its habitat between curious glances at her.

"The quetzal is a shy bird; they make their nests high in these trees. You can hear them sing in the morning and at dusk when they mark their land. Some tribes believe they symbolize the Quetzalcoatl—the god of the sky, sun, and wind." He stooped to snap a leaf off a plant and put it to his nose. "Others say he is a trickster."

"What do you believe?" she asked, watching him draw the plant from its roots.

"Grandfather says he is a wisdom teacher. He calls on the quetzal for guidance as part of a ritual. If he sees one, it's a sign the ceremony will be successful." Benjamin collected a bunch of the crisp aromatic leaves. Louise opened the sack for him to deposit them and turned her face to the cloudless sky.

"My father is very worried about Maud. She's been ill for some time."

"Don Pedro is a powerful awa. If your sister is willing to receive the songs, chances are good she'll be cured."

Their path narrowed alongside a buoyant stream. Across the way Charles watched them fixedly. Benjamin cleared the overgrowth with his machete; Louise trailed a few paces back. The contrasts between the young man and his grandfather were great: Benjamin's physique was longer, his skin fairer, his profile sharper. Most of all, his eyes were golden while Don Pedro's were coal black. When the trail widened and they walked side by side again, she spoke her mind.

"You're very different from your grandfather."

"How so?"

"Well, you're much taller for one."

Benjamin grinned.

"The Nrvai are not very tall people. I take after my father. He was a Spaniard."

Her puzzle solved, Louise eyed him again and recognized bits and pieces of Spanish conquest carved in his face. *Mestizo.*

"Did you grow up here in these beautiful hills?"

"Yes and no. My mother was living here when she met my father. He was a hard Christian missionary, very strict. She fell in love with him, but he refused to marry her unless she renounced her Nrvai beliefs and grandfather's shamanism." He chuckled softly. "My father called it 'devil's work.' When my mother consented they married and moved to a big house in San Jose, where I was born." He chopped a limb off a spindly tree and scraped at the bark. "I knew nothing about this place or the Nrvai until I was twelve years old, when my parents died."

"I'm sorry! I didn't mean to—" Louise thought she was prying, but he continued.

"Our house caught fire one night. I was pulled from my bed by an unknown visitor." Benjamin divided the branch into three logs. "Grandfather said it was Sibo who sent a dwalok spirit to save me from the flames. Then I came here with my grandfather. I had never met him before. That was nine years ago." He stomped his feet; caked mud crumbled off the sides of his boots. "Grandfather knew I would be with him someday. He believes I am the only one who can learn his methods and pass them on." Benjamin swung the sack brimming with plants back and forth at his side like a pendulum. She felt compassion for him, but she could see he didn't need it. Apparently he had cast off the past. His brow was unfurled, his gaze calm and present.

"When did your mother die?" Again his golden eyes poured deep into her, like a liquid sunset.

"Eight years ago. I was twelve, too. Since that day my life has never been the same."

He slung the bulging sack over his shoulder, its shape like that of a crouching jaguar.

"Grandfather says one has to die for another to be reborn. That's the nature of the Creator. It's what the elders told him and what he told me."

The sun was lower in the sky, and a lavender mist colored the trees surrounding the dwelling when they returned. Charles paced in front of the doorway.

"What took you so long? Maud has fallen asleep!"

Louise peeked inside. Maud lay deep in the hammock, snoring loudly. Benjamin answered before Louise had a chance.

"Sleep is good. She'll be more receptive during the healing ceremony." Charles stepped back as Benjamin thrust his machete in the wall of woven palms. "We found everything Grandfather needed." He took the sack off his shoulder and smiled at Louise, his mouth favoring one side.

"Well then, let's get on with it." Charles said, tired of pleasantries.

They went inside. Don Pedro was waving a fan made of feathers over glowing embers in the hearth. He clapped his hands when Benjamin approached him with the sack. After exchanging a few words the awa opened the bag and shook its contents on the raised wood floor. He squatted down to inspect each vine, leaf, root, and flower, murmuring to Benjamin beside him. The two separated the plants into piles; a potpourri of heady scents filled the space. The heat of the day lifted and a cool draft blew into the hut. Charles took his post by Maud's hammock. Louise looked down at her shoes: mud encrusted them almost to her ankles. Prickly thorns, green burs, and splinters formed a wild pattern on the hem of her shift. She sat on a stool and tucked her feet under her skirt, wondering what Benjamin thought about her. Did she appear too much of a city girl, shallow and precious, like those girls at home whose lives revolved around fashion and galas and fancy doodads from abroad, like her sister Maud? She touched the loosened curls around her cheeks and decided not to contain them at the back of her head. Her eyes followed Benjamin around the room. She watched him pick out a drum, a carved gourd rattle, and a small, stripped log and place them by the fire. Don Pedro hummed, Maud snored, and Charles gaped at his pocket watch.

"Benjamin, when will the ceremony start? How long do you expect it to last?"

Grandson and grandfather exchanged glances.

"Curing ceremonies have no time limit. It takes as long as Grandfather needs for the required effect," Benjamin replied.

"But the carriage will be waiting for us at half past seven! Might we be finished by then?"

Benjamin explained the dilemma to his grandfather. The awa swung his arm in the air.

"It's over when your daughter is better!"

Charles held his head in distress. Louise tried to console him.

"Father, we need Maud to get well regardless of the time it takes. Right now Don Pedro is our only hope."

Charles had not planned on being delayed in these remote hills yet was frantic to help Maud, worried that if he didn't act quickly her health would continue to fail. Louise remembered the day when an associate at the commission told Charles a miraculous story of how Don Pedro had cured his jaundice. She was surprised when Father decided to see the awa. Shamanism was beyond his comprehension. At first he called it barbaric superstitions, but this colleague's restored health was living proof. Charles would not stand by and helplessly witness losing his daughter as he had he lost his wife. Now she watched her father tear himself to pieces with worry over the waiting carriage and the dangers of traveling down the mountain in the dark and Maud's condition and…

Don Pedro interrupted her thoughts with a sudden outburst. The awa strode to and fro by the hearth, its smoldering glow punctuating the animation in his eyes.

"I have been very successful in my ceremonies—not every awa can say that." Don Pedro wagged a knotty finger at Charles. "You are fortunate to have found me. I know the stories about how this and many other sicknesses were formed. It was my mother, Tukitima, who taught me. Yes! My father did not know she was an awa. She kept it hidden. I was a little boy, but she revealed the stories and the sacred songs to me. By and by, I learned all. True healing takes time!" He snatched a mug of water off a stool. Louise and Charles looked at one another. Maud was unstirred by the awa's exposition. Benjamin sat a short distance away, his face hidden in the shadows of a beam. When he had quenched his thirst, Don Pedro continued.

"I taught my grandson the language only shamans can understand. He is ready now. He knows Sibo's songs. He has his own sacred stones. He can ask the right questions, too! I taught him as only a master can."

There was a rustling outside. Charles put his hand on the pistol in his breast pocket. A tiny woman entered the dwelling and halted at the sight of the pale visitors. Benjamin greeted her, gave her the package they brought for the awa's payment. The woman spoke briefly to Benjamin before going about preparing a meal. His lecture over, Don Pedro began parceling the herbs, chanting unintelligibly. His lips were in a constant state of motion, as if he were reciting some oratorio. Benjamin, collecting scraps of plants, would often nod and hum along. Soon the smell of stewed chicken, rice and beans, and plantains wafted through the dwelling. Louise inhaled deeply, hoping the smell would satiate her a little. The woman reappeared, carrying plates of hot food for Charles and Louise. However, for Don Pedro, Benjamin, and Maud, she brought only a bowl of mashed plantains. Louise immediately stood and offered her plate to her sister.

"Maud can have my portion."

The awa dismissed her with a shake of his head.

"Plantains and water! That's all she can have until the healing is victorious!"

"This is ridiculous! Get your things Louise. We're leaving." Charles said.

Just then Maud awoke. For the first time since they left home no cough sputtered from her lips. She rubbed her eyes and looked around. Charles dashed to her side.

"Maudy darling! Are you all right?"

"Oh Papi! I dreamt I was at home in my bed," Maud said, her eyes glossy with sleep. "Mother was there, and she brought me some plantains to eat. They smelled so good, and I was so hungry."

Charles could not conceal his astonishment. The bowl of mashed plantains rested on a trestle. Don Pedro picked it up and gave it to Maud.

At dusk, after everyone had eaten, the ritual began. Stars appeared one by one against an indigo sky. Don Pedro explained to them the special significance of twilight.

"When night buries the day, the ancient memory of spirit prevails. It is time to talk to mediators and to Sibo, who owns everything you can see!"

He dropped a bundle of leaves, roots, and vines into a cauldron of boiling water on the hearth. Stones of various sizes and shapes tumbled out of a small canvas bag onto the ground. The awa started to sing. He interspersed his song with questions and then blew on the stones.

He shook the gourd rattle as if to cleanse the air. Benjamin sat on the floor softly beating a drum between his knees. To Louise, it was like the heartbeat of the verdant countryside. She could not help staring at him. Moonlight danced across his hands as he played. The uneven shadows cast by the fire on his face gave it an ethereal, painterly quality. At that moment Louise became aware of her sister, who had been watching her. She quickly diverted her attention to their father. Charles, leaning low in his chair, was fighting sleep. Outside a chorus of creaking frogs and crickets seemed to harmonize with Benjamin's soothing rhythm. Her gaze wandered back to the awa's grandson.

The ritual went on a long time. To Charles's relief, a local boy was sent to the river to tell the carriage to come back in the morning. Soon Louise's head grew heavy and the ceremony began to fade. She was resting against a wooden pillar when she heard Benjamin start to sing. The clarity of his voice rose in the fragrant evening air. Through glazed eyes she saw Benjamin give Don Pedro the log he had stripped earlier, the one she heard him call an "ulu." The awa scrawled drawings on the log with a piece of charcoal. From a distance it looked like all sorts of crude stick figures and abstract symbols. *You're an artist.* Benjamin's words echoed in her ears. There was something fascinating about him, in the way he moved and spoke to her. Somehow Benjamin and his grandfather were able to speak the language of nature, of healing; a language Louise did not understand but could sense its truth and goodness.

The little woman came back again, this time offering blankets and hammocks for Louise and Charles to sleep in. It had grown quite cold and late. His first inclination was to refuse, but Maud had already been instructed to lie down in the hammock nearest Don Pedro, who, after covering her with a blanket, returned to his chanting. Maud, at last, slept soundly. Charles had no choice but to accept the offer. Benjamin sat cross-legged and still on a mat, assisting his grandfather in meditation. Louise got up from her stool, her limbs stiff from sitting so long, and swung her worn body into the first hammock near the fire. She fell asleep almost immediately, the netted bed more comfortable than she had expected. A multitude of stars, cushioned by the dark heavens, lulled all but the shaman and his grandson to sleep.

MORNING CAME, BRINGING WITH IT a cacophony of rural life: the rooster's crow, the bellow of mules, the grunts of pigs. Don Pedro was just concluding the ritual, his voice hoarse from singing through the night. Benjamin held a large gourd filled with coffee for his grandfather. Charles too was awake, standing over Maud, watching her sleep. Louise could smell breakfast cooking somewhere. When Maud finally awoke her face glowed, her eyes were brighter than they had been in weeks. Charles helped her out of the hammock. The woman appeared and handed Maud another bowl of boiled green plantains. Don Pedro, solemn and pensive, drank his coffee before giving his final analysis.

"The ceremony has driven out the external forces that have attacked your daughter's *wikol,* her soul. That's good, but it is not over."

All eyes were on the awa.

"Two more nights are necessary to complete the long-term protection…maybe more."

Charles blanched at the prospect. "Don Pedro, I'm grateful for your hospitality and Maud's results are impressive so far, but I must start back today! I have business to attend to. We can't possibly stay another two nights."

To this the awa shook his head and replied, "Failure to continue the ritual will destroy all hope of getting better."

Charles spread his arms wide. "But we've come so far! Surely there must be a way to solve this dilemma!"

Don Pedro closed his bleary eyes. The lines in his face seemed to have multiplied since last night. He paced the floor. He took his grandson aside. The awa spoke in hushed tones; Benjamin listened intently, but his demeanor changed at his grandfather's words. He glanced at Maud. Was he uncertain about something? Benjamin started to counter, but Don Pedro placed his bony hand on Benjamin's shoulder. Benjamin stared at his feet, nodding. Finally the two looked up at the Lindo family, who awaited their verdict.

"There is a way to complete the healing," Don Pedro announced in a gravelly voice. "Benjamin will carry out the rituals at your home." The tired awa patted Benjamin on his back. "He knows what has to be done." Don Pedro turned to Charles. "I will decide on the payment for these special services."

"Excellent solution! I knew we would come to an agreement." Charles shook Don Pedro's hand and embraced Maud. Louise was happy too, but inside, the plan came as a shock. It never occurred to her that Benjamin might finish the awa's work—and in their home! She blushed at the thought of him in the carriage. *Where would he sit? What would they say to each other? How long would he stay? Where would he sleep?* She imagined him in their great arched doorway, passing the potted geraniums on the tiled floor. Was there bread and tea in the cupboard? Would Rosa be there when they arrived? Benjamin packed his belongings in a cloth bag. He bundled the leaves, roots, flowers, and the log the awa had drawn on last night and put them in a large sisal sack. A bucket of water was brought for them to wash their face and hands. Louise helped Maud put on her shoes. She shook the burs and dried grass from her sister's skirt. Maud was talkative now, but Louise paid her no mind. She strained to hear Charles and Don Pedro's conversation outside the hut. The awa called for Benjamin to join them. Soon they were all shaking hands. Father, quite pleased with himself, strutted over to where she and Maud were tidying themselves for the trip home.

"It's all settled," he gloated, "for a payment of ten pounds of flour, three boxes of nails, and a pair of scissors."

The four made it down the mountain terrain before the heat of the day set in. Guaria morada orchids and countless guanacaste trees stretched their shade along the path. Maud, lively in spirit but still weak in the body, draped herself over Louise and Charles's shoulders. When they finally came upon the canoe, tied to a post by the river, Benjamin swept Maud up and carried her across the slippery landing to the boat. Mud from her shoes flew and caught Charles on his sleeve. Louise brushed the soil off her father, who was flustered at the sight of the young man's forearm around Maud's waist. Benjamin stepped into the canoe and lowered Maud onto the wooden seat; her arm lingered a fraction too long around his neck. He then reached out to Louise to help her aboard; his firm hand made her think of last night's drumming. Charles stepped in last, relieved to be on his way back to civilized society in Panama City. Benjamin untied the rope from the post and pushed off from the riverbank, freeing them from their mystical harbor.

Halfway across the river, Louise saw a flicker in the sky. A scene from the ceremony came back to her.

"Father, look! I saw those birds last night!" She pointed to a pair of colorful birds flying overhead. Everyone looked up. The small birds with their iridescent red, green, and yellow feathers were stark against the morning sky. "They circled around and around while Don Pedro sang, like they were dancing!" Louise waved her hand in the air, as if she could flag down the birds.

"Birds?" Father yawned. "That's absurd, Louise."

"I saw many of them! The patterns they formed were quite beautiful," Louise insisted.

"It was the quetzal." Benjamin had been silent for most of the trip. "They can appear in numbers during a ritual of significance," he said, dipping the wooden oars in the water. "Not everyone can see them."

Maud and Charles looked at Louise. So she wasn't dreaming. Benjamin took out the bone whistle he had shown to her by the ravine. He blew into the delicate instrument, and again the notes bobbed lightly like her reflection on the river. A delicious thrill rushed through her. She glanced at Benjamin. The sun caught threads of bronze in his hair.

As they approached land the sight of their coach in waiting reminded her of home. She pictured the narrow labyrinthine streets of San Felipe, lined with humble Spanish terra-cotta-roofed homes that butted up against grand French architecture; the iron balconies that overflowed with bougainvillea vines. She blotted out the inquisitive neighbors who would openly stare at Benjamin and his sack of herbs; her thoughts were wrapped up in the details of his stay. She slid closer to Charles and carefully chose her words.

"Father, we should have Rosa prepare the upstairs guest bedroom for Benjamin. It's closer to Maud's room than the one downstairs, so he can better care for her. That way I can also assist him and observe her progress."

Charles mulled over his daughter's suggestion.

"I suppose upstairs would be best. It's only for a few days… Rosa will be there." He rubbed his bloodshot eyes, pressing his fingers into the sockets. "While I'm at the office you'll be in charge, Louise. Start a medical journal immediately. Take meticulous notes and keep me informed on all that transpires."

"Yes, of course! I'll create a log of Maud's treatments," she replied, remembering her drawing pad wedged between the carriage door and seat. They soon left the canoe, boarded the carriage, and began their journey back to the old mansion in Panama City.

2OOI

Brooklyn, New York

FIVE YEARS OF MOTHERHOOD FLEW BY, bringing to light a new set of skills for Sheri to master alone. Diaper rash and cradle cap, potty training and sippy cups gave way to kindergarten, reciprocal play dates, and hovering peewee soccer moms. Since her promotion to creative director she rarely got home before dark. It was a demanding position; she was part of a consummate boys' club with long hours wasted in pointless meetings and schmoozing clients that left her little time for herself. In a black town car Sheri took long blinks between traffic lights. She needed a wife. At least she had Leatrice, her trusty babysitter. Where would she be without her? A paper bag with warm french fries balanced on a pile of work she brought from the office. She touched it and thought of Zig.

The car pulled up behind a Fresh Direct truck double-parked in front of her building.

"You're home, Sheri. Lemme know what time you want to be picked up tomorrow night."

Jimmy drove her home so often he was practically her private chauffeur. The balding Irish man gave her a voucher to sign, along with a sympathetic look. He was forty-four—four years older than her and he already had two sons in college.

"Pick me up at six, Jimmy. Tomorrow's Friday—if I'm not in the lobby by five after, come and get me."

Cell phone handset hanging from her ear, she dumped a large portfolio, laptop case, and an oversized handbag onto the sidewalk. The french fries! She reached back in the car to grab the greasy bag, suddenly aware of her growling stomach, the power bars she'd eaten for lunch having long worn off. A blustery wind made her shiver, but she didn't bother to put on her hat. Instead, she craned her head to find her apartment window among the string of identical ones. There it was—her Glo-Ball lamp. From the sidewalk the floating opal was like a lighthouse tower guiding her way. It meant Zig was still eating dinner with Leatrice. Sheri would surprise them. She hurried around the idling Fresh Direct truck and started down the long walkway to the front entrance. She barely saw her son by the light of day; only on weekends when she wasn't traveling could she see his sweet face in natural sunlight. She checked her watch: seven twenty-seven. Inside the lobby Juan was surrounded by boxes. He jabbered on, his Dominican accent ricocheting off the art deco ceiling. A deliveryman crossed names off a sheet of paper. Some of those boxes had to be hers. Point-and-click grocery shopping was how she spent her meager downtime at the office. She pictured immigrant workers tossing bananas, boneless chicken, and canned soup into boxes without a thought to checking expiration dates or dents or the rotten carrot on the side of the three-pound bag. Juan spotted Sheri and yelled.

"*Mami*'s just in time for her deliveryyyy!"

He came from behind the front desk— he was barely a foot taller than it.

"All of this is for you!" he said, waving his hands at a tall stack of boxes. "What are you feeding that boy? For a five-year-old he eats like a man!"

"Five years, five months, and two weeks." she replied with a brief smile. It was best not to engage Juan in any extended conversation, especially after his evening joint. She waited for the delivery guy to load her boxes on a hand truck, resisting the urge to hurl her heavy bags on top of them. Juan assumed his pseudo doormanlike authority.

"Okay. Ride up with Miss Lambert to 7B. *Mira,* you want me to watch the truck? The cops are out."

The delivery guy wheeled the boxes toward the elevators.

"Nah, there's another guy out front. He'll move it."

Juan swore under his breath, always in pursuit of a tip. The delivery guy shoved the cart into the elevator like he was schlepping file cabinets instead of food. His skin had the dull cast of someone who ate bodega sandwiches for breakfast, lunch, and dinner. She caught a whiff of crushed basil and oranges and counted off five boxes—did she really order that much stuff?

When the elevator doors opened the guy rolled the cart down the hall behind Sheri. Her keys jingled as she unlocked the door, and right away, she heard the familiar sound of Zig's chair scraping the floor as he pushed away from the table.

"Mommeee!"

The door swung open before Sheri had a chance to turn the knob. Zig wrapped his little arms around her waist, almost knocking her into the delivery guy.

"See? I told you my mom would come home early today!" He glared triumphantly at Leatrice. She was picking up bits of food off the floor under his chair.

"Right you are, Zig! He was telling me all day you would be here before eight o'clock."

"Hi, Leatrice. Yes, I managed to escape early today."

Sheri stepped aside with Zig dangling from her body so the young man could wheel the boxes into the kitchen. When he finished unloading them she tipped him five dollars. He thanked her, the bill disappearing into his meaty fist.

She dragged her cumbersome portfolio in from the hallway, leaving the door ajar. The living room smelled of wet socks and rubber boots. She threw her handbag on the leather Eames sofa and straightened one of the matching chairs in front of her glass Noguchi coffee table. Though they were scratched and showing signs of age she never tired of them. The mid-century furniture's simple, modern lines concealed nothing yet revealed everything about the daring pop art on the walls, art she had lovingly amassed over the years.

Zig had dried ketchup on his chin and on the sleeve of his sweatshirt. He was holding his favorite toy—not one of those newfangled electronic gadgets, but an old wooden canoe that she'd found at a stoop sale, its patina dull from constant coddling. He pulled Sheri to the sofa.

"You smell like french fries! Did you bring me some fries?"

"French fries? Hmmm…let's see." She opened her handbag and slowly lifted out the fries. "Whoa! How'd these get in here?"

Zig snatched the paper bag and ran to his room with glee. Sheri glanced at her smiling babysitter cupping crumbs in her hand.

"Did he finish eating, Leatrice?"

"He et all except de broccoli," she replied in broken patois.

Sheri called out to Zig.

"No fries until you eat a little broccoli, k?

"K…," he called back, mouth already stuffed.

"How was his breathing today?" Sheri passed Leatrice a small waste paper basket for the crumbs.

"Pam said he was okay in the playground. He 'ad one nebulizer treatment afta school and another one at seven o'clock."

There was no shortage of West Indian nannies in Brooklyn. Raised in Grenada, Leatrice was sincere and steadfast, especially regarding Zig's asthma. If she couldn't babysit on weekends her younger sister, Desiree, who also did housecleaning, was Sheri's backup. They both had a proper air, the formal residue of British colonialism. After grilling several babysitters from a host of nanny agencies, Sheri had hired Leatrice when Zig was just three months old. Calm and collected, her face never betrayed any uncertainty; you could hear palm trees sway in her graceful movements. Pulling her thin jacket on, Leatrice quietly reported some news as Sheri walked her to the door.

"When we were coming home from school today Zig asked me if I loved him."

Sheri froze.

"Oh…what did you say?"

"I told him yes, I love you."

Sheri looked everywhere but at Leatrice, afraid of what she would see. But Leatrice was still smiling, her brown lips ashen from a missed meal. She'd said the right thing, whether it was true or not. Guilt tightened its grip on Sheri's throat.

"Thank you, Leatrice," she replied, barely above a whisper.

"Good night, Zig! Have a good evening!" Unaffected, Leatrice made her usual cheerful exit, venturing deep into Crown Heights in hopes of seeing her own three kids before bedtime.

Sheri closed the door and tried to shut out her wounded pride. Should she ask Zig about it? He ambled into the living room, relishing the last of his french fries. She collapsed on the sofa and yanked off her suede boots. No, she let it go. Right then, all she wanted was to sprawl there and admire his beaming little face.

"Why didn't you eat your broccoli, Z?"

"I ate *some*. Broccoli is so pointy." He tapped her gold elephant drop earrings, an impulse buy from the Met gift shop and a favorite of his.

"Pointy! You have the weirdest way with words—the makings of a good writer. How're tomatoes again?"

"Hot rocks on my arm." He wrinkled his nose in distaste. "Yuk."

Sheri laughed. Though his face had changed much over the years, his golden eyes still flickered like tiny embers. At two his hair started to curl and now he had a head full of untamable cowlicks and waves. The color of bark, it shot out in every direction like some Japanese anime cartoon character. His nose was changing too; the cute pug shaped itself into a graceful line. And he had a knack for talking to total strangers—newspaper-stand men, little old ladies, bike messengers, disabled kids—as if he had known them forever. Pam, his kindergarten teacher, called him the Mayor. Zig unhooked Sheri's earrings and played with them on his lap until an idea made him draw a sudden breath.

"Hey! You can give me a bath tonight!" His eyes shone at the prospect of being bathed by his own mother.

"Oh Z," she moaned, "how about a nice hot shower instead? I'm beat."

He pleaded nonstop for a bath. She drew a weary finger across the glass coffee table. *How'd it get so dusty already?* Tired and hungry, she went into the kitchen and opened a box of groceries. A bar of fair-trade organic dark chocolate was on top of a "heat and eat" dish of Chilean sea bass with tomato-fennel broth. She grabbed the chocolate, tore into it, and gave in, her decision garbled by a waxy chunk in her mouth.

"Okay! Okay! Go turn the water on!"

Zig raced to the bathroom, peeling off his clothes on the way. While the water was running, he recounted his play date with Caleb.

"Caleb ripped leaves off a plant because he couldn't blow bubbles in the house."

"That was no good! He could hurt the plant."

"The leaves will grow back."

"Maybe so." Sheri ran her fingers through his wild hair. Once Leatrice took him for a haircut and he came back looking like the Dalai Lama. She'd have to pencil in a trip to the barber.

"What did you do today when I was at school?"

Hmmm. What didn't she do?

"Well, I mostly sat in meetings listening to people blab on and on. Then I looked at a lot of pictures of makeup ads."

"Like gunky lipstick and girlie stuff?"

"Yeah—stinky perfume, too."

"Did you like any of them?"

Sheri shrugged her shoulders. "It's the same old stuff. Nothing new."

Zig was quiet for a long moment.

"Why don't you paint or draw anymore, Mom?"

Sheri laughed at the suggestion, feeling the presence of her father in the room. She was uncomfortable with him even in memory. *Art is a waste of time, not a profession.* He took a deep drag on a cigarette, let the fiery smoke coat the rest of his thought. *She'll never make any money. Picasso she's not!* She had heard him say it over a hair-raising *Carmina Burana* aria blasting on the stereo. Sheri's mother threw her resentment into a pot on the stove. She wouldn't dare challenge him. He was always right.

"I haven't done that since college, Z. That was a *looong* time ago."

"You don't remember how?"

"No, I remember. It's just that I'm too busy."

"Busy doing what?"

"Busy giving you a bath, that's what! Busy tickling you, that's what!"

Zig crouched as she tickled his sides, his giggle like the peal of wind chimes. She turned off the faucet and checked the water temperature before giving him the go-ahead. Tittering, he swung his skinny legs over the edge of the tub and sunk into the warm water with a sigh. One arm surfaced to sweep toy boats and action figures lined up against the wall into the water. Where'd the Spiderman and Pokemon come from? The glow of his olive skin contrasted with the cracked white subway tiles. She poured water on his head with a plastic beach bucket, watched it bead in his long dark eyelashes. How simple and perfect he was. Zig rambled on about everything: the new DVDs and toys he wanted, the afterschool shows he was banned from watching that all his friends watched, how he'd had fun at the birthday party with everyone except Andre.

"What happened with Andre?"

"He didn't want to play with me."

"Why not?"

"Andre likes to pile up blocks and then he throws them at you if you get too close. He doesn't really play with anybody. But I knew that from before."

"Before when?"

"Before when I was in heaven."

He was waving a washcloth in the water, the ripples swooshing back and forth in steady movements. Sheri paused, a bottle of lavender shampoo in her hand.

"You remember when you were in heaven?"

"Uh-huh."

"Really…" She squeezed out a dollop and began to lather his hair. "What were you doing up there?"

He didn't answer right away. When he did his tone was factual, as if it happened yesterday.

"Waiting to jump. All my friends were waiting with me. Caleb and Ruby and Andre wanted to jump, too."

"Jump…from where to where?"

"From heaven down to earth, to their moms. We had to choose our mother. I chose you, but I had to wait."

Sheri felt a tingling in the back of her scalp. She stopped scrubbing his hair. Suds slipped down his temple into his ear. Zig squinted at her.

"What, Mom?"

His expression was blank. She studied his face.

"You had to wait?"

"Because it wasn't my turn. Sibo said no. He whispered to me very gently. If He said it louder, the whole world would shake!" Zig thumped his arms in the bathwater to demonstrate, causing a small tidal wave.

"Who's Sibo?"

"The One who made everything you can see."

She dropped the shampoo on the floor. What was this? They had never talked about these things before. Maybe he picked it up from a kid at school? Heard it on TV? She pushed up her wet sleeves, sorting through the questions whirling in her mind.

"What does this have to do with Andre?"

"Well, Andre couldn't decide who he wanted to be his mommy. Sibo lets you choose your own mom. He doesn't tell you who to go to. You just say what you want and He might say, "Okay, good." Or He'll say, "Are you sure?" Andre wasn't sure if he should jump, but Ruby was getting impatient. She wanted a mother to love. So because of Ruby, Andre jumped."

Sheri thought about the logic of his answer. Ruby and Andre were twins.

"I guess they had to jump together."

Zig shook his head.

"No. Ruby is Andre's little sister. He had to jump first."

He was right. The twin's mother told Sheri they were six minutes apart. Andre was the firstborn. Zig's fingers and toes were getting waterlogged. Sheri was riveted.

"So what did you do?"

"I told Sibo I chose you."

"You could see me?"

"Of course! I could see through everything. I saw you cooking in the kitchen. Not this kitchen, a different one. You were angry sometimes."

"I was angry? About what?"

"You wanted a baby and you couldn't get one. But you weren't ready anyhow. So I just waited until you were ready!"

Sheri looked down at her soggy hands on the edge of the bathtub. The same hands that shook five years ago as she unwrapped the pregnancy test stick in the bathroom stall at work, her fate held in its little plastic window.

Please be blue
little boy blue
bluebells, blueberries
blue heart bleeding

She sat on the toilet seat and held the wand in a stream of urine between her knees. A blue smear slowly appeared. Liane burst into the ladies room searching for her. Had she forgotten about the internal meeting? No, she hadn't forgotten.

Zig dunked himself underwater, pinching his nose shut. Another question plagued her.

"Did you see anyone else?"

She immediately regretted asking. She hoped he hadn't heard her. Zig emerged with his rubber duckie, squeezing it hard to suck bath water into its beak.

"I saw my daddy."

Sheri fell silent. Zig sprayed streams of water out of the bird's beak.

"He had red light all around him and bouncing gold balls, bouncing high and low. I saw his arms moving really fast like this..." He twisted left and right. Water splashed all over her jeans. He stopped abruptly.

"Mom! Are you crying?"

She was just as surprised as he was. Why was she crying? He'd never asked about his father. Sheri had an answer ready, but the question never came. She wiped her eyes with wet fingers, water and tears streaming down her cheeks.

"It's okay. I already knew about Dad. It's O-KAY!"

Zig faced her squarely. She wanted to know more.

"What happened next?"

Zig spun around in the tub, his toys swirled around him.

"Sibo said I could jump. So I held on to the string. It was a little scary, sliding down, down, down."

"You slid down a string…Where did you land?"

"I went right through here, to here." Zig quit spinning, reached over and touched the crown of Sheri's head. He traced his finger down to her navel.

"Wow, Zig, that's…that's…"

She stared at him. He yawned, following a long blink. She wondered about the stories they were reading at school. Excelsior Prep was a prestigious private school in Brooklyn Heights, highly regarded and with no religious affiliations. She had him on the waiting list before he was born to get in there. Would they dare teach this kind of mystical stuff? She wracked her brain trying to remember if there was a memo in his backpack, something about a guest speaker or school trip, but if the topic were religion she would have remembered. There were no e-mail alerts, no announcements on Excelsior's Web site. Where was this coming from?

"Did you read a story like this at school?"

"No."

"At the library with Leatrice?"

Zig wrung water out of his washcloth.

"It's not a story."

Distant church bells rang nine times. Nine o'clock. He had been in the tub for an hour.

"It's late, sweetie. Let's get you out of the tub or you'll be Zig soup!"

He climbed out and into his favorite towel with a huge Haring *Radiant Baby* in the middle. Sheri draped it over his head and shoulders like an Arabian cape. He tiptoed to reach her neck and hugged her tightly; his little pruned fingers pressed her skin. Lukewarm bathwater trickled down her sweater.

"I'm glad you chose me, Z."

"There was nobody else but you, Mom."

Zig's bedtime routine continued as usual. He stood in his bed and pulled on his flannel pajamas, singing a new nursery rhyme he'd learned at school. Sheri read his pop-up dinosaur book for the hundredth time. Even so, she felt different, as if something had shifted between her and Zig.

When she turned out the lights, he said in a dreamy voice, "Do you remember when you were in heaven?"

"No, Z. I don't."

She could hear him thinking.

"Do other people remember?"

"I'm not sure. I've never asked anyone."

He drifted off. She sat beside him on his bed, watched his breath become slow and deep. A hush crept into the room, enveloping her like blanketed arms. She kissed him and got up to leave.

"Mom, will you try to remember?"

She looked over her shoulder. His eyes were closed.

"I'll try."

In the kitchen were groceries to unpack, food to store, boxes to flatten, a dishwasher to load and set. The alien-green power light on her laptop beamed from the granite counter. Glancing at it made her inbox fly open in her mind and thirty-five new e-mails lash out. If she didn't take care of them now, by tomorrow they would metastasize like cancer. Next to her laptop stood a foot-high deck of bills, a credit card game waiting to be shuffled and dealt. She turned off the lights. A black hole swallowed the picture, creating an interior pause button. She pushed open a window in the living room and let the wintery air sweep over her drained face. It felt good. In the moonlight the treetops in

the Brooklyn Botanic Gardens were like feathery fingers pointing at the night sky, waiting patiently for spring.

I chose you.

Those three little words stood out, solid and incorruptible.
She pictured Zig swirling in the tub; when he spoke his eyes
were clear, steady. There was no hesitation in his voice. *What if
it were true? What if he'd had a choice?* Maybe he was fated to be
her son. But why her? She had little to offer him by way of spiritual means. Unexplained mysteries brought her back to ninth
grade. Sitting in algebra class, Sheri would watch Mr. Green-
stein's bearded mouth flap up and down, her stomach in knots,
his equations like endless gibberish. Her parents were atheists
who raised her without any awareness of God. They taught her
to value what was logical, what made sense (death and taxes).
Even so, there was always a deep longing within her; she was
sure there had to be more.

One Sunday, when she was sixteen, she had waited in front
of the sprawling St. John the Divine cathedral to see the pa-
rishioners pour out the Gothic doors. She combed their faces for some expression of divine wonder and inspiration, not
sure what she was looking for, and found only crabby children,
chatty mothers, and bored fathers. College twisted her into a
skeptic. She came to view life as if it were a marketing plan—a
quagmire of personal objectives, strategies, and goals. But the
longing did not let her go. Building a successful career, acquir-
ing all the right things, even motherhood could not satiate her
hunger. With the volume set on high in her head, she drowned
out the persistent ache she could not name, like her true identity.

On the living room walls her Keith Haring prints hung like
hip, sarcastic friends, their hard-edged black lines and saturated
colors exaggerated by the ghostly light from the street. Across
the room were her Basquiat and Max Ernst birds and her cov-
eted Frida Kahlo portrait, art she bought with the money she
made from the sale of her parents' co-op almost twenty years

ago. Friends thought she was crazy, but Sheri had to have them. She felt something transcendent when she looked at these abstract pieces. She was drawn to their primitive nature; their almost childlike compositions were like live wire, bursting with an underlying current of meaning and complexity. The Haring and Basquiat reminded her of the drawings she used to make as a little girl, figures that still showed up now and then as mindless doodles on scraps of paper. In the Kahlo portrait she saw a raw image of herself. Not only did Sheri resemble her physically, but also she identified with the brutal honesty, the endurance of life's cruelties that lay bare in the artist's expression. Living with her collection was the closest thing she got to a religious experience. If God existed, perhaps He was hiding there between the brushstrokes, behind the electric inks that stirred her emotions, in the feeling she used to get when she poured her heart onto a blank page.

Predictability and order were also important. Knowing Duane Reade would always stock Zig's asthma medication and his favorite tear-free shampoo. A pack of Chips Ahoy had twenty cookies that tasted the same as the first. She could count on her babysitter, her doorman, her routine with Zig, her reputation in the business. These things gave a sense of security, of belonging.

Then came 9/11.

It had been five months since the collapse of the World Trade Center towers and life as she knew it. The somber march across the Brooklyn Bridge, the powdery fall-out dusting the faces of stunned pedestrians, the brilliant sunshine on the darkest of days was ever vivid. When she finally got to Excelsior Prep to pick up Zig, she was one of the hordes of desperate parents trying to control their anxiety, trying not to bolt down the hallways. She found him sitting on the floor in his classroom playing with a friend, his backpack like a parachute on his back. He seemed oblivious to all the commotion, even though he knew what had happened. Zig saw the first plane crash from the rooftop playground, before the teachers knew, before they rushed the children back down to their classrooms. Something he said stuck in her mind. *Don't be sad, Mom. Those people had to jump out of their bodies today, but they'll get a new one. Then they'll come right back down again.*

The tragedy of that day crushed her personal truths. Mayor Giuliani's televised speech haunted her; how his face twitched as he urged New Yorkers to carry on a normal life—to keep shopping, as if shopping were a balm to soothe us, console us, and sustain us as a people. It was a defining moment that pushed her to the edge of her own burning edifice, with no hope or God or faith to comfort her. Night after night she would lie awake, too afraid to sleep, frightened at the bang of a garbage truck or the slam of a gate. Curled up on his side, Zig would slip easily into a tranquil slumber. When she reached out and held him tight his peace was with her. Zig's love was transcendent; it was the only thing that kept her sane. He was what truly mattered. He was her reason for living.

SHORTLY AFTER 9/11 he began telling tales about being an Indian.

On and on, day after day, he would recount endless adventures of his past indigenous life—foraging for food, animal conquests, tribal initiations, even details of his dwelling and his crude weapons. She listened with half a mind, juggling deadlines and terrorist news headlines. Life went on despite the turmoil in the city. Still she indulged him, thinking what a great storyteller he was, and maybe he'd be a writer someday. But something else nudged her. Zig was special in ways she couldn't fully understand. These were more than just stories to him.

Sheri heard the thermostat click and the heat come on. How long had she been standing there? The living room was ice cold. She reached up to close the window. Out of nowhere a helicopter appeared, swooping and hovering in the sky, choppers whipping the air. Her body tensed up in panic. She quickly shut the window. The helicopter zoomed up over her building and out of sight.

She took a deep breath and closed her eyes.

I waited until you were ready.

She thought about Zig lying in a tender sleep in bed and wondered what kind of dreams he had.

1899

Panama City, Panama

THE POUNDING OF HORSE HOOVES on stone streets awakened Louise. She opened her eyes to find Benjamin staring at her. Louise hastily looked out the carriage window, her heart racing. The city was upon them. Their carriage mirrored others moving swiftly through San Felipe, carrying passengers eager to be home for supper. Despite the noise, Charles and Maud slept on, their heads bobbing like marionette dolls. Benjamin sat next to Charles and opposite her. Was he still watching her? Shadows dipped in and out of the coach.

"What's that?"

Benjamin pointed to a broad stretch of dilapidated bricks and stones.

"Those are the remains of the old seawall," Charles answered suddenly, as if he'd been wide-awake all along. "Eons ago the notorious pirate Henry Morgan looted San Felipe and burned it to the ground. A massive fortress was built to protect residents from future attacks."

"A fool's wish," Benjamin said, amused. Louise glanced at him curiously.

"Indeed! Fires destroyed it anyway, along with the country's confidence," Charles replied, yawning.

"When someone wants something, no wall can keep them at bay," Benjamin added, but Charles wasn't listening. Louise shifted in her seat; a smile crept across her face.

The carriage barreled off Avenue Alfaro and their elegant French mansion came into view. Casa Bella Vista was where Louise was born and had spent all her twenty years. It was a grand house; she loved the twelve-foot ceilings and intricate tiled floors, the brightly painted frescoes and the cupola's rounded windows that were flooded with sun by day and bathed in moonlight at night. Charles had purchased the property for a song from a noble family who had all but abandoned it during the failed French canal efforts. It was his prized possession. But with the canal in financial transition, budgets had been cut and positions eliminated. He was fortunate to have kept his employment. The past few years had been leaner and the house suffered—the foyer needed a coat of paint, stones were loose in the entrance walkway, the roof needed repair. He worked long hours at the canal on the administration changes and kept himself preoccupied from sunrise to sunset. Tonight their street was empty except for one coachman waiting for his fare. The air was warm and salty when the gleaming glass-paned door opened. Rosa, their housekeeper, greeted them with slippers and hand towels. Short, stout, and stiff-lipped, her smile faded as Benjamin stepped into the foyer.

"Rosa, this is Benjamin, Don Pedro's grandson," Charles announced. "He will be staying with us for a few nights, attending to Maud and her asthma. Please see to his needs." He wiped his face and hands on the cloth with a sense of conciliation. "After dinner prepare the guest bedroom upstairs. We are all famished and tired as well."

"Sí, Señor Lindo." Rosa paused, looking perplexed. "Buenas noches," she said dryly, handing Benjamin a towel.

"Buenas noches, Señora. Gracias," Benjamin replied politely, touching the towel to his forehead. Rosa looked him up and down with suspicion. Louise could plainly read her thoughts: a working-class *mestizo* from the rain forest—a so-called shaman. Native Panamanians who embraced Christianity shunned shamanism and its culture, at least until their health failed and they could not afford the costly doctors' fees. Rosa had worried about Charles taking Maud to see an awa. She too pandered to her delicate little mistress.

Before dinner was served Maud said she was not feeling well and went directly to her room. The night air disturbed her breathing again. Louise instructed Rosa to boil sweet plantains for Maud to eat in bed. At the dinner table Benjamin ate nothing. He appeared to be listening closely to Maud's sporadic cough. When Rosa came out of the kitchen with Maud's supper he excused himself and followed her upstairs, leaving Louise to dine in silence with her father.

A second night of drumming and chanting began. The rhythmic sounds spilled out the open windows to the streets below. Passersby would stop and look up at the terrace in wonder, straining to see who was beating out the magnetic tempo. Eucalyptus and other strong herbs boiled in pots on the stove, the scent adding an atmosphere of mystery to every corner of the house. Charles, catching up on paperwork in the library, had shut his door to the ritual happenings. Louise sat in a corner of Maud's room. Her sketchbook on her lap, she dutifully took notes, as Charles had instructed, keeping track of Maud's treatments. But after a few pages she tired of words. No longer focused on the ritual, her eyes took in the smoothness of Benjamin's skin, his lean and graceful movements around the room, the intensity of his concentration. Her pencil began to drift, outlining the subtle curves and shades of his face in the mellow lamplight.

Though he seldom spoke, his face was quite expressive. There was an honesty and confidence behind his closed lips. He passed the carved mahogany settee in the parlor, the eight-foot gilded mirror by the front entrance, even the imported French dresser and headboard in Maud's bedroom, without noticing their luxury. The young shaman attended to Maud with a single-minded coolness. Louise sketched an outline of his profile in quick strokes. Every so often he caught her watching him, and she automatically scribbled a few words on the page. His eyes would linger a moment on her. How must she look with her unruly hair and bushy eyebrows? Charles's appearance in the doorway put an end to her musing.

"How is Maud feeling?" He strained to see in the faintly lit room.

"She's stable now, her cough has quieted." Louise closed her sketchbook.

"I've given her a tea to help her sleep," Benjamin said.

Satisfied with the answer, Charles went back to the library. Maud finally fell asleep with a low rattling in her chest, and Benjamin and Louise went into the hallway to talk.

"Your sister's spirit is willing, but the hostile forces surrounding her are strong." Benjamin tightened the bundle of herbs and picked up his drum. He showed no signs of fatigue, though he had little rest.

"But she is getting better—I can see that. It's just a matter of time." Crushed leaves tumbled out of Benjamin's sack onto the floor. They both reached down to pick them up and bumped heads. Pardons were promptly exchanged, and this time she didn't blush. He smelled like the rich earth from his village.

"I can't judge how long it will take. I only know Sibo's signs. So far I have seen a few, but not all."

Rosa had gone home for the evening and left tea and biscuits on the small table in the front parlor.

"You must be very hungry. Won't you have some tea?"

Benjamin accepted, though he confessed he could only help himself to tea during the ritual. They sat down at the table.

"I can't thank you enough for traveling so far from your home to help my sister. Father is very grateful." She leaned over to pour him a fragrant cup of hot tea, glad Rosa had not used the chipped china.

"Grandfather said it was a good time to test his teachings." Benjamin held the delicate cup with as much assurance as he did when selecting plants in the rain forest.

"Is it a tradition that's passed down only among family members?" Louise asked.

"Not always, but many times it's in the same family for generations. In my grandfather's case his mother was an awa."

Louise pondered his statement.

"But how does someone know if it's their calling?"

Benjamin sat back in his chair.

"I only know what grandfather told me. He said sometimes a child gets a mysterious illness that no one can cure. That's what happened to him. His sickness brought him near death in order to cleanse his soul—to wash away all that was bad and weak within him. It was part of his initiation." He massaged his right arm. "Grandfather says if the sickness doesn't kill you it transforms you."

She sipped her tea, wondering how this could be. "But what if he were to have resisted? What if he was unsure?"

Benjamin replied, "The spirits of a dead shaman call the chosen one out to follow the path. If they choose not to accept their duty to heal and help others they may suffer the rest of their lives...or die."

"That seems so extreme, so rigid. But the same did not happen to you."

"I was supposed to die in the fire with my parents. The Great Spirit pulled me out. I was found unconscious on the street a half a mile away from the house. No one knows how I got there." Benjamin touched the linen tablecloth, his eyes distant. "We had a room very much like this one…I don't remember the fire."

A loud crash from above startled them. Several thuds and the sound of breaking glass followed. Charles hurried into the parlor. The sound had come from Maud's room.

The three raced upstairs. When Charles reached for the doorknob Benjamin intercepted him.

"Sir, I should go in first. Spirits do not take kindly to intruders."

"*Spirits!* Someone has broken into my daughter's bedroom! Charles gripped the brass doorknob, his anger tinged with fear. Benjamin's hand was firm on his arm.

"Your life may be in danger…"

The ruckus stopped. Charles glared at Benjamin. His hand fell from the doorknob. Benjamin opened the door.

The tall narrow bookcase facing the bed had fallen and caught on the edge of the footboard. Books were scattered everywhere; torn pages danced around the floor, some stuck to the wall as if by magic. Maud's porcelain dolls lay smashed underneath the fallen books; shards of their gaily painted faces still smiled. Maud slept serenely, unmoved by the commotion. Neither the fallen books nor the dolls nor the bookcase had touched the bed. Chanting low in his native language, Benjamin found a path through the debris and sat down on the floor near the head of Maud's bed. A sliver of moonlight inched over to where Louise and Charles stood in the doorway. She could barely see Benjamin; his figure became a deep, shapeless mass, his intonations a haunting lullaby. Were there really spirits that caused the mayhem? How could he have known? Charles, trying to be stoic, took repeated steps back and forth, muttering something about Rosa forgetting to close the windows, the strong evening breeze this time of year…

Louise sank down to the floor in wonder. The house was so completely still that she became aware of her shallow breath, her fists pressed against her chest. Slowly her fingers unfurled listening to Benjamin and his song.

2006

New York City

THE CONFERENCE ROOM WAS STIFLING. Vents in these old loft buildings never worked well. The offices were as cold as a meatpacking warehouse, while the wide hallways and meeting areas remained morbidly hot. Sheri untied the Hermès scarf around her neck and stuffed it in the pocket of her wool suit. In the post-9/11 advertising world, budgets shrank to half their sizes and so did agencies. Aeon moved its offices from high-rolling midtown to the humbler Flatiron district, where rents were lower and ominous dust clung to exposed ceiling pipes. She gave up her corner office with sweeping views of the East River for a cell in the middle of the hall sandwiched between the CEO and the CFO. It didn't bother her as much as she thought it would. In fact, things that used to get her riled up at work had little effect on her these days. Liane dragged the meeting out with her usual strategic drivel.

"The 2006 Response Rate Trends Report helps us develop comprehensive, results-oriented campaigns…improve overall marketing performance…increase JetSet sales, leads, traffic…"

PowerPoint screens flipped page after page of numbers while Sheri drew black inky doodles in the margins of her yellow legal notepad. Elaborate swirls, squiggles, and stick-figure designs eventually took over the whole sheet of paper. She had lost her patience for long meetings and spent more time doodling than taking innocuous notes, even at a presentation as important as this one. The drawings reminded her of the original infamous logo she had designed for JetSet. Unbeknownst to Sheri, the logo prompted uproars from a native tribe who claimed it was a revered symbol in their culture being used for profit. She quickly made revisions while JetSet apologized with a sizable donation to an Indian college fund. Then it had seemed like just a freak accident, and she didn't give it a second thought. The angry letters stopped years ago. Why was she thinking about them again? Zig.

She masked a yawn and checked the time on her Black-Berry—over an hour already and they had not gotten to the creative portion of the meeting. Across the cherrywood table sat the three Brits—Thom, Jude, and Karston. They were slender men with pallid complexions, around the same age and height, wearing navy blue suits and flat expressions. JetSet Airways pins shone on their lapels. Sheri knew this account inside out. It was her ad campaign that catapulted the tiny boutique airline to fame, more than tripling the budget in less than five years. Karston Roberts, JetSet's senior brand manager, was at the far end of the table. He scratched his nose and avoided her eyes. Karston had tried to kiss her after too many hours together on a shoot in LA and too many drinks. Even when he was drunk he was a humorless bore. Sheri twirled her pen between her fingers. She had no intention of mixing business with pleasure, no matter what the cost. Now, despite the fact that Aeon had put JetSet Airways on the map, they were thinking of taking their business elsewhere. The first telling sign was the audit. Quiet little men with calculators sat in their offices every day for weeks amidst rumors of misappropriation of funds. Aeon's president blamed the CFO and fired him, hoping to quell the suspicions. Then came Karston's amorous advances. It was hard to blot the embarrassing scene from her memory; JetSet was the agency's biggest account. If they lost it half their revenue would be gone. Staff would be cut drastically, and Sheri could be among them. Other agencies were invited to pitch the business. Most were of no consequence; Ogilvy was the one she was concerned about. She glanced at Roland and Marcus. Their legs were casually crossed but their jaws were clenched. Everyone felt the pressure. She had been up half the night editing spec TV spots for the meeting. At 2:00 a.m. she took the executive committee—Roland, Aeon's senior VP account director; Liane, senior VP media director; and Marcus, the president and CEO—through the new campaign. It went over budget but the work was outstanding. Marcus and Roland were ecstatic, convinced that Aeon would win them over again. Sheri wasn't so sure.

The door creaked open and a stream of light entered the dark room. Grace, Sheri's new assistant, crept in to hand her a note. Sheri strained to read the tiny handwriting.

Jacqueline Dodson from Excelsior Prep called and wants you to come to the school ASAP.

Sheri looked around the table. The others were still in the marketing twilight zone. She got up and walked calmly to the door. Once outside she quickened her pace. Grace met Sheri halfway down the hall.

"What happened? Is Zig okay?"

Grace walked backward toward her desk, cracking her knuckles.

"I'm not sure…She wanted to talk to you. I told her you were in a meeting…"

Sheri stared at the note in her hand. What did he do this time? Did he get into a fight? She imagined him rolling around on the rubber matting under the monkey bars, wrestling with a red-faced kid. Did someone tease him? Bullies called him "asthma boy" and "maskhead" when he went to the nurse for a nebulizer treatment. *Come to the school ASAP.* Her head pounded. Grace waited, her nervous eyes searching Sheri's for orders. On Grace's desk a red candle shaped like a devil had *I've Got the Hots for You!* printed across its belly. Next to it was a clock radio with a huge neon-colored digit display. 11:48 A.M. Excelsior Prep was just over the bridge, less than half an hour away. She could make it back in time for lunch with the client. Roland would have to present the creative campaign. Sheri dashed to her office with Grace at her heels.

"Tell Marcus and Roland I had an emergency—I'll meet them at Gotham for lunch. Call the school; say I'm on my way. Cancel my 4:00 dental appointment and check my calendar to reschedule early next week."

She snatched her handbag from under her desk and adjusted the straps on her sling-back shoes. Through the grime on the wide loft windows clouds in the sky appeared thick and muscular. Grace was still standing in her office. Sheri gave her a deadly look and she scurried away.

She took a gulp of her hours-old Starbucks coffee and blotted her lips on the back of her hand. Lack of sleep was wearing on her. Not having to present to Karston gave her some relief. Now she just had to endure him through lunch. The screen saver on her computer flashed a slideshow of Zig making funny faces. She grabbed her coat and umbrella off a hook behind her door and rushed to the elevator. He had gone too far this time.

A cold mist started to blow when she hailed a cab on Broadway. Things had gotten out of hand these past few years. Zig could act wild and rebellious. Maybe she let him get away with too much. At times she even admired his stubbornness. He was fearless and she encouraged it. However, letting an obstinate ten-year-old go unchecked is asking for trouble. "Conduct Needs Improvement" and "Unsatisfactory" were written all over his last report card. How could he get straight As and be such a bother? Now it was raining. She put the window up and became instantly overwhelmed by the sickly sweet car deodorizer dangling from the rearview mirror. The windshield wipers swooshed and blurred the bodies of people huddling under umbrellas into a melancholy smear.

This all started with Zig's crazy Indian fantasies. Dr. Breen was wrong—it was not a boyhood phase that would eventually peter out. On the contrary, as Zig grew older he became more obsessed with it. Wearing sandals in the dead of winter… the pouch made out of a lost leather glove to collect feathers and stones…the constant search for some ulu stick that drove Leatrice crazy. Zig would wander into remote areas in Prospect Park looking for broken tree limbs to drag home. He fought fervently to keep his so-called ceremonial sticks, demanding that Sheri let him whittle the bark off with a penknife. Watching him hop up and down in bed to demonstrate his tribal dances was sweet at first. When it didn't stop she began to worry. She had to find out where this was coming from, and soon. The JetSet review that bogged her down for months was coming to a close. Funny enough, just today she remembered the issue with the old logo…

She made good time to Borough Hall; no major traffic. It was just 12:15 p.m. The sidewalks were spotted with trial lawyers hunting down their lunch. Sheri pushed open Excelsior's ornate brass doors. Mrs. Johnston, the usually jovial receptionist, greeted her with solemn civility and directed her to the headmistress's office. Sheri's heels clopped on the marble floor, the hollow sound echoing in the Ancient Greece–inspired moldings. Around a column she caught sight of Zig slouched on a sofa opposite Jackie's oversized, intimidating desk. He twisted the hem of his polo shirt, his eyes lowered. Jackie was busy writing in a notebook. A polished woman in her early sixties, Jackie had been head of an elite school in North Carolina before coming to Excelsior a year ago. Excelsior wanted to change its image to attract more families from the city, bolstering a pseudo Ivy League exclusivity that Sheri was not thrilled about. Jackie never married and had no children. In her pale green tailored suit she appeared as frosty as a mint julep. Bifocals magnified her watery eyes. She peered over them when Sheri entered the room.

"Sheri! Thanks for getting here so quickly. Please, sit down."

The office was spacious and furnished with tasteful antiques, yet it exuded a pretentious lifelessness. Sheri walked to the stiff, upholstered sofa thinking how ironic it was that Zig ended up in a snobby private school just like the ones she'd felt out of place in as a child. She wasn't zoned for the one decent public school in the area, and private schools were her only resort for the small classrooms, afterschool programs, and peace of mind she desperately needed.

"Hey, sweetie!" She reached out to squeeze Zig's hand. He pulled away, his lips tight. "What's going on?" She didn't like the way he looked.

"During recess today there was an accident in the playground that involved four children. Zig, would you like to tell your mother what happened?"

Not a word came out of his mouth.

"All right then. Some of the children were playing pretend games—I believe it was based on that TV cartoon called Avatar, wasn't it, Zig?"

Again he was silent.

"Yes, that's it. Anyway, Zig called their game ridiculous and proceeded to teach them *his* game. They sat away from everyone in a circle with Zig in the middle. The children were quiet for some time. The teachers thought they were playing cards or telling stories. Then a girl, Francesca, got up and started screaming, waving her arms in a panic. When the teachers rushed to help her, Francesca fainted and fell to the ground. An ambulance took her to the hospital. Her parents were notified and are with her now."

Sheri looked from Jackie's concerned expression to Zig's closed face.

"We are not quite sure what happened; the other three children won't talk. Zig hasn't told us anything, either. We're hoping you can help us find out what went wrong." Jackie leaned forward on her desk, folding her hands.

Sheri was taken aback at her insinuations. "Why do you think Zig had anything to do with her fainting? It could happen to any kid!"

"Yes, but the game was his idea. Francesca fainted while they were playing together. We're just trying to understand why. She's never fainted before and has no medical condition. Her parents are looking for answers. We don't know what to tell them. I'm hoping you can talk to Zig."

The headmistress was obviously shaken. Her perfectly coiffed, beauty-parlor-silver hair gave her an embalmed look. Sheri leaned down to Zig's ear.

"What sort of game were you playing, Z?"

He fidgeted in his seat. "We were just pretending. Only real pretending."

"What's 'real pretending'?"

Zig paused and swung his feet at the headmistress's desk. "It's like remembering the past, that's all."

"How exactly do you play 'real pretend'?" asked Jackie in a lyrical yet prickly voice.

Zig threw up his hands. "You just *concentrate!*"

"Con-cen-trate…" Jackie jotted down a few more notes. "On what?"

"On who you are and who you've been, that's all."

There was an awkward silence. Sheri feared it might come to this one day. It was just a matter of time before he introduced some of his wild ideas to his schoolmates. Why did she put off the talk she planned to have about his imagination, to remind him that not everyone would appreciate his stories and musings? The headmistress flipped through pages in her notebook.

"I recall Ms. Herman telling me about your fantastic Indian stories."

Shit. Sheri held her breath.

Zig looked up at Jackie. "What did she say?"

"Ms. Herman said your colorful accounts of indigenous life were somewhat accurate, but your outbursts about actually being an Indian were quite disruptive to the class." Jackie read from her notes.

Zig grumbled.

"Excuse me?"

He didn't answer. Jackie pursed her lips.

"So tell us, Zig—how do you play the real pretend game? You were sitting on the ground with Francesca, Daniel, Kwami, and Jacob…"

Silence.

"Zig?" Sheri prodded him gently.

"She yelled at me!" He cried, finally looking at Sheri. His mouth tightened again. Jackie continued taking notes.

"I'm sorry if you thought I raised my voice!" Jackie replied, as genuine as NutraSweet. "Let's just try to get to the bottom of this. You were concentrating…How do you do that?"

He hesitated for a moment. "We all closed our eyes and crossed them in our head until."

"Until what?"

"Until we saw something."

The headmistress stopped writing. Sheri twitched in her seat. Where was he going with this?

"Daniel was the first to remember. He said he was a Viking soldier and his armor was heavy and stinky."

Jackie glanced at Sheri.

"What happened to Jacob?" said Jackie.

"Jacob said he was a tall man with a long beard wearing a turban and a long white robe. He said his sandals were funny looking and hot sand kept getting on his toes."

Zig twisted the middle of his shirt.

"And Kwami?"

"Kwami was in a barn with lots of horses. He said it was real hot and hard to breathe, said he had a hammer and was hitting something hard."

"Hmm. And you were?"

He shifted his eyes. "I was an Indian sitting by a fire, singing songs."

A pained expression came over his face, frightening Sheri. She put her arms around his shoulders, pulled him to her. Jackie's hand moved swiftly in neat, even lines.

"What about Francesca?"

He was silent again.

"Go on…" Sheri tried to smooth his springy hair.

"She didn't say anything. At first."

"No?"

"She just sat there with her eyes closed. Then she started moving like this." Zig rocked from side to side.

"Did she say anything at all?"

"Well, after a while she was going "Ahhhh…ahhhh…" really low, and then she started getting louder."

"And what did you do?" Jackie grilled him.

"I said, 'Francesca, who are you?' But she kept on moaning. Then she started screaming *Vesuvius! Vesuvius!*"

The headmistress put down her pen.

"We tried to stop her but she ran away screaming and swinging her arms and smacking her head and pulling her clothes." Jackie pushed away from her desk, sat stiffly in her chair.

"Francesca's face and arms were flushed when she fainted. One of the teachers heard her cry out. She recognized her words as something in Italian."

Zig pulled on his shirt. "It was Latin. Francesca said, 'Hercule serva nos,' which means, "Hercules, save us."

Jackie raised her eyebrows.

"Do you know Latin?"

Zig looked away. He sunk back into the sofa. *What was this?* Sheri stared at him, trying hard not to show her surprise in front of Jackie. *How did he know that?*

"Zig, I'd like to speak to your mother for a moment. Would you please wait outside in the lobby? We'll be just a few minutes."

Zig sauntered out of the room, eyes downcast. The heavy door closed like a vault. Sheri prepared herself for Jackie's reaction. Her son was just a witness to this unfortunate event; he didn't give rise to it. Zig made up a game and shared it in the playground. He didn't touch the girl. He didn't hurt her. It wasn't his fault.

After a pregnant pause, Jackie spoke.

"Zig has quite an imagination. Does he play that game often at home?"

Sheri thought about the many times Zig talked about his Indian life. She straightened the raincoat on her lap.

"No, I…I'm quite surprised. I don't know what to say."

Another pause.

"Sheri, at the last parent-teacher conference Ellie noted that she discussed Zig's behavior with you." Jackie's blue-veined hand removed papers from a folder with Zig's name written in bold letters.

"Yes, she did. I thought it was under control." Sheri felt the skin on her chest tighten. Jackie continued, "As you know, Zig is one of our top fifth-grade students. He completes his homework on time, received As on most of his class projects, and scored high on the ERBs. You must be very proud. However,

Ellie says she still has trouble getting him to cooperate with class rules. I think he has a problem."

"What sort of problem?" Sheri crossed her arms; the dead air in the room burned her throat.

"He repeatedly disrupts the class to ask questions, sometimes to the point of harassing Ellie on various subjects but particularly history and social studies. Then at times he is reluctant to participate in class. Some days he sits at the tables with classmates in the dining hall. Other days he sits alone on the floor in a corner, away from everyone." She slid the papers back into the folder. "How are things at home?"

Sheri thought about the crunch she had been going through preparing for the JetSet presentation—the late nights, the weekend meetings…

"I've been working long hours at the office lately, but he hasn't been acting any differently at home." Her phone started vibrating in her handbag.

"We're a bit concerned. That's why I'd like Zig to see Bruce Schumer, the school psychologist. Bruce will get to the root of what's going on and help him work on his behavioral skills. Zig is a very bright young man—we want him to reach his full potential at Excelsior."

"Jackie, we're talking about a children's game here. It was clearly make-believe. Maybe Francesca is the one who needs to see a psychologist!" Sheri was defensive even though she was starting to have doubts about what constitutes a fantasy.

"I understand your concern; however, a child is in the hospital and Zig was intrinsically involved. As headmistress I need to be assured that nothing like this will ever occur again. Bruce is quite competent, patient, and caring. Everyone will benefit from the evaluation."

Sheri dug her heels into the gaudy flower designs on the thick piled Victorian rug. Jackie was not letting up. She had to appease Francesca's parents with something. Sheri felt trapped.

"It's the right decision, I assure you." Jackie picked up the receiver and pressed a button on her phone. "Margaret, would you set up an appointment for Zig Lambert to see Bruce this afternoon? And please tell Bruce to drop by my office when he's done." She placed the receiver back on the handset. "I would encourage you to stay, Sheri, but parents are not allowed to sit in on evaluations. It's school policy."

Her head was killing her. Sheri's cell buzzed again. The glow on the screen showed two missed calls—no messages. It was almost 1:00 p.m. Damn! If she left now she might get to Gotham before the entrées arrived. She would deal with the school later.

"I have to leave. Can Zig go back to his class now?"

"It's been a hectic morning. I so appreciate your taking the time to come in." Jackie walked over to a tall bulletin board and studied a tacked-up schedule. "They're in the middle of science lab right now. He can play outside until class is over. Bruce will meet with Zig by three this afternoon." Jackie held the office door open while Sheri collected her belongings. "I'll be in touch with the results of the evaluation."

"I'll be expecting your call."

Sheri went out into the stone lobby, glad for the fresh air. Zig was spinning around in the piazzalike open space; his light feet made no sound on the solid floors. At the back of the lobby a foyer led to the courtyard playground. It had stopped drizzling. The playground was empty except for a maintenance worker sweeping up leaves under the swings.

"Honey, I have an important lunch appointment. We'll talk this whole thing over tonight."

"She yelled at me, Mom. I hate this school."

"We'll discuss that later—"

"Everyone is so stupid. They don't know shit." He kicked a soggy soccer ball against the courtyard wall.

"What!" Sheri looked around to see if anyone had overheard him. She grabbed his wrist and pulled him aside.

"Don't ever talk like that again, you hear me?"

"You say it. I hear you on your cell phone."

"We're talking about you right now! You better straighten up and cut the crazy games, okay?"

He kept kicking the ball into the brick wall; it thumped and rolled back to him like a rotten cabbage. Sheri yanked on her coat and shook out her umbrella.

"What is it with you? Why can't you just play like the other kids?"

"Their games are about nothing but bogus superheroes."

"You like that Airbender Avatar!"

"It's a *cartoon*. The story's okay—a boy with powers—but it's not a true story. I was trying to show them how to use their own powers."

Sheri watched him dig up a stone with the tip of his sneaker. The late October wind raked through his wild hair. He looked like a regular ten-year-old, but he spoke like no one she had ever known. She couldn't wrap her mind around it just yet.

"I've gotta go, Zig."

"You always gotta go." Zig stomped on the soccer ball until it cracked.

"I promise to be home early tonight."

"Will you tell me a story then? A true story?"

"I will. Promise."

"Promise promise?"

"Promise promise. Leatrice will pick you up. I'll see you at home."

TUCKED AWAY AT THE END of a long hallway on the second floor was the school psychologist's office. Bruce Schumer sat reading a typewritten transcript while he sipped his twice-warmed mug of coffee. He looked closely at several paragraphs before turning the page. His office faced the courtyard playground, making it quieter than the offices that overlooked the busy two-way traffic on Adams Street. Between reading the report, he glanced out the window at a boy in an orange shirt kicking a dead soccer ball into the side of the building. The hollow thud was almost rhythmic, the kicker's movements precise and steady. When the thumping stopped, he looked out the window and the boy had gone. A few minutes later the boy in the orange shirt walked into his office.

"Hey, Zig! That was you out there in the playground smacking that old soccer ball."

Zig looked at the sun-faded Monet posters on the wall in the narrow office.

"Ms. Dodson told me to play outside until science lab was over. Then she said you wanted to see me."

Bruce searched the boy's distant eyes.

"Yes…I'd like to talk to you, Zig. I have just a couple of questions to ask. It's not a test or anything ugly like that, and you won't be graded. So you can relax."

Zig had no reply.

"Okay! Sit anywhere you like. Would you like some water or juice?"

"Just water, thanks."

Bruce stood up, a tall, lanky man with large hands and feet and a gentle nature. His shoulders were slightly rounded from bending down to meet kids and most adults somewhere midair. He grinned at Zig.

"Water it is. I'll be right back."

The pastel walls and landscape prints gave the narrow room a cozy atmosphere. A loveseat sofa was next to the psychologist's desk, which fit exactly into the tight space under the sole window. A leather director's chair stood opposite the sofa. Zig sat down in the chair and placed his arms lightly on the armrest, his feet dangling a bit above the bare wood floor. Jackie's southern accent was heard trailing out in the hallway. *Francesca's mother just called. Franny is okay. She came to an hour ago and doesn't remember anything. She'll have a CAT scan in the morning. Is Zig in your office now? Good. Let's get to the bottom of this."*

In a few moments Bruce walked back to the office looking distracted.

"Here's your water!"

He handed the cup to Zig and folded his body into the swivel office chair. He shuffled through the pages of the report he had been reading, and said,

"You're in the fifth grade now, right, Zig?"

"Yes."

"How's school this year? You've been here since kindergarten."

"Preschool."

"Preschool too!"

He turned over a couple more pages.

"Wow! Almost seven years! How do you like your teachers?

"They're okay."

"Fifth grade is a different ball game. Most kids complain there's way too much homework. But you seem to be doing really well in Ms. Herman's class—all As on the last report card. Think the work is challenging enough for you?"

Zig shrugged. "I dunno. I guess so."

"The reason I ask is because sometimes if the work is too easy a child gets bored. And when he's bored he does things he might not ordinarily do just to avoid boredom."

Zig fell silent again. Bruce turned to his report.

"I have here a copy of the discussion you had with Jackie and your mom today. It says you and four friends were playing a game of 'real pretend' during recess, a game that you—"

"What's a psychologist?"

Zig was looking at a metal plate on the door with the words Bruce Schumer, Child Psychologist engraved on it. Bruce exhaled and leaned back in his chair.

"What's a psychologist…well, Zig, a psychologist is someone who studies the inner workings of a person's mind—mostly their emotions and behavior—and tries to understand why they do the things they do."

Zig thought for a moment. "So if you can understand why a person does what they do, that means you believe the reason why they do the things they do, right? You believe in them."

"Well, sort of. I guess you could say that, though I've never quite put it that way."

Zig swung his legs. Bruce chewed on the end of a pencil.

"So, tell me about this game, 'real pretend.' It sounds very interesting. Can you teach me how to play it?"

Zig eyed him and shook his head. "It's too hard a game for grown-ups to play."

"Really? How so?"

"They have way too much stuff going on in their head."

"What does that have to do with playing the game?"

"In 'real pretend' you have to forget everything so you can remember who you are and who you've been."

"Hmm, why do you suppose that's true?"

Zig mused. "I don't know."

Bruce gazed at the bushy-haired little boy with the shirt that was too long in the sleeves. He nodded and spoke aloud, as much for his benefit as for Zig's.

"Makes a lot of sense. Kids can play 'real pretend' because they aren't so stuck on their thoughts and what people think of them yet. They can easily free their minds and become more… receptive. Yes, I understand completely." Bruce leaned forward in his chair toward Zig. "Now, be a sport and tell me exactly how the game started."

Zig relaxed a bit in the chair. "Well, Jacob, Daniel, Francesca, Kwami, and I went behind the basketball court. It's pretty quiet there. We sat down in a circle and I told them to close their eyes and then cross them."

"Cross them? Why would they cross them?"

"Because when you cross your eyes you can make both eyes one. It makes the game work faster."

Make both eyes one. Bruce pulled up to his desk to jot down some notes. "Go on."

"Then I said, 'Picture yourself when you were five years old, then two years old, then the moment you were born, then when you were growing inside your mother's stomach, back to when you were just a speck, then make the speck disappear. After that I asked, 'Who are you?'"

The psychologist stroked his chin, wondering if this was some kind of hypnosis. "Jackie's report said Daniel spoke first—"

"He was a Viking soldier."

"Interesting…was he turning red or having trouble breathing?"

"I don't know. My eyes were closed."

"What about Kwami and Jacob? What happened after they said who they were?"

"Everyone sat still."

"But Francesca had a different experience."

Zig said nothing.

"Why do you think that was?" Bruce asked.

Zig scratched the back of his head. "Well, everyone has so many lives. Thousands and thousands of them. Right now, everything you do and even think shows up in your next life. For reasons you already know but can't remember."

Bruce nodded. *This was a fifth grader? Where did he get these ideas from?*

Zig drank his water and continued. "I think Francesca forgot she lived when that volcano erupted—"

"Mount Vesuvius," Bruce offered.

"Yes, that's the name. She brought back to her mind that time in her life."

"It must have been terrifying for her. She fainted in the playground."

"But that's just it—she's still here!" Zig gripped the armrest. "Nothing really happened to her, back then or now. She's here again, this time in Brooklyn."

"So you're saying…"

"It's just like a dream! A very, very, very long dream. We keep dreaming these different lives and adventures until we wake up."

"Wake up?"

"Then we don't have to be thousands of different people doing a thousand different things anymore."

Bruce put his notes to the side. He stared at the boy.

"Zig, do you belong to a church?"

"No."

"Have you had any religious instruction?"

"Er, no, just swimming and tennis."

"Yet you believe in God?"

Zig jerked his head back. "I don't have to be taught what to believe. I know what I know!"

Bruce massaged his jaw with his big hands. There was one question he was eager to ask.

"What about you? Says here you were an Indian man—"

"Singing songs by a fire."

"Could you see your surroundings? Were you alone?"

Zig looked down at the floor.

"No, I wasn't alone, but everyone was asleep."

"Can you remember the song?"

"I think so…"

"Would you mind if I recorded you singing the song? For my report, of course."

Zig shrugged. "I don't care."

Bruce hastened to open a file cabinet under his desk and took out a small portable cassette recorder. He opened the deck and removed an old tape, rewound it on the end of his pencil, put it back into the machine, and closed the lid. Then he pressed the red and black record buttons and moved the cassette deck close to Zig. Zig closed his eyes and began to hum, then to sing, a soft, tuneless lamentation, his voice unlike a child or a man's. It was as if an instrument flowed through him from a faraway land.

At once the sound transported Bruce to another time and place. The air was thick with herbal smoke. He saw himself peeking through a slit in a tent, watching, listening to a tribal ceremony, taking notes on a damp piece of paper, the ink skipping, notes he needed for his dissertation…

When the singing ended Bruce stopped the tape. Fascinated, he looked at the boy. Zig was motionless.

"I'd like to talk to you some more about this, Zig. Zig?"

1899

Panama City, Panama

IT WAS PAST MIDNIGHT WHEN LOUISE and her father finally went to bed. Charles continued to grumble and cling to logic. Seeing that Maud was stable at once pleased and baffled Charles, and convinced him not to disturb Benjamin's service. Louise found it impossible to sleep thinking about all that had happened. She replayed scenes in her head, picturing Benjamin's rigid expression when he grasped Father's arm. At dawn she tiptoed from her room to Maud's doorway and found Benjamin sitting in the same place she had left him—his body statuelike, unflinching. Louise was afraid to enter the room when he opened his eyes.

"Are you all right?" she whispered.

His face glowed. "Everything was just like Grandfather said."

He was exhilarated and she sensed it, too. He spoke of how through his song he had communicated with the spirits that beset Maud well into the night. Louise hung on every word.

"Were you able to drive them out? Are they gone for good?" she asked, inching over to him.

"Only time will tell. Grandfather said I must feel it to know. There can be no doubt." Benjamin skimmed the disheveled room.

"But he taught you the way to heal."

"About herbs and songs—yes. He also told me that in Sibo's world there is no teaching or learning, because there is no belief. There is only certainty." He paused for a moment, then added, "When one becomes the flute, the song of healing can flow through to others."

She looked down at the scratched wood floor.

"I don't think I'll ever understand."

"But you do. Because you are here with me, you do."

He was looking deep into her again, past her eyes and face, past her insecurities and heartache and emptiness. He looked until she felt something real, a point of light inside her. She felt the gentle warmth from that small beam spread over her entire being.

MAUD'S PROGRESS WAS STEADY but slow, making Benjamin's stay longer than expected. He awakened in Louise a passion for drawing despite her father's claiming it a frivolous activity. Rosa got used to the smell of boiling herbs in the kitchen alongside her pots of stew. Charles reimmersed himself in his work at the canal. Even Maud, feeling better at last, resumed her natural state of coquetry, soaking up the attention of the handsome young shaman and making eyes at him when he rubbed her forehead with his tinctures. Louise made her medical journal entries, but more and more her descriptions veered from words to portraits of Benjamin. As the days passed they grew more comfortable around each other. Benjamin started recalling bits of his early childhood in the city before he went to live in his grandfather's village. While lingering in the garden one afternoon he had a sudden memory.

"I remember running along a thicket of bushes that led to paned doors...very much like the ones here." Deep in thought, he turned his head as if he saw himself run by, his expression softening into that of a child's.

"Perhaps our garden is similar to the one you grew up in. These courtyard designs were probably typical in San Jose, too," Louise said, thinking how fate took him out of the stifling atmosphere of colonial customs and society and brought him to a magical place. How lucky he was.

A week after the bookcase fell there was another strange occurrence. It was Independence Day, and Louise, sorry that her sister was missing all the colorful costumes and dance, returned early from the grand *fiesta patria* with silky ribbons and a bouquet of torch ginger flowers to surprise Maud. As she entered the house she was shocked by a queer sight: an enormous sea turtle was parked in the middle of the parlor floor! On clumsy legs the olive leathery creature stood its ground, blinking its ancient hooded eyes at her with a dreamy wisdom. She too blinked, frozen in her steps. How could it have gotten inside? Where did it come from? At that moment Benjamin came in through the garden door. He saw her confusion first, then the turtle. Immediately his excitement grew. He spoke rapidly, emphatically, while Louise tried to piece the meaning together:

a great honor…the sign he was waiting for…the Primal Mother is here…a reminder that She provides for all our needs…just as the turtle cannot separate itself from its shell, turtle magic helps unite heaven and earth…awaken the senses on both a physical and spiritual level…now he is seeing what he should…hearing what he should…sea turtles carry the symbolism of water…

Louise's head was spinning. "What is the symbolism of water?" she asked.

He took his eyes off the reptile and focused them on her. "It's the power of the female energies, of reproduction."

She watched as Benjamin knelt down and murmured gently to the turtle, thanking it for its message. She felt transported in his presence. He had a reverence for all of life that she found utterly alluring, tender and romantic. She wanted to stand closer to him, to touch him. He said he had to help the turtle get back to the sea. He coaxed the creature out of the house and she stared after him until he disappeared from sight. She was in awe of him. She was in love with him.

"what are you drawing?"

Louise shut her sketchbook.

"Benjamin! I didn't know you were there."

It was just after breakfast. He had come up behind her while she sat outside on the terrace, drawing. She'd thought she was alone.

"May I see it?"

"It's nothing."

"Please? I'd like to, if you don't mind."

"You won't like it…"

Louise opened the book to a half-finished portrait of him. She viewed it with him looking over her shoulder as if someone else had drawn it. She did not recognize the complexities, the intricate detail and emotion that flowed from her into the drawing. She saw not an idle sketch but a sensitive work of art. More than that, it was evident that she was in love with her subject. He stood behind her for what seemed an eternity. Her face became hot.

"Is this how I am to you?" he asked.

Louise opened her mouth but no words came out.

"Then I must show you how you are to me."

Sweet notes from his flute encircled her head. Gentle, lyrical notes danced into a sensual yet mournful melody. It seeped through her skin and flowed in her blood, its beauty making her dazed and dizzy with the notion that he, too, felt the same for her.

at daybreak the next morning Charles appeared outside Louise's bedroom impeccably dressed in a morning coat and matching waistcoat, dark trousers, white turnover shirt collar, and black floppy bow tie. His hair, moustache, and beard were neatly trimmed and smelled of pomade and bay rum.

"I have some urgent business to attend to in Balboa. I shouldn't be long, but tell Rosa not to expect me for supper." He removed a stack of papers from under his arm and straightened them on the hall railing. "I'll be dining with a colleague in town before returning home. Rosa will stay here with you and Maud until—"

"Oh, Father, Rosa needn't stay!" Louise cut in. She reached out to straighten his tie, sure that the colleague was a lady. "I am more than capable of taking care of myself."

"Rosa will stay." He brushed her hand away and tucked the papers back under his arm with a militant air. "How is Maud this morning?"

Louise turned her back. Four months had passed since her twentieth birthday. He expected her to be an exemplary young lady—when would he treat her like one?

"Well enough. She wants to have breakfast on the terrace."

"Excellent! My little Maudy! Can she take the stairs?" Charles gleamed beneath his spectacles.

"You needn't worry. Benjamin and I will help her down."

"Good! Now I can send that young man back to his grandfather. A rig will take him to Guabito by the end of the week."

Louise felt the color drain from her cheeks. "Friday is too early! What if Maud has a relapse? Do we want to be left to the whims of the local doctors again?" She wrung her hands. Would the dour hospital image change his mind? Charles gazed at his shoes, stroking his beard.

"No, I suppose not. But if she's well enough by Friday he will return to his village without haste." He fingered his timepiece through his suit pocket. "I must go. Tell Maud I'll see her before bedtime. Promise." He patted Louise on the arm and hurried away, shoulders bent as if he were some commander rushing off to battle. When would her life cease to be at his mercy? She kicked her door closed and dragged the bedroom curtains aside. Down in the garden Benjamin was trimming a vine of flame-colored flowers.

2006

Brooklyn, New York

RUSHING TO THE SUBWAY SHE RANG both Roland and Marcus several times—their cell phones went directly to voice mail. Her text messages went unanswered. Grace's line bounced to voice mail, too. Was the whole agency out to lunch? For Marcus and Roland to be unavailable was not good. In the dank station she reorganized the contents of her bag and picked invisible flecks of lint off her raincoat. Forty minutes late to the restaurant. Gotham had been her recommendation, too. She was sick of the starched power scene at Sparks and at Smith & Wollensky, the medieval slabs of bloody meat hanging over the edge of heavy plates. Hopefully the artsy Greenwich Village energy would help revive Aeon's declining image. There would also be a good supply of hip young women to keep Karston's eyes busy. She peeled a scrap of milky nail polish off her thumbnail and checked her cell for the umpteenth time, despite there being no signal underground. Why won't they answer? She wondered how the creative presentation came off without her. The international campaign was by far some of her best work—sexy, clever, right on target for JetSet's new branding. All night long she'd edited a barrage of speculative commercials; the booming music track still throbbed in her head. The No. 4 train pulled into Union Square. It was raining again. Outside, wet drops pelted her umbrella and sounded like a staccato dialect. *"Hercule, serva nos."* Zig quoted Latin. It's not offered until seventh or eighth grade at Excelsior. Water trickled in long stringy streams off her umbrella. What else did he know? She imagined him playing "real pretend," leading his friends in a game so real one of them actually passed out. She imagined the panic on the teachers' faces, pictured Zig scrambling off the ground, dazed, and then his stoic silence. Maybe he sees things other people can't see. To him this was not make-believe. Gotham's triangular awning came into view, prompting a sharp twist in her gut. Something had gone wrong.

Sheri strode into the airy restaurant filled with a stylish lunch crowd. The maître d' appeared just as she spotted Roland at the end of the crowded bar. Roland, a fair-skinned African-American man with freckles and velvety brown hair, and Sheri were the stars that won the JetSet account ten years ago. He was the kind of account guy every client wants on their business—smart, always available, and malleable. In the muted light his complexion appeared sallow; his freckles more like an outbreak of the measles. He was alone. Twirling a drink in his right hand, his cell phone pressed to his left ear, he listened intently to whoever was on the other end. Could they have eaten so quickly? Sheri moved past the tables toward his slight figure. Skilled waiters balancing bold plates of vertical food crisscrossed in front of her. Her eye caught the wasted gaze of a woman in a 1960s Diane Arbus photo. *Girl in a Shiny Dress.* Sheri tossed her bag on the bar and slid onto the stool next to Roland. He did a double take when he saw her and changed his posture.

"She just walked in. Yeah. Right. Okay. See you at two-thirty." He flipped the phone closed and laid it on the bar.

"That was Marcus. JetSet went with Ogilvy. We lost the account."

Roland picked up his drink and took a long swallow. His full lips twitched and darkened when he was stressed, and he compulsively pushed his glasses up on the bridge of his nose. His declaration hung in the air, as incomprehensible to her as Latin.

"Ogilvy! How…how could that be?" She glanced around to anchor her thoughts. "We were in the final round of—"

"Karston saw their presentation yesterday. Apparently Ogilvy blew him away. He raved about their test commercials. Said they would 'blaze the trail for the next phase of JetSet Air.'" Roland stomped the bar's brass footrest. "I knew it. I knew something was up. It was obvious when they canceled lunch. Ours was just a courtesy presentation."

Roland drained his glass. A cautious bartender found a lull in their conversation and wandered over.

"Would you like a drink, Miss, or would you like to see the menu?"

The last thing Sheri had was a swallow of black coffee.

"I'll have Absolut and tonic."

"Same here." Roland flicked the empty glass away from him. The bartender swept it somewhere under the counter and hurried to prepare their order. Sheri was speechless; the news cut like a knife. Moments later the bartender reappeared and placed two generous drinks in front of them.

"What was their reaction to the creative? The TV campaigns?" Her hand shook as she took a sip from her glass. The liquor felt good flowing down her throat.

"Jude and Thom were amused at times, but you could feel the tension. Karston just sat there; he never cracked a smile. Asshole." Roland snatched up his cell phone, scanned it for e-mail, and tossed it back on the bar.

"I called and texted you guys a million times."

"I got your text message—right in the middle of Marcus ranting like a freaking lunatic. What happened anyway? You ran out of the meeting like a bat out of hell."

"Zig got into some trouble at school. I had to get over there."

"Isn't he at a private school? What kind of trouble could they have? Shit, you pay them to keep your kid out of trouble. Marcus was pissed."

Sheri glared at him. "It's not like you guys never presented creative to Karston before. Those spots were award winners! They could easily sell themselves!" She steadied her elbow on the bar, ran nervous fingers through her hair. Marcus, with his skinny head and Nazi chin, couldn't care less about the creative process, about turning a slither of an idea into beautiful pictures and words. He hinged his bets on his close relationship with Karston. They both went to Stanford, played golf at the same country club, took vacations together, attended each other's weddings. She couldn't tell if Marcus knew about Karston's advances.

"What about the music? Did you tell him Sting agreed to do the final cut?"

Roland spread his arms.

"We couldn't get the CD player to work."

"What! I cued it up!"

"Marcus accidentally pressed the power button. The settings were lost and nobody knew how to reprogram the damn machine. Karston took a call on his cell while Marcus was scrambling."

Her eyes met Roland's. They both knew what fate had in store for them. A third of the agency's staff was devoted to working on JetSet business. Come Friday thirty or more people would be let go, Sheri and Roland included. All the stress she had been dealt today—at work, at Zig's school—was so surreal, so bizarre it was funny. She took another gulp of her drink. Laughter burst from her lips. It was infectious. Roland joined in.

"Looks like curtains for us, huh, partner?" He took off his glasses and rubbed his eyes.

"Speak for yourself." The vodka loosened her tongue.

"You won't survive the boot. You're not that cute."

"That's all right. I just have to be cuter than you."

"Karston won't be checking you out anymore either."

Sheri stopped laughing. "What's that supposed to mean?"

"Oh, come on. Everyone knows he's hot for you. He was all over you after the shoot at Celadon."

"You weren't there…you went back to the hotel."

"Aha! That's what you thought! On my way out of the restaurant I spied a cutie at the bar and hung around for a little while. When her date came back from the men's room I got up to leave in time to see Karston breathing down your neck."

"So why didn't you rescue me, Batman?"

"A multi-million-dollar piece of business? Unlimited expense account? Two-week shoots in LA? Hell, I wasn't gonna mess that up. You're a big girl. You could tackle him."

"I wish his effing wife would tackle him."

Roland threw his head back and howled. A group of Japanese tourists nearby turned to stare. He groaned. "This is just great…just fucking great."

She was frightened and at the same time relieved. The relentless grind was coming to a screeching halt. What was called "a living" had to be redefined whether she liked it or not. She had every reason to be concerned. There were huge credit card bills. Tuition. A mortgage. Health insurance costs. But for some reason instead of worry a weight lifted off her. She felt like she was floating, watching the drama unfold from afar.

Roland snatched his coat from the bar counter.

"I gotta get out of here. There's a two-thirty meeting on OfficeMax."

She started to say why bother but changed her mind. She needed some space.

"I'll stay and finish my drink."

"Whatever. See you at the guillotine." Roland went to pick up the tab. Sheri put her hand on his arm.

"I got it."

"It's about time! Thanks, Mother Teresa."

"Don't mention it, Judas."

He flashed a half-sarcastic smile, dug in his breast pocket for a Marlboro Light, and popped one in his mouth. She watched his slim silhouette glide along the bar and out the entrance. The lunch crowd had died down; there were just a few couples hurrying to order from the prix fixe lunch menu before it expired. The dynamic atmosphere abruptly changed to solemn, as if it were almost closing time. She called the waiter over and gave him her AmEx. This might be her last receipt to put in for reimbursement. Sheri finished her drink and headed for the door.

BLACK FRIDAY CAME AS PREDICTED. News of the JetSet Airways loss blew through the office like wildfire. Staff stumbled around in a paranoid daze, whispering in corners, awaiting the final doom. Everyone pitied her, rubbernecking whenever they passed her office, looking for signs of emotional wreckage. Late that afternoon Marcus charged into her office and shut the door. She barely heard his ill-rehearsed speech; her thoughts revolved around all the years she spent at Aeon, building the small, unknown shop into a powerhouse creative agency, only to watch it backslide into its original heap. In less than a year he would be begging her to come back to salvage the ruins. No way. She was done with Aeon, regardless of how bleak the job market looked. Marcus's dry lips moved but the audio was off in her head. She noticed how blank and rubbery his forehead was; how vacant his icy blue eyes were. He mumbled on about downsizing the department… some new executive search firm…six months' severance…

Sheri stood up from behind her desk.

"Save it, Marcus. Just give me what I'm entitled to and I'll walk."

He sprinted out of her office. The sense of liberation she had before was still with her. She opened her writing journal and scribbled all over the page, easing her tangled nerves with swirling spirals and hangmanlike stick figures, spindly trees, and snake-ish vertebrae. Drawing like this comforted her, reminded her of when she was a little girl lying on her stomach on the living room floor, squares of golden afternoon sun framing her as she drew, making the figures seem to leap off the paper. It kept her loneliness at bay, being absorbed in the detail and placement of every shape. Strangely enough, her very best ideas all started with these simple lines. Her eyes drifted over the neat white office. She was so used to her place here, the space she carved out for herself. At forty-six, could she work for someone new, learn a whole new company culture, new accounts, new bureaucratic BS? The thought was grim. And what about Leatrice? She'd have to let her go. There's no telling how long it would take Sheri to find a job. Tears welled up in her eyes, but she quickly blinked them back. She would never give anyone at Aeon the benefit of seeing her cry.

Sheri took a last look at her wall of metal friends—the unbending Andy and Clio Award statues, the One Show Gold Pencils, the winged man on the London International Award. Each stood gleaming under archaic track lights, reflecting years of endless nights in editing sessions and hunched over light boxes staring at photo slides. Zig's face floated by on her computer screen saver—fresh, alive, spirited. He was not just another trophy. Not just another title she could add to her name. Her love for him was the greatest joy in her life. It was the only thing that mattered.

The room dissolved. She pictured those mothers who went on field trips and carried pretzels and M&M's in Ziploc bags. Mothers who barely combed their hair and wore the same jeans every day, who knew all the supermarket guys by name, who faithfully dropped their kids off at school and picked them up at 3:00 P.M. Could she be one of them? Even for a little while? She got six months' severance. She'd get something from unemployment and could borrow from her 401K. Their lives would have to downsize drastically while she figured out her next move. But this was the chance she had yearned for—time to spend with her son. And with what was happening at school she needed to be available for him, physically and emotionally. By being at home more she could keep him grounded; then maybe he wouldn't have to escape to a fantasy world of "real pretend." Yes, at last she could sort out his inexplicable behavior, find the meaning behind his amazing stories. Though her mind sailed into rocky, uncharted waters, somehow it felt good. It felt right.

Sheri closed her journal, spun around to her computer, and pressed a few keys on the keyboard. In seconds her entire history at Aeon vanished into cyberspace. Soon after, the HR woman came by with flattened cardboard boxes for Sheri to fill and exit papers to sign. While she was reviewing the forms the IT guy snuck in to remove her computer. As soon as they left Sheri pushed the boxes behind her door, cleared out her file cabinets, bookcase, and desk and threw everything in the trash. She walked out of Aeon the way she walked in thirteen years ago—with a bag on her shoulder and a coat over her arm.

1899

Panama City, Panama

IN ANOTHER BEDROOM MAUD WAS GETTING DRESSED with the help of Rosa. She insisted on wearing her French silk gown with embroidered trim, a fancy dress usually reserved for dinner parties. After lying in bed listless and ill for weeks, she itched to get out the house. Louise started to knock on her sister's bedroom door when she overheard Maud's catty complaining.

"What's the use of having fine dresses if you can't wear them whenever you like?" Maud argued.

"But, niña, you don't want it to get soiled outside," Rosa replied weakly.

"I don't care! I look pretty in this dress! I'm sick of night-gowns and robes." Louise imagined her twirling in front of the standing mirror, admiring her reflection. As usual, Rosa submitted to her wishes.

"Aye, whatever you want, niña."

"No no no! Leave my hair out—in long ringlets. Only Louise has to always wear her hair up else it would be a big frizzy mess."

Louise narrowed her eyes and rapped on the door.

"Aren't you ready for breakfast yet, Maud? I'm famished!" She twisted the doorknob.

"I'll be right out!"

Rosa was placing the last ringlet behind Maud's ear when Louise opened the door. The sight of her painfully slim sister so formal and perfumed caused her to stop. Maud's eyes were as pale as her skin. Light, bouncy locks hung away from her small face, accentuating her pointy nose and pinched lips. She reminded Louise of the trumpet-shaped white lilies that grew wild in the bush, the kind with a clawing sweet fragrance that traveled for miles.

"Maud! That's your new silk dress!"

"So? I won't be cooped up in nightgowns another day." Maud shook her shoulders to puff up the mutton sleeves. Louise watched her sister fuss and tried not to grin.

"If Father saw you he'd—"

"Papi's gone on business. He'll be back late tonight." She pushed past Louise to the stairs and stopped short. Not only was Maud still weak, but she would surely stumble without her glasses. She refused to wear them.

"Just wait—Rosa and I will help you down."

Rosa's tight mouth appeared tighter than usual. In addition to her house chores she had the burden of policing the Lindo sisters and Benjamin while Charles was away.

Rosa and Louise walked Maud to the terrace where breakfast dishes were laid out. The early morning air was humid; the skies thick and overcast. Benjamin stood by the table with a cluster of purple foxglove in his hand. Maud blossomed when she saw him.

"What lovely flowers, Benjamin! Are they for me?"

Louise pretended not to hear the question. Out the corner of her eye she saw Benjamin give the flowers to Maud. Who were they really for?

"You're looking well today, Maud," he said, amused by her candor. Maud glanced sidelong at Louise. She took a whiff of the flowers before jamming them into the vase on the table.

"Why, thank you!" She spun around for his benefit, then glided waiflike into the garden chair he held for her. "I feel wonderful!"

"You should—you've had the very best doctor," said Louise, unhooking a mountainous fluff of dress that had caught on the leg of Maud's chair.

"It's not my doing. True healing comes when you allow it." He pulled out a chair for Louise and then sat at the table, his hands folded in his lap. His usually wavy hair was combed flat and smooth.

"Well, most times I had no idea what you were singing or doing, and some of those tinctures were just awful, but I never felt better!" Maud fingered her scant, golden-coiled hair.

"Of course you are." Benjamin seemed pleased. Was he enjoying her sister's unabashed admiration?

"Some café, niña?" Rosa brought a steaming kettle to the table.

"Yes, please! And I'll have tortillas with eggs and cheese and *hojaldras* with lots of sugar and—"

Benjamin stopped her.

"Maud, we've been successful so far, but you should continue the diet for this last morning."

"More boiled plantain! I'll die of starvation if I continue this way." Maud's tiny pout was like those painted on the broken heads of the dolls in her bedroom. The thought reminded Louise that Maud never knew about the fallen bookcase. It was promptly replaced with all the books stored as they were before, and the mangled dolls were hidden away in Louise's closet.

"Just one more morning," Louise said, "then Rosa will make *sancocho* for supper—your favorite! Won't you, Rosa?"

Rosa shot Louise a hot look. Even though her "little niña" was better she still struggled with the whole shamanic discipline. Maud stared at Rosa.

"Promise?"

"Sí, niña," Rosa purred.

Rosa set a large bowl of mashed plantains in front of Maud. Maud frowned then turned the conversation to dances, garden parties, fairs, outings, and the latest fashions. Benjamin listened to her idle chatter with the courtesy of a tourist. Could he be interested? No, Louise decided. She helped herself to another *hojaldra*, sprinkling sugar on top of the plump pastry. Never had she met anyone so detached and indifferent to superficial things. Maud ran a hand over her ruffled sleeve.

"What do you think of my dress, Benjamin? Louise and Rosa did not want me to wear it." Maud took a sip of tea and coughed.

"I've never seen anything like it," he said with a sly smile.

"It's imported from Paris," Maud said, puckering her lips, "made with the finest French silk." She coughed again. Louise spied a tea stain on Maud's bodice.

"Let's go in—it's so humid." Louise got up. Benjamin was looking at the sky. Dark clouds were beginning to swell, blotting out the sun.

"A storm is coming. We should bring everything inside." A gust of wind flipped a plate to the ground. Rosa rushed over to pick up the shards before they blew into the garden.

"You go help Maud. I'll clean up."

"But I don't want to go in! The fresh air feels so good." Maud took a deep breath and launched into a coughing fit. A breeze blew under her gown, lifting it around her ankles like a hot air balloon.

"May I escort you in?" Benjamin touched Maud's elbow, and she immediately changed her mind.

"You may!" Her pixie face brightened as he led her into the house. Rosa glared at Maud's back, muttering under her breath. Louise watched them walk off as she gathered the coffeepot and condiments in her arms. For a moment she wished she were

Maud, feeble yet bold enough to show her affections. Maud coughed once more, leaning heavily on Benjamin.

As the day wore on the sky turned dark and angry. Swollen clouds pressed down on the rooftops of homes as far as Louise could see. The sea and sky became one through the heavy mist, and a sickly green tinge coated the countryside. Birds disappeared; animals abandoned the fields for shelter. It was close to three o'clock. Louise worried about her father traveling in this weather. She turned to the windows overlooking the sea. The wind picked up, causing the fronds on the coconut trees to bend. San Felipe's climate was usually predictable; hurricanes were rare but not impossible. If the roads flooded Father could be stranded for several days. Once when she and Maud visited Aunt Esther in Colón a storm passed through the day they planned to leave. For two extra nights they stayed inside waiting for the storm to ease, listening to the howling wind and Aunt Esther's colorful tales of her childhood with their mother. They baked *panderas* and sang some of Mother's favorite Ladino love songs. The sensuous blend of Spanish and Hebrew, the passionate, lamenting choruses still moved her. How she missed her mother!

Between cooking and tending to Maud, Rosa kept drifting over to the window with great apprehension.

"This looks bad." She twisted the dishrag she held into a knot. Rosa had to be concerned about her own family. She'd agreed to stay here while Father was away, but early this morning there had been no threat of a storm.

"Rosa, I know you're worried about your children. Leave now before things get worse. Maud and I will be safe here. Benjamin will help us."

Rosa shook her head vehemently.

"No, Louise. I promised your father I would stay."

"That was before the storm clouds appeared," Louise argued. "If Father were here he would insist you leave right away."

"But I promised!" The sky rumbled; her resolve wavered.

"Rosa, go. Your family needs you. Father won't ever know."

A clap of thunder smacked the roof, surprising both of them. Rosa was as frightened to stay as she was to go. Louise was scared, too. Father would reproach them for having no chaperone, but she wanted to prove she could take care of herself and Maud. There was no time for propriety. Rosa should leave. It was the right thing to do. Louise took the dishrag from her and steered the reluctant housekeeper to the front door.

"There's not a moment to lose. Go!" She draped Rosa's shawl over her head and practically pushed her out the door. The solid woman sprinted down the empty street, dodging heavy raindrops that were beginning to fall. At once Louise regretted what she had done. Seeing Rosa leave reduced her to a small girl, terrified of what was brewing inside and outside her door. Where was the confident young woman who defied her father's rules? Where was Benjamin? He had helped Rosa close all the windows. She last saw him studying the drawings on Don Pedro's ulu stick, measuring portions of roots and plants, preparing special extracts. What about Maud? Could Louise rely on her not to tell Father? Would she act up with both Father and Rosa away? It was too late, Louise had made her choice. The three of them were alone.

2006

Brooklyn, New York

OUTSIDE AEON'S OFFICE ON PARK AVENUE SOUTH the brisk October air renewed Sheri's spirit. Halloween was on Monday, and all around her New Yorkers were gearing up for the city's grandest love affair with fantasy. The thought of taking Zig trick-or-treating thrilled her. She hadn't done that in years; fall was always packed with last-quarter ad deadlines. Climbing steep brownstone stoops, ringing doorbells with glow-in-the-dark paper witches taped to glass-paned mahogany doors, nibbling fistfuls of corn candy from goodie bags. What did he say he wanted to go as this year? This time she could enjoy finding his costume instead of the usual last-minute dash to grab whatever the stores had left. Maybe she'd even dress up—but who would *she* go as? Along Sixth Avenue costume stores appeared out of thin air. In one window an array of life-sized rubber masks lined the shelves, wearing expressions that seemed to heckle passersby: a cross-eyed pope; a brown-toothed Rudy Giuliani; Siamese twins of Cheney and Bush; the head of John the Baptist on a floppy golden platter. A block over she saw a sneering Joan Crawford mask, cigarette dangling from oversized red lips. No costume of a woman, interrupted; woman out of a job with no prospects. But she could go as a stay-at-home mom, a costume she hoped to wear long after Halloween until she got Zig under control.

Citibank was on the corner near the subway. She went to the ATM and took out five hundred dollars. She didn't remember the ride home or the walk to her building. When Sheri got to her floor, she noticed a few white feathers stuck in the carpet just outside her door. She unlocked and pushed open the door to see a cluster of downy feathers floating lightly along the parquet floor. Leatrice rushed over to greet her, waving a noisy hand vac.

"Zig, your mother is home!" she exclaimed, breathless. "Sheri, he is not behavin' 'imself at all dis evenin'!"

Flustered, Leatrice recounted her dilemma on the way to Zig's bedroom, punctuating her story with stops to suck up clumps of feathers.

"I went to fix his dinner and 'im say he wanted to play a little in his room first so I said okay. When I put 'im plate on de table and called 'im out he didn't come or answer. So I ran see what 'appen and dere he was sitting on the floor with him pillow ripped open."

Sure enough, Zig sat cross-legged in the middle of the rug in his room, absorbed in a task Sheri could not comprehend at first. Around him were billowing tufts of feathers mined from his pillow. Large feathers, separated from smaller ones, were grouped between his legs. Several long, thin cardboard strips were scattered around him. With a strip in his hand, he painstakingly glued feathers one by one onto the cardboard. A bunch of Magic Markers lay beside one completed strip of feathers colored with black, brown, and gold streaks. The room was blanketed with feathers.

"Mom! You're home early!"

"What's going on here, Z?"

"I'm making my Halloween costume."

Leatrice turned on the hand vac to clear some of the feathers from under his bed. Zig started to holler.

"*Stop! Stop!* I need those feathers!"

"Hey! What did I say about yelling—especially at Leatrice! Say you're sorry."

He pasted down another feather and tried to shake one off his thumb.

"*Now!*"

"Sorry, Leatrice."

Sheri stood there, feathers dancing around her feet, not knowing what to make of her ten-year-old's unusual mess.

"What are you making anyway?"

"My headdress." He blew lightly on a glued feather to dry it.

"Oh. An Indian headdress." She remembered Jackie's flat reaction to Zig's statement that he was an Indian, and how much trouble he got into for constantly correcting his teacher when they studied the Iroquois. *But Haudenosaunee is the right name, Mom. Iroquois means "real snakes." It's a nasty nickname they got from their enemy, the Algonquians. Ms. Herman can't even pronounce Haudenosaunee. She's so stupid.* These days he was a self-proclaimed authority on all indigenous groups.

"That's why you need all these…feathers."

"I need *white* feathers. I didn't have enough in my collection. But I did use some of the others." He showed her a strip of cardboard that had several pigeon, swan, and duck feathers he had gathered from around Prospect Park Lake stuck to it. In the center of the strip was a tall reddish feather.

"Where'd you get that one?"

"He saw it in the middle of de road comin' home from school. The wind blew it under a car and him wouldn't budge until he could reach it!" Leatrice said, perplexed.

"I'm just about done with the top part—then all I have to do is connect everything," he announced, hard at work.

The sight bewildered Sheri. "When you're done you're gonna have major clean-up duty. But first you have to eat."

"I'm not hungry."

She threw up her hands, too weary to fight him.

"All right. I'll put your plate in the fridge for now."

Leatrice ran around the living room and dining room picking up as many feathers as she could. Sheri stopped her midway.

"It's okay, Leatrice—I'll take it from here. Let's go into the kitchen for a minute."

Leatrice turned off the hand vac and placed it back on its charger in the pantry.

"Sorry about the mess, Sheri." She looked guilty.

"It's no problem at all, really." The awkward pause induced a change of subject. Sheri almost choked on her words. "Starting Monday I'll be at home full-time, Leatrice. I got laid off and I'm not sure how long I can keep you on. I just heard today."

"Oh…" The expression on her babysitter's face turned from shock to confusion to numbness. Sheri saw in Leatrice a swift reflection of her own ruin. It killed her to have to alter this woman's life as well. She felt tears coming on and quickly took the wad of cash she got from the ATM out her wallet, handing it to her as if it were a packet of Kleenex.

"Here's your pay for this week. Take Monday off, Leatrice. It's Halloween. I'll take him to school in the morning and pick him up at three. Of course you'll still get your regular pay. You've been like family to me and Zig for the past ten years, Leatrice. I don't know what I'll do without you."

Leatrice folded the bills and put them in her sweater pocket. Sheri could see her planning her future right there in the kitchen, figuring out which bills to pay and which could wait. She turned and looked behind her.

"I haven't told Zig yet. I need some time to figure this whole thing out."

She only nodded, looking off to the side.

"I'm so sorry, Leatrice."

"I'm sorry too," she said.

Leatrice turned mechanically and didn't seem to know where to go. She walked up to the coat closet, removed her jacket and tote bag, pulled on a fuchsia knit hat without saying another word. Sheri could barely hold herself together.

"If you need references please feel free to give out my phone number. I'll also give you a written recommendation if you like. You're the best, Leatrice."

None of that seemed to register with her; it was just a matter of time before her money would run out. Even so, she said what she always said every night for the past ten years.

"Have a good evening."

Leatrice left the apartment without a backward glance. Sheri shut the door and leaned heavily against it, her body caving under the emotional stress and strain. For the first time in a long while she cried. She was devastated. Losing her job was one thing. The thought of losing her caregiver—the one person she could trust and rely on, who was there every day, rain or shine, the humble woman who played a big part in helping raise her son—was more than she could bear.

"Mom! Where are you?"

She grabbed a dishtowel and swabbed her face.

"In the kitchen…are you done?"

She smoothed her hair and steadied her walk back to Zig's room. He was standing up facing his dresser mirror with his back to her, fastening the headdress to his head.

"No more playing, Z, it's time to—"

He turned around. A striking crown of feathers cascaded from his forehead onto his shoulders. Sheri blinked. For a second his face aged; a glint shone in his eyes like that of an old sage. He reminded her of a photography exhibit she'd seen long ago—dramatic sepia portraits of chiefs and shamans from various tribes around the world. Little bells, attached to the ends of some feathers, tinkled when he moved. A bluish hue seemed to extend from the feathers. He smiled, apparently pleased with her reaction.

"It's not exactly the same, but it's close enough."

SHERI PROMISED TO HELP ZIG make the rest of his costume after dinner. Reheating his dinner and defrosting a meal for her was completely unappetizing.

"Let's order in tonight, babe."

"Yayyyy! I want Thai food—sticky rice and pad see yu with chicken! Don't forget the extra hot sauce."

Every month Zig consumed a bottle of the hottest pepper sauce on earth. He fancied himself a connoisseur of the pepper species and their countries of origin. She even gave him a boxed set of international hot sauces for his tenth birthday. It was the first thing he reached for at every meal; he slathered it on eggs, popcorn, even candy bars. He said it killed germs in his body. Salt, black pepper, ketchup, and mustard were the only condiments she had as a kid; she couldn't get used to the burning sensation that he had such a passion for. She phoned in his order and chose kratieum prik thai, grilled shrimp, for herself.

The food came and Zig dived into his entrée with glee. Sheri joined his enthusiasm. This was a good time to tell him the news.

"Guess what, Z—I'm taking you trick-or-treating on Monday!"

He looked up from his plate wide-eyed, cheeks packed with brown flat noodles. "You're taking me? Woo-hoo! You got the day off?"

"Well, actually I'm going to be home a lot more often now."

"Really? What happened? You got fired?"

She shot him a glance. "Downsized. I got downsized from the agency. They lost some business and couldn't afford to pay me anymore."

Zig chewed and considered her choice of words. "So down-sized is kinda like being fired, isn't it?"

"No! Sort of. Let's just say I would still be working there if they didn't lose their biggest account."

He paused to swallow. "Did they lose it because of you?"

She told herself he was just curious. "Absolutely not. JetSet was on their way out—it was a long time coming."

"Oh." He looked at her and gulped some water. "Is Leatrice still gonna come every day?"

"For a little while. Then it'll be just me and you.

"Will you take me to school?"

"Yes, I'll be taking you to school."

"What about pickup?"

"Picking you up too."

"How about soccer practice and games? And swimming?"

"I'll be there."

"For how long?"

Sheri put down her fork. He seemed anxious, like he was carefully calculating her responses as if he had some kind of agenda. She stroked his cheek.

"For as long as I possibly can."

Zig nearly knocked over the table. He threw his arms around her neck, his saucy fingers tangled in her hair. She gathered his narrow body in her arms, not realizing just how much he missed her, how much she missed him. He never complained, spending every morning, afternoon, and most of the evening with his babysitter. Day after day, he held in his emotions for her sake. Sheri pressed her cheek to his. How would she ever be able to leave him again?

"Things will be different from now on, sweetie. Everything will be better."

Zig rubbed his eyes.

"You have to tell me a story tonight, like you promised on *Wednesday*."

"I'll tell you a story every night. Promise."

They finished eating dinner heartily; both agreed that take-out Thai food never tasted so good. Sheri even put a glob of hot sauce on some noodles and slurped them down the way he did. He helped her wipe off the table, and before shower time he picked up every feather from the far corners of the apartment, placing them in his special leather pouch with the rest of his collection.

"You'll still help me finish my Indian costume before Halloween, right, Mom?"

"We could save time and just buy one, you know."

He stuffed more feathers in his pouch. "Real Indians make their own clothes."

Sheri bristled, recalling the incident at school. But Halloween was all about make-believe; she had to oblige him. "Well, okay. What do you need?"

"I already got most of it laid out on my bed. Come see."

He took the dish towel from Sheri and pulled her over to his room. To her dismay, there on the bed was his brand-new wool sweater cut open down the front in a jagged line. The sleeves, on the floor at the foot of the bed, were hacked off to create a vest. The pillowcase that contained the feathers was ripped to shreds. Long tails were colored red and blue and brown, some were left uncolored. Sheri turned to Zig, who was beaming with pride.

"I just bought that Gap sweater for you last week!"

He looked at the butchered sweater and then back at her.

"Don't worry, Mom…I'm gonna wear it!"

FRIDAY WAS THE LONGEST DAY of her life. Sheri could hardly wait to swallow the one Ambien left in the medicine cabinet; the faster she could get to sleep and blot out her troubles the better. She sat cross-legged on Zig's bed, his cut-up sweater on her lap, threading a needle to sew cloth shreds onto the spots he marked with a pencil. Zig lolled back on his pillow as he directed the creation of his costume.

"The big ones go over the big dots—"

"And the small ones go on the small dots. I know, you told me three times already." Missing the eye of the needle, Sheri squinted and tried again.

"Good! Now you can tell me a story while you sew my costume."

She was hoping he'd be too tired or would just not remember. Sheri peered at her lounging boy. He had one hand behind his head, the other up in the air waving a fist full of strips like the tail of a kite. He was wide awake.

"All right. Once upon a time—"

"Wait! Is this a story about when you were little?"

"It's about when I went to summer ca—"

"You told me that one already. I want to hear a story when you were an *Indian* girl."

Sheri glanced at him. He was watching her, waiting for some grand recollection to leap from her mouth. "Don't confuse my story with yours, Zig. You're the Indian, not me."

He sat up on his elbows and jutted out his chin. "You're wrong. I came from you so you're an Indian, too."

Her patience was running thin. She'd had enough confrontations for one day.

"I'm not like you, babe. I don't remember any stories from—"

"Yes you do!" he yelled. "Anyways, you're a *"creative"* director. Make it up!"

There was no mistaking his sarcasm. Sheri threw his sweater aside.

"Just who do you think you're talking to? You better watch your mouth or you can forget about a story tonight." Her nerves were fraying fast. Zig lowered his eyes and dropped back on his pillow.

"Sorry, Mom." He pulled at the strips in his hand. "Could you tell me a story…please?"

She didn't want to think anymore. Her head hurt like hell. But a promise is a promise, and bedtime stories would be a good way to renew their bond. Sheri looked around the room for ideas.

"Once upon a time there was an Indian girl who—"

"What was her name?" he interrupted her again.

"Right, she needs a name. It wasssss…"

She moved Zig's costume off the top of her latest issue of *Vogue*. Tina Turner, *Sexy over 60,* was on the cover.

"Tina!"

"I don't like Tina—reminds me of bad-breath Christina in 5B. She's always flipping her hair around like this." He held the strips on top of his head and flicked them away from his face with his other hand, batting his eyes at the ceiling.

Sheri laughed and her body slowly began to unwind.

"Okay. How about…Ti-ma. Is that better?"

He paused. "Tima is a nickname. What's it short for?"

"It's not a nickname."

"Yes it is!" he argued. "It's only part of a name—like Tina and Christina."

Sheri's mind went blank.

Zig answered. "Tima is short for Tukitima."

When he spoke the name she liked it right away. It had an exotic, almost magical ring that sounded familiar, but from where? He curled his lips into a smug smile, the little know-it-all.

"Once upon a time there was a girl named Tukitima…"

Zig wriggled under the covers, at last content with the story's beginning. Based on the collage of magazine clippings he had tacked to the corkboard by his desk and taped all over the wall behind his bed, Sheri weaved a tale of an Indian girl's life in her village. There were photos of rain forests and waterfalls, rustic Indian dwellings, an assortment of pottery, tools, and weapons;

portraits of families and boys and girls from different nations. Tired as she was, Sheri surprised herself at the ease in which she conjured up the story; the more she imagined, the faster and easier the story came. Or had she heard it somewhere before?

"Tima's parents had died. Her grandfather raised her."

"*Great*-grandfather. He was *really* old."

"Well, she just called him Grandfather. He was short and feisty but also very kind and he let her roam in the forest. Tima didn't go to school—her grandfather taught her everything, as if she were a grandson instead of a granddaughter."

"Stuff like how to hunt tapirs and jaguars. She learned how to make hammocks from vines and cord bags, and bows and arrows from pejibaye wood. But there were other things he taught her, too…right?" Zig added. He fought a yawn; his eyelids grew heavy. The length of the day suddenly weighed upon Sheri, too. Her focus started to drift.

"Yeah, Tukitima was a tough little girl. One day she went into the rain forest alone and…and…something terrible happened…"

"What happened to her?" His glassy eyes shot open.

"That's the end of chapter one—we'll find out what fate awaits Tima in chapter two."

"Well, okay." He hugged his pillow and pulled the covers up over his shoulders. "Now you have all day to think about chapter two since you don't have to go to work."

She had happily forgotten her situation for the past hour or so. The bleak reminder came back to her.

"Right, I've got all the time in the world."

He fell asleep before she sewed on the final ragged piece of cloth. She held up the woolly costume to see if she missed any spots. The colorful shreds fringed the edges of the vest and bunched like a tail in the middle of the back. How symmetrical and striking the effect was. Zig lay sleeping with a couple of strips still clutched in his fist. Sheri gently opened his hand and slipped them out. She kissed his ear, breathing in his sweet, soft innocence mingled with the faint vinegary smell of stubbornness. He moaned and rolled to his side. She hung his costume on the clothes tree near his bed, stood up, and turned off the light. Amazingly, her headache had disappeared without the assistance of the codeine painkillers she had leftover from a root canal. She undressed, fell into bed and into a deep sleep.

THE EMERALD RIVER WATER GLEAMED; viscous ripples tingled between her toes, wrapped themselves around her ankles. Her foot splayed and distorted in the water, changing to prismlike shapes. She was certain they were there again, circling round and round, above her head. She kept her eyes on her feet and the shapes, fearing what she would see if she looked up. With every pore she fought the beautiful silken strands of the birds' call, fought the urge to lift her face…

In the middle of the night Zig's footsteps hurrying down the hall awakened her.

"What's the matter, Z?" She sat up quickly, swung her legs over the side of her bed.

"I'm wheezing."

Shoulders high and chin tucked in, he labored to catch his breath. She pressed her ear to his chest. The tight, squeaky noise was not unlike the sound she made as a kid, blowing into empty boxes of Mike and Ike candy or Red Hots. In her night table drawer was an extra inhaler—one of several she had in almost every room in the apartment. She turned on the lamp and took out the small plastic pipe that housed an aerosol cylinder, removed the cap on the mouthpiece, and shook the tube vigorously. She gave it to Zig. He put it in his mouth and pumped out two puffs of mist.

"Hold it in for as long as you can…one, two, three, four, five, six, seven, eight…"

At eight Zig exhaled, pushing all the air out of his lungs. Sheri watched closely for the result. *What could have triggered it this time? Was he catching a cold?* She touched his forehead—no fever. Maybe she should put him on the nebulizer. She listened to his chest again. A weak whistle eked through his pajama shirt.

"How do you feel?" She searched his face in the semidarkness.

"I'm okay now."

He gave her the inhaler and she pushed the cap on. She placed it back in the drawer, next to vials of Albuterol, foil packages of Pulmicort, and an empty prescription bottle of Prednisone. Albuterol is taken every three to four hours, Pulmicort twice a day, both in the nebulizer. *Take three Prednisone tablets by mouth in the morning and three in the evening for three days.* The dosages were engraved in her mind after last fall's harrowing ordeal. Zig had to be admitted to the hospital for four days to get his breathing under control. She spent sleepless nights next to him in a hard hospital cot. He was on steroid medications through January and missed two weeks of school. Worst of all, it came smack in the middle of her working on a grueling new business pitch. She vowed never to let that happen again.

"Why don't you stay here with me, Zig—just in case?" She would lie half awake the rest of the night anyway, listening for his footsteps.

"I'm all right, Mom. I'll sleep in my bed."

Sheri stumbled back to his room, tucked him in, and sat on his bed, watching the rhythm of his chest rise and fall. Should she call Dr. Breen? That would mean enduring his depressing stats: how much gunk was in the air, how many asthmatic kids he currently had in the hospital, how many more would be admitted before the end of the season. Then he would immediately start him on the meds again. Zig hated taking that stuff; he said it made him feel spacey and light-headed for months. She moved to his beanbag chair and rested her feet on the bottom of his bed, covering her legs with his dragon print bathrobe. The room seemed a bit chilly, but she was too exhausted to get up and change the thermostat. She wouldn't leave his side, not even with the slightest wheeze. She stayed until she heard birds twittering and the swell of traffic in the plaza circle. *Birds circling round and round, above her head…*Zig's breathing was regular, no sign of distress. She got up to make breakfast.

1899

Panama City, Panama

LOUISE WATCHED UNTIL ROSA was out of sight. Wind whipped through the brick-paved streets and along the plaster facades; hanging flowerpots creaked in neighboring balconies, and fragments of branches skipped into doorways. Louise pressed hard against the door, which slammed shut with such a force that Benjamin came rushing in.

"Is everything all right?" His eyes darted around the room.

"Yes, everything's fine." She turned away from the door, not knowing what to do with her hands. "I was concerned about Rosa and sent her home to her family. How's Maud?"

"The humidity is too much for her. I gave her a tonic to quiet the cough. She's resting now."

An awkward silence stood between them.

"I'm afraid supper will be up to us this evening. Rosa made *sancocho*. I'll see what else is in the pantry."

"I'm not hungry." His arms were motionless at his side. He looked taller and broader. His cotton shirt was loose; its sleeves rolled up to the elbows. The lace curtains stirred. Mother's figurines in the curio cabinet held their patient poses. She tried to smile, though she could not breathe. Benjamin looked at the floor.

"I can help you set the table. For later."

"Yes! Thank you." Heart pounding, she hurried over to the china closet, glad to be moving. "The dishes are right here."

His nearness was exhilarating. When she opened the china closet and reached inside the storm clouds finally relieved themselves. A deluge of water pelted the clay tile roof, followed by piercing cracks of thunder.

"Rosa!" Maud cried out in fear.

"I'm coming, Maud!" Jolted from her enchantment, Louise left Benjamin standing in the dining room and headed up the steps. She soon froze at the staircase window. A strong surge had thrown over the garden furniture, which began to tumble about.

"The chairs and table!" Louise yelled.

"I'll put them in the shed." Before she could protest Benjamin was out on the terrace. Louise raced up the long flight of stairs to see Maud crouching at the window. She wrapped her nightgown around her; the silk dinner dress lay discarded on the floor by the bed.

"Maud, come away from there!"

Maud gasped and pointed out her window. While battling the violent wind with the garden table in tow, a tree limb hurled from the sky, striking Benjamin on the head. He let go of the table and fell to the ground. The iron chairs danced dangerously close to him. Louise ran downstairs as if in a dream. The French doors were flung open; Benjamin lay wet and still. She rushed to his side in spite of the turbulence. Blood flowed from a gash on his forehead. The table had landed on him, pinning his leg to the ground. She began to push the table when he stirred.

"Louise!"

Benjamin struggled to free himself. Louise pushed with all her might until the table finally dislodged, tumbling away in the wind like a wild animal. Twigs and palm fronds scratched their faces; they crawled on hands and knees to the doorway. Benjamin inched inside first and then reached back to help Louise. Behind her a chair hurled toward the door.

"Give me your hand!"

Benjamin's powerful fingers dug into her forearm as he hauled her in. With a loud crack the chair lodged itself in the wooden moldings around the doorway. Benjamin shoved his back hard against the garden door and shut out the vicious torrent. His chest heaved; his trousers were drenched and ripped at the knee. She noticed another gash on the back of his hand. Panting, Louise slowly sat up on the floor. For a long moment they stared at each other, unable to speak.

"You're bleeding," Louise said, breaking the silence. She went to him trembling, the hem of her wet dress smearing spots of blood on the floor. Taking his stiff fingers in hers she examined the wound.

"Louise, where are you? Where's Benjamin?"

Maud's frightened voice pealed over the banister. Louise glimpsed her barefoot sister creeping down the steps, coughing along the way. She let Benjamin's hand drop and quickly stepped aside.

"I'm here, Maud. We're both safe," she called out. "Don't come down—it's wet and slippery! And stay away from the windows! Anything could break through!"

"But I can get the mop and…"

"Maud, stay in your room!" Louise warned. "I'll be right there!" Her sister did as she was told and hurried back upstairs.

"We need something to stop the bleeding."

She hurried to the kitchen and rifled through the cupboard drawers. She snatched up the dishcloth she'd taken from Rosa earlier. Benjamin followed her and sat on the housekeeper's stool with his wounded hand between his knees; his other hand was cupped underneath to catch the steady trickle of blood.

Blood from the slash on his brow ran over his eyelid and cheek. Shocked at his ghastly sight, she immediately pressed the cloth to his knuckles and wrapped them tight. Though she was still stunned from the chaos in the garden, the sensation of manipulating his hand, her fingers in contact with his, sent a thrill through her body. He watched her as she bandaged him. She could feel her wet shift clinging to her skin, her tangled hair pasted to her neck.

"Thank you," he said, his voice calm and intimate. "I'm not sure what happened…"

"You took a nasty fall when a branch struck you." She was surprised at her own composed tone. Outside, the wind screamed like a lost child. Louise combed the drawer for another cloth to blot his oozing forehead.

"Storms like this are very dangerous. You put yourself at risk for me." His amber eyes caressed her face. Her insides vaulted.

"Fortunately the gash is not too deep." Afraid to return his gaze, she touched his cheek instead, tilting his head so the wound would catch the failing light. "Besides, you pulled me out of the way of that chair, too." Louise studied the jagged cut; flecks of dirt were lodged in the swollen flesh. It needed to be cleaned. But wait—she had forgotten to wash his hand! It could become infected! She dropped the cloth and untied his hand.

"We have to wash your wounds first before dressing them." Louise led him over to the kitchen sink; the feel of his hand excited her again. She turned the cold brass knob on the faucet. Water thundered out the pipe, rushing like her pulse. When she rinsed his knuckles over the enamel sink Benjamin slipped his fingers between hers. He pressed his palm to her palm. Her knees weakened; heat rose to her face. Their hands blurred under the running water until she could not distinguish one from the other.

"Last night I dreamt about you."

His whisper melted her. She turned and met his lips. The kitchen became a kaleidoscope, a spinning palette of metal bowls, spoons, and kettles colliding with each other. Inanimate objects seemed to bear witness to her desire: a bowl of papaya gasped on the sideboard. The polished wall clock clanged in protest. The bloodstained rag ogled her from the edge of the sink. His kiss tasted of the wind and rain, the pounding drum, of the soaring quetzal painting the sky with iridescent wings, of freedom.

Someone called her name. Far away she heard it once, then again. People and places slipped back into her mind. It was Maud. Their hands were still joined under the running faucet. Awakening from his kiss, Louise turned off the water. Neither one wanted to move.

"Louise, where are you? You said you were coming! Louise! My lamp won't light!"

The power had failed. Though it was late afternoon storm clouds darkened the room as if it were evening. There was barely enough daylight left to find the oil lamps.

"I'm coming, Maud!"

Her voice sounded stark and shaky—did it betray her kiss with the young shaman? In the semidarkness Louise and Benjamin groped the kitchen shelves for the squat glass of the oil lamps. Louise found one next to a box of matches.

"Here it is!" She slid it off the edge of the shelf. Benjamin moved closer, turning the little knob to lengthen the wick. He struck a match and lit the lamp. The flame grew long, illuminating the dado on the walls and making his eyes glow. The split skin above his thick brow was red and puffy. He moved closer still until she felt his lips on her neck. Again she sunk deep into an intoxicated state; Maud's panicked voice sifted through the air.

"Where's Rosa? She's not in her room! Louise!"

2006

Brooklyn, New York

THE WEEKEND WAS DEVOTED to throwing out hoards of Aeon paperwork she had brought home over the years, purging herself with every print ad, TV storyboard, and presentation folder she'd stuffed into neon blue garbage bags. Disillusion had grown into an emotional tumor; discarding her lifework made her feel like a cancer patient on chemo, losing all her hair, exposing her naked pain to the world. Things had to get worse before they got better.

Zig helped her haul everything down to the recycle bin in the basement, glad to make space in the living room closet for his precious stick collection. He'd put the finishing touches on his costume Sunday night and selected an ulu stick to bring to school. Excelsior Prep allowed children to wear their costumes all day as long as they weren't too scary or hindering in the classroom. On Halloween morning she played his valet, assisting with the tying on of his impressive headdress. He was very particular about how and where the feathers should fall. Then he carefully put the vest over a T-shirt, adjusted the dangling colored fringes so they hung straight, and placed his feather pouch strap over his shoulder. After insisting on wearing moccasins he ceremoniously picked up his stick, and the transformation was complete. For a moment, watching him admire his reflection in the hall mirror, smiling broadly, as if he had just created a masterpiece, she wondered if she was wrong. The way he constructed his outfit, his exact specifications, and the startling result—it was too detailed for a child's creation. It made her think twice about what he had been claiming for years. *Maybe his was not all a fantasy.*

Zig didn't talk on the way down in the elevator. He held on to his pouch and his stick while Sheri lugged his school backpack. The morning was unusually warm for Halloween, and he was glad not to wear a jacket so he could show off his creation. Passing through the lobby, Sheri saw another mother and her two costumed children leaving for school. A tiny girl waved a silver sparkly wand like Tinker Bell. She followed her big brother, who swung a black vampire cape about him; plastic fangs hung out of his mouth and fake blood dripped down his chin.

"Look, Ma—an Indian!" the boy exclaimed as Zig walked by. Even Juan got up from his desk.

"Indian? That's a *shaman*! In my country, when we see a guy coming like that—with feathers and bells and a big stick—everybody move!"

Zig held his head high. Sheri caught the reactions from people on the street. Some commented; some only stared and smiled. Tapping his stick on the ground, Zig strutted along, humming to himself. He wasn't looking around to see who was looking at him. On Plaza Street they passed a group of do-ragged teenagers chomping on candy and dropping wrappers in their wake. They gurgled when they saw Zig; some cupped their hands over their mouths to mimic a call:

"Wooo wooo wooo wooo wooo...."

At the Grand Army Plaza subway station the neighborhood panhandler was parked at the bottom of the steps—a cheerful guy who wore a black eye patch and had the nonstop chatter of a used-car auctioneer.

"Whoa! Don't tell me, don't tell me—you must be Injun Joe or Sitting Bull or—no, I got it—White Cloud! I know there was a Red Cloud, but you look like White Cloud to me!"

Zig slowed down to scope out the man, as if he too were wearing a costume. The man turned to Sheri.

"Can you help me out with somethin'?"

Sheri picked some loose change out of her pocket and dropped it into his dirty paper cup.

"Bless you, Miss! Happy Halloween!" To Zig he added, "You be good now! Don't jab nobody with that Injun stick!"

The No. 2 train came quickly. Sheri and Zig stood in the middle of the car holding on to a pole. She could count on one hand the times she had ever taken the subway with him to school. An elderly woman sitting in front of them tapped Zig on the arm.

"Did you make that costume, young man?"

"Yes. My mom helped, too."

"Homemade costumes are the best. I was just admiring your headdress. What Indian nation are you supposed to be?"

Zig looked thoughtfully up at the straphangers. "I'm not sure exactly. I know I'm not from here. It's too cold."

"Maybe from Florida then, like the Seminoles?

He shook his head definitively. "No, I mean, not from this country."

"Oh!" The woman smiled at Sheri. "Well, it's a very unique costume. Enjoy your Halloween!" She hobbled off at Atlantic Avenue.

Zig muttered under his breath. "It's not a costume."

They got off at Borough Hall and walked to the front gate of Excelsior. Downtown was in full swing with people pouring out of the subway. It was interesting to note the brand of professionals in Brooklyn—lawyers and middle managers, teachers, shop owners and city workers. Brooklyn's energy was different. The people seemed weary from the start, not as crisply pressed and dry-cleaned; the suits were last year's cut; the shoes unpolished and not as trendy. Yet they seemed more authentic to her now that she was a mere observer of the plight to the office. Men and women with a purpose whizzed by, pressing buttons on their cell phones, sorting through voice mail, e-mail, and text messages, deleting, saving, deleting. Suddenly she felt estranged, thrown out of the club. Pangs of despair gripped her as she held her son's hand and led him to school. She couldn't help feeling lost in the homemaker role. This morning she had pulled on the same sweater and jeans she wore yesterday, but when she got to school she fell in with very few of the mothers dropping off their kids. One woman dressed in a pin-striped suit rushed off, kissing the air, leaving her twins on the sidewalk by the school. Another in running clothes pried herself away from her daughter's clutches. Some carried yoga mats and skipped off for their morning class. There were fathers too, a limited variety but more than she expected : the amiable and aimless L.L. Bean men in khakis and polo shirts. Skinny-jeaned Dumbo gallery guys. And the any-business business-men—clean-shaven, pepper-haired, faceless. Sheri searched the drop-off scene for someone like her, another jobless single mom, terrified and defiant. A group of three women stood off to the side. They looked ancient, more like grandparents; no doubt the ones whose clocks ran out and either adopted or spent a fortune for an egg donor, bravely giving birth on the brink of fifty. Haggard yet happy, they got their gift late in life, these women who reminded her so much of her mother. She felt more kinship with them than with anyone else.

Across the lobby a stoop-shouldered man had been watching them since they came in. He finally walked over, grinning with enthusiasm.

"Awesome costume, Zig!"

"Hi, Bruce. Thanks."

"Did you make it yourself?"

"My mom helped a little."

"Just a little." Sheri crossed her arms.

"I'm Bruce Schumer." The man extended his hand. "I left a phone message for you on Friday regarding Zig's evaluation."

"Right! You're the psychologist! Sheri Lambert." She shook his hand; the call had completely slipped her mind during those last dark hours at Aeon. "Sorry—Friday was insane. I meant to give you a call."

Just then, three boys raced over to greet Zig. The stocky blond boy wore a cardboard placard painted with an elaborate silver design suggesting body armor. He had a matching cardboard helmet with a plume stuck on the top and detailed silver-painted shin plates over black boots. Another taller boy wore open-toed leather sandals revealing long stringy toes. He held a corner of his flowing Middle Eastern robe and glanced up at Sheri beneath a towering turban of gauze. A third, brown-skinned boy wore a long apron spotted with black oily stains; black smudges were on his cheeks and chin, and he carried an old wooden mallet.

"Hey, Zig! Cool headdress!"

"Hey, Daniel. Your helmet's cool too. Did you make it?" Zig peeked at the back of his friend's head.

"It took me all weekend."

"What's up, Jacob! Hey, Kwami!"

The four boys created quite a contrast to the commercial superhero and princess costumes that filled the lobby.

"That's interesting…Sheri, do you know these boys?" Bruce asked, leaning into her ear. Sheri shook her head.

"They were all part of that incident last week." He paused to look at her, to see if she understood. "They're dressed as the characters they saw themselves as when they were playing that game."

Bruce and Sheri gazed at the boys in silence. They were like actors cast in a play of their own lives, glimpsing their history, each one a snapshot of the past that Zig had identified as theirs. They weren't at all scared. She thought they would be after witnessing Francesca's horror. Instead, they seemed energized, empowered. Was their silence that day out of fear or solidarity? There was no goofing around, no jokes thrown about. Nothing but a small sense of belonging, and a certain deference to Zig, who introduced them to this underground game.

"Looks like that afternoon is still playing itself out," Sheri said, nervously adjusting the strap of her bag on her shoulder. "Zig has a good imagination…he takes after me that way."

"Really? What do you do?"

She flinched. She hadn't prepared an answer for that question just yet.

"I'm going up, Mom." Zig turned to wave good-bye.

"Okay, sweetie." Sheri hugged him, careful not to disturb his headdress. "Meet you at three."

Children piled into the elevators; a Mardi Gras display of squished costumes and masked faces disappeared behind brass-plated doors. Minutes later there was scarcely a parent or child in sight. The psychologist stood by her side.

"So what line of work are you in?"

"I'm an artist." The words fell out of her mouth without a thought to their absurd meaning. Why did she say that? Flustered, she quickly changed the subject. "How did the evaluation go?"

"Very well! Jackie got the report on Friday. We'll go over it today." He looked down at his feet. "Sheri, do you have a minute? There's something I'd like to show you."

Sheri started for her BlackBerry out of habit and corrected herself. She zipped her bag shut.

"Sure, I've got time."

They crossed the empty lobby and stepped into the elevator. Frank, the elevator operator, nodded at Bruce.

"Hey, Frank! Good weekend?"

"Eh, if you like raking leaves. Second floor?"

"Second floor."

The man pulled a lever to close the heavy brass doors. Bruce turned to Sheri.

"I had a fascinating conversation with your son last week."

"Really? I couldn't get Zig to say much about it." Sheri readied herself for what might follow. He had his hands clasped behind his back and a thoughtful look on his face. The elevator door opened.

"Thanks, buddy." Bruce stepped aside to let Sheri off and continued, "Zig came to see me right after your meeting with Jackie. I had some of Jackie's notes to go on when I talked to him about what happened."

At his office door Bruce pulled out a wad of keys and selected one to unlock it. The narrow room smelled stuffy but not unpleasantly so. Papers were in neat piles on his desk, and rays of morning light brightened his sole window. She got the impression he burrowed himself as much as possible in this cubbyhole, away from the school staff and bureaucracy.

"Please sit anywhere you like." He threw his satchel on the sofa, opened a file drawer, took out an old black cassette player, and placed it on his desk. Sheri sat down on the edge of a chair nearest him.

"I was expecting to hear the usual playground complaints—somebody threw something at somebody, name-calling, fighting, yada yada yada. Instead, I discovered that Zig led his friends in a relatively innocent but complex game of what he called 'real pretend.' 'Real pretend,' as I see it, was a kind of guided meditation or hypnosis."

"Guided meditation?" Sheri repeated, pondering the words.

Psychologists were a curious bunch, employing a mishmash of ancient belief systems and modern science to arrive at a good guess. "Zig described the game when we met with Jackie."

"Right, you heard the whole story. However, what was amazing to me was when he spoke about his own character—"

"The Indian."

"Yes…has he mentioned this before? That he remembers a past life as an Indian?"

"Zig's been telling me this story on and off since he was five. It started right after 9/11. All of a sudden he was like a walking encyclopedia, rambling nonstop with facts and anecdotes about his native upbringing. Frankly, I've been concerned. Have you ever come across anything like this?" There. She had admitted it. He was a psychologist—maybe he would have some answers.

Bruce rubbed his hands together. "Kids will have great emotional responses when they're exposed to scary news and violence. They can do things like attach themselves to strong hero types in a movie or book or even a video game, idolizing these characters as a way to escape reality. " He looked off to the side for a moment. "But I don't feel that's the case with Zig."

The old wood-framed window rattled in the wind. Sheri folded her arms, trying to read the psychologist's face. *What if he says Zig needs extra medical attention? Hints at some psychosomatic disorder and recommends prescription drugs to control him?* Nowadays doctors prescribe Ritalin as the childhood cure-all. She knew of two boys in her building who were on ADHD drugs. Maybe they were out of control before, but now to her they walked around as if they were looking at the world through one small keyhole in their mind.

"When I was in grad school I did some ethnographic research on the Guaymí, a group of native people in Costa Rica. I lived with a Guaymí family for almost a month, studying all aspects of their daily lives. It was a tremendous experience, but the thing I remember the most was their music." He fingered the handle of the tape deck. "They sang often and had a song for every task, each one with different tonal qualities that told stories or reflected their beliefs. When I asked Zig if he was doing anything specific when he saw himself as an Indian, he said he was singing by a fire alone late at night while everyone else was asleep. I asked if he remembered the song, and he said yes. I then asked if I could record him singing it. He agreed." Bruce looked at the tape recorder. "I'd like to play it for you."

Sheri glanced at the machine with skepticism, this Pandora's box that might threaten Zig's standing at the school. Yet at the same time she was curious about what the tape contained. Would there be something concrete that could help her?

He pressed a button. A mature, raspy voice started out humming low, then built to a rhythmic chant. Unusual tones reverberated like a gong; she followed the sounds until they echoed and died into silence. For a moment after it ended neither of them spoke.

"That couldn't...that didn't sound anything like Zig! Is it possible for a boy's voice to drop to a man's voice like that?"

Bruce pointed to her chair.

"He sat right where you're sitting and recorded it last Wednesday. Afterwards he wouldn't open his eyes; he was in a trance-like state. I got a little concerned when he quickly snapped out of it. But what struck me was where I had heard those sounds before." He ran his hand over his forehead. "I wracked my brain and it finally came to me. It was a day when the village shaman came to perform a blessing ritual. I remember him singing all through the night. By dawn his voice was hoarse. Something about Zig's song reminded me of him."

Sheri squeezed herself. "So what does that mean? Are you saying it could be true? That he actually once lived as an Indian?"

Bruce sat back in his chair. "I don't know. I'm not that familiar with past-life phenomena. All I know is, he probably could not have made the song up." He pressed another button on the recorder to rewind the tape. "It's been fifteen years since I did the study so my memory is a bit rusty. But when he started singing my hair stood on end." The machine stopped and a button popped up. "It means something, Sheri. His experience was quite real."

Sheri stared at the tape deck while questions flew through her mind. "That's bizarre…perhaps he saw a documentary on the National Geographic Channel? Could it be a new trading card game like that dreadful Yu-Gi-Oh thing?"

"I doubt the media could do an in-depth documentary on any indigenous clan in Central America. These people are very private and insular. I was honored when they let me stay with them." He gazed at Sheri. "If you don't mind my asking, where are you from?"

That question used to be a painful one for Sheri, but over the years she came to realize New Yorkers have to know what ethnic group they're dealing with at all times. They need to categorize people according to their bias of race and class so they can get on with their day. It wasn't so obvious with Sheri. She recalled the hours she spent searching collections at the library on Panamanians, her vague resemblance to the pictures she found, how she tried to feel some kinship with the people of that country. She did not speak Spanish, nor was she exposed to any Latin culture. As a result, she didn't fit in with the handful of Latinas in high school or college. She was attractive in a nondescript multinational kind of way; her olive skin, deep brown eyes, and chiseled cheekbones were mathematically matched to almost any continent short of Asia. When she was with Italians she looked Italian. Traveling in Egypt she passed as an Arab. In Paris she was asked for directions by Americans. She browsed street markets in Rio and never got hassled by vendors. Hassidic Jews in the park blew their horn for her during Passover. If she flat-ironed her hair she might even pass as Irish.

"My adoptive parents were Jewish. They brought me here from Panama."

"Oh." Color rose to his face. Bruce was Jewish. He quickly added, "So you do have some Latin American roots!"

"Well, yes. I guess so. My mother died when I was born. I don't know of any biological relatives."

"Still, there must be some kind of link. There're some pretty good genealogical Web sites—better yet, I just remembered something..." Bruce grabbed a chunk of papers off his desk and hurried through them on his lap. He pulled out a limp, photocopied brochure and passed it to Sheri. "I'm on the mailing list of the International Indigenous Leaders. I get notices of all their events, especially when elders come to speak. Here's one that's giving a talk this week. You might make a connection there. These lectures are always inspiring and draw people from many different nations."

Sheri took the flyer, never bothering to say she had long given up hope of finding any real information about her roots. But Bruce was encouraging. Could she open herself to the possibility again? Would it amount to anything? For her or Zig?

"In any event you'll get a copy of my report by the end of the day or early tomorrow, and just FYI, I did not include the tape in my report," Bruce added.

"Oh!" That came as a relief; still she looked at him cautiously.

"It would raise too many eyebrows. I recorded it more out of curiosity from my anthropology days."

"Great, I appreciate that." But she wanted to know. "What did go into your report?"

"In a nutshell it says he was playing an innocent game and Francesca had a bad reaction to it. He was not at fault for anything deviant."

Sheri nodded with enthusiasm. "That's exactly how I saw it, too. Glad we're on the same page." She swiftly gathered her belongings to leave should he add any caveat. She had one last request.

"Bruce, since it's not an issue, would you mind if I took the tape?"

"It's all yours. In fact, it may be very useful in identifying the tribe. You might find someone who can help at that elder gathering."

He flipped open the top of the tape deck, removed the cassette and gave it to her. Sheri closed her fingers around the plain black plastic tape. It weighed nothing in her hand compared to the gravity of its echo in her mind.

"Don't worry about Zig. Just listen to him, let him express himself without being judged. Perhaps it will make sense one day. Or else it'll fade away and he'll forget all about it. You'll see."

Sheri thanked Bruce and left his office. The hallways were sleepy and silent on the administrative floor; the classrooms were all upstairs. She walked back to the elevator with her thoughts churning. Then she saw Zig's teacher, Ellie, hurrying toward her from the other end of the hall.

"Oh hi, Sheri! Nice to see you! Zig's costume is just amazing; he said you helped make it, too!"

"Thanks, Ellie. Halloween is in full swing."

She was balancing a huge plastic pumpkin stuffed with Halloween goodie bags on one knee. Sheri could see why Zig did not care for Ellie. Wild-eyed and hyper-perky bordering on neurotic, Ellie was of the thin-skinned variety who could go from sunny and warm to dark and foreboding at the drop of a hat.

"Did Zig tell you about our trip on November fifteenth? I'm sending home a reminder note today. We're going to the National Museum of the American Indian in Lower Manhattan to culminate with our study of the Iroquois Indians! I could really use some parent chaperones—are you available?"

"I'll have to check." She looked at the tape in her hand, as if it had all the answers.

"Don't forget to sign the consent slip, too. Whoops! Gotta get back with the goodies! Hope you can make it!"

Ellie dashed to the stairwell, taking the stairs two at a time. Sheri pressed the button for the elevator. She had never gone on a school trip with Zig. What would that be like? A bunch of kids throwing balled-up paper at each other, crunching chips and spilling juice, texting friends and trading cards on the sly. Could she handle it?

PARK SLOPE'S SEVENTH AVENUE HALLOWEEN PARADE begins at dusk. Today she and Zig turned onto Seventh Avenue and Park Place at 6:30 p.m.—plenty of time to walk up to the center slope and join the parade coming back down the avenue. Her son beamed, happy to have his mother with him for once on Halloween. The streets were packed with colorfully costumed children and adults. A group of swarthy pirates went by, waving plastic swords and yelling, "Aye aye, Captain" to a boy wearing a huge three-cornered hat. A horn honked and a blond curly wigged Harpo Marx ducked and dived between the crowd, chased by a cigar-tipping Groucho Marx. King Tut, all of four feet high, with smeared but expertly drawn indigo eyes and a gold painted face, walked like an Egyptian while his mother jogged along snapping photos. The assortment of characters was endless; Sheri couldn't believe she had missed the spectacle all these years. Two Grim Reapers on Rollerblades appeared, gliding like ghosts, menacing in their stark white hockey masks and black hooded capes, wielding a fake sickle in the air. When one came Sheri's way she stepped aside to let it pass. Instead, the Grim Reaper skated right up to her, raising its sickle over her head. Sheri screamed. The stupid thing gave her a good scare. She laughed to cover her embarassment, but Zig did not find it funny.

"Don't worry, Mom. It's not time to go yet. When you're number's up it's up. That guy has no control over it."

"Okay, Z, don't be so morbid."

"I'm not morbid! Halloween is the day when spirits come out to play, when magic is the most powerful." Zig spread his arms in wide reference to the crowd. "Some of these may be costumes…and some of them may not," he joked, doing his best *Twilight Zone,* Rod Serling imitation. An impish grin spread across his face.

"You can't scare me Injun Joe!"

Sheri went to grab him but he ran ahead of her. Then she noticed how his shoulders were hiked up to his ears. The weather had changed sharply since this morning; leaves flew like a flock of geese in the cold, brisk wind. Was he wheezing again?

1899

Panama City, Panama

THE SPELL LIFTED.

Louise instantly put a proper distance between her and Benjamin. She forgot Maud didn't know Rosa had gone home.

"Keep this pressed against your forehead for now," she touched the twisted dishcloth to his brow and replaced her hand with his. "I'll get the gauze and iodine." Louise started for the stairs with the lit lamp, her head still spinning. Maud met her at the top of the landing.

"Is Benjamin badly hurt? Where's Rosa?"

"Rosa's gone home. I told her to leave before the storm got under way." A thin, creaking noise came from Maud's chest. Louise tried to lead her sister back to her bed. She resisted.

"Gone home! Father told her to stay here with us until he returned!"

"I know, but Rosa has a family, too. They would be worried sick about her, and she about them."

Maud hesitated before she got under the covers. Louise placed her lamp on the nightstand next to Maud's unlit lamp. Matchsticks littered the floor.

"So it's just me and you and Benjamin…"

Maud waited for a reaction. Louise ignored her and turned up the lamp; the flame brightened the bedroom walls. She spied a candle behind the nightstand and picked it up.

"How is he? I saw him lying on the ground outside."

"He got a smart bruise on the head, but it's nothing that—"

"Good gracious! He needs my help!"

"Maud, you must stay in bed. Fretting like this will only make you worse. Why, you're wheezing again already!" Louise busied herself with tucking Maud in. Maud studied her sister.

"Why didn't you answer me when I called you?"

"What do you mean? I answered you right away."

"I called out three times before you replied."

"Maybe I didn't hear you, what with all the wind and my looking for the lamps..." Louise avoided Maud's inquisitive stare. She took the glass shade off the lamp to light the candle.

"Where's Benjamin now? In his room?" Maud coughed after her question, a racking cough that lasted through Louise's answer.

"He's down in the kitchen waiting for me to bandage his hand and head. Afterwards I'll fix us some supper and—"

"Let me help you." Maud threw the covers aside and started out of her bed.

"No! You stay here. I'll tell Benjamin to—"

"It's not you he likes, Louise. He fancies me!"

Louise cast a wary eye at Maud and bit her tongue to keep from mocking her. Maud lay back, pulling the covers under her chin.

"Ask him."

Louise ignored her challenge. The humid evening air always brought on a worsening of Maud's condition and her attitude.

"I'll light the rest of the lamps and get supper ready."

The storm continued to beat against the roof and windows. Louise got up to leave, taking a last look at her little sister covered up to her neck in bed sheets. Her limp, blond ringlets were pressed flat on the plump pillows. Her mouth, slightly open, sipped at the air. Several books were facedown and pushed aside. Maud fixed her gaze on the pouring rain. She had a childlike fear of foul weather. Maud worried Louise as much as she annoyed her. Prior to meeting Benjamin she wished her sister's asthma would go away for good. Now she hoped her recovery would take all the time in the world.

She left Maud and went to fetch the iodine and bandages from the medicine cabinet in the hall bathroom. Benjamin surprised her at the foot of the stairs.

"How is Maud's breathing? I heard her coughing again." He looked grave and concerned. Louise pictured Maud's smug face.

"She's a bit congested, maybe more so with the storm."

Branches tapped an eerie tempo on the windows in the parlor. Maud coughed loudly, ending her spasms with a moan. Benjamin took swift steps up the stairs. Louise blocked him.

"Let me bandage your head first." She poured a bit of medicine on the gauze and gently wiped his brow. "What Maud needs more than anything is a good night's rest. Perhaps you can give her that…the tea that makes her sleep quite soundly?"

She taped a bandage over his wound. Under the weight of his stare she felt both desirable and disgraceful.

"Yes, the storm is taking its toil on her. She should rest. I'll prepare the herbs."

Louise lowered her eyes and tugged on her damp gown, her fingers cold and shaking. She could hardly believe what she had proposed. All she knew was she had to be alone with him again.

"I'll get supper ready. I promised her Rosa's soup."

Without a word Benjamin went up to his room to retrieve his parcel of herbs. Louise went into the kitchen and took the kettle off its hook.

2006

Brooklyn, New York

ZIG DARTED THROUGH THE CROWD, under the arms of a giant clown on stilts and around a clan of shrieking witches.

"Slow down! Wait!" she yelled.

Heads turned to Sheri's frantic call. Cold fall evenings had a way of messing with Zig's lungs, especially if he started running around. And just the other night he'd had a hard time breathing. Where did he go? It made her nervous not to be able to see him, even for a few seconds. There he was, crouched behind a fruit stand, laughing his head off. She grabbed him tightly under his armpit and lifted him from his hiding place.

"It's not funny, Zig—I told you to stop. If you won't listen to me we're going home." The smirk fell off his face. Just as she feared, he was struggling to catch his breath and began to cough.

"Get your inhaler out and take a puff right now."

Zig's eyes glinted in the early evening light. He patted down his front pants pockets. Giggles escaped from his lips in little spurts between coughs. He patted his back pockets.

"Uh, I think I left it in my backpack."

"What! I asked you if you had it before we left home!"

"I thought I put it in my pocket."

A festive mob was assembling to start the parade a few blocks up. Where were they? She squinted to read the nearest sign: Twelfth Street. Sheri filled all Zig's prescriptions at the Duane Reade near her office in the city; they should have it on file here in Brooklyn, but the closest store was on Flatbush Avenue, almost a mile away. Zig sat on a fire hydrant to catch his breath, his cough building in intensity. He could have a full-blown attack in no time. They had passed Methodist Hospital on their way up at Sixth Street. Much as she loathed the emergency room scene, it was her best option. She reached into her bag for a bottle of water.

"Here, take a drink, then climb up on my back. We're going to the emergency room."

Zig wagged his head. He swallowed a mouthful before picking words through a wracking cough. "Piggyback?" his said, his voice hoarse. "Daniel *(cough)*, Kwami *(cough)* are gonna see me!"

Sheri took the bottle from him. "It's too far for you to walk and we've got to hurry. C'mon!"

Zig glanced around covertly; he couldn't bear to have any of his buddies see him scrambling onto his mother's back. She hoisted his thin legs around her sides and he clasped his arms under her chin. At ten years old he still felt light but was cumbersome to carry. His cough went deeper. She could feel his chest rising and falling rapidly against her spine. Sheri wobbled along, dodging the throngs of trick-or-treaters darting in and out of stores, grabbing cheap foreign candy. She had to stop to redistribute his weight every couple of feet. Carrying him six blocks would take forever. According to Dr. Breen, almost half the kids in New York City had asthma; it was as common as pimples. Someone out here had to have an inhaler. She searched the crowd for anyone who was coughing or dragged along or jumping around, the way Zig got when he took his medicine. Today all the kids fit that description.

"I can't believe you forgot your inhaler, Zig! How many times have I told you—"

"Mom, stop! There's Kwami!"

He pointed to the boy she had seen at school this morning, the one dressed as a blacksmith. The boy spotted Zig at the same time. He and his mother, a plump, buoyant woman in a Yankees baseball cap started for them. Could they have an inhaler? Zig slid off Sheri's back; her shoulders numb. She hurried to meet the mother on the curb.

"Hi, I'm Sheri, Zig's mom."

"Hi, I'm Gina!"

"This may sound like a strange question, Gina, but would you happen to have an inhaler? Zig forgot his and he's having trouble breathing."

The woman's smile faded. "Oh, gosh no, I'm so sorry!" Her posture hung forward in apology. "Great costume!" she said, praising Zig in his haggard state. "You should win a prize for that one." Zig covered his mouth, hacking his reply. Gina watched him struggle. She put her hand on her cheek.

"Inhaler...oh! Daniel! He carries one."

"There he is—over there!" Kwami exclaimed.

"Which one is Daniel?" Sheri craned her neck to see above the crowd.

"He's the gladiator—see the helmet with the long plume?" Gina pointed. "Clara is his mom."

Sheri dashed across the avenue, leaving Zig behind on the sidewalk with Gina and Kwami. She followed the plume waving above the crowd, pushing her way through. The boy's mother was straightening his helmet.

"Clara! Clara!" she yelled. "It's Sheri, Zig's mom."

"Oh hi! We were just looking for Zig. Daniel talks about him all the time. He's dying for a play date."

"I'm in a bit of a dilemma, Clara...Do you have an inhaler on you? Zig forgot his and I think he's having an asthma attack.

Kwami's mother told me you might have one."

Clara read the desperation on Sheri's face as only a mother with an asthmatic child could. "Yes, I'm sure we have it."

"Can I trouble you for a puff or two? It might help me avoid Methodist's emergency room. I'll pay for the cost of the inhaler—"

"No, that's okay, it's no problem." Clara looked down at her son. "Daniel, can Zig borrow your inhaler? He needs a puff."

Daniel's pert little face appeared beneath the cardboard helmet. "Where is he?" he said, digging deep in his pocket and handing Sheri his inhaler.

"He's right across the street." Sheri looked back through the crowd. Zig was doubled over, half gasping. She ran to where she left him with Gina and Kwami. Clara and Daniel followed her.

"I told you we were supposed to meet *here!*" Daniel chided his mother, running over to Zig. Gina was patting Zig on the back and looked relieved when Sheri returned.

"He's not doing so great," she said, stepping back so Sheri could see him. His face was red; veins rippled in his neck.

"It's okay! Daniel had his inhaler! Hurry, Z!" Sheri immediately shook the inhaler and pushed it into his hand. Zig hesitated.

"Go on! Take a puff!"

He just sat there on a milk crate, eyes closed and head bowed. Sheri became frantic. "What's the matter?"

In the near distance the peal of African drums cut through the commotion. The parade stopped. Everyone grew quiet and stood on their toes to see what was going on. Drummers dressed in flowing batik gowns with matching caps marched up the middle of Seventh Avenue. The count appeared endless; fifty or more musicians advanced steadily like an army of sound and fury.

"Zig, please hurry! Why are you waiting?" She shook him by the shoulders; still he made no move. Was he losing consciousness? At once the noise was maddening; there were too many people, not enough air. She wanted to sweep him up above the scene and carry him to safety. Suddenly he tilted his head as if he were listening. The force of the drummers' rhythm stunned her; the vibration was so powerful it nearly threw her to the ground. But the sound had the opposite effect on Zig. He moved toward its thunder. Lips parted, he seemed to be breathing, in time, to the beat.

The drumming ended as abruptly as it started. People in the crowd exchanged looks of wonder.

"Whoa! I've never seen African drummers at the Halloween parade!" Gina gazed after the performers.

"Me neither! Where did they come from?" Clara too was straining to get a last glimpse of them.

"Take a puff right now, Zig, before you have another attack!" Sheri demanded, trying to contain herself.

"I don't need it." He put the cap on the inhaler and gave it back to Daniel.

"What're you talking about?"

Zig shook his head. "I don't need it."

Sheri pressed her ear against his back. The two women waited for her reaction. Sure enough, his lungs were clear, completely clear. She pulled her head back. How could that be? He looked into her eyes. Feathers hung limp around his head; shards of cloth blew wildly at his sides. Zig was like an Indian warrior on his last leg, weary from facing a long battle. Sheri faked a smile and fingered his headdress, her hands shaking. She glanced nervously at the other mothers.

"Maybe I was overreacting. Maybe you weren't as bad as I thought."

"Overreacting!" Gina blurted out. "I was terrified waiting for you to come back—he worried the heck out of me!"

Clara looked at Sheri. Zig got up, dusted off the seat of his pants.

"I needed some help, so they came."

There was a pause. The two mothers bent down to his level. Kwami and Daniel moved in.

"Who?" Gina asked.

"Sweetie, it's getting late—"

"The drummer spirits! See, it's kinda like the inhaler...I sucked in the beat and the silence between the beats, and the pain in my chest stopped. The drumbeats beat the cough out."

Sheri observed the two women, wondering what was percolating in their minds. Gina pushed up her baseball cap. Clara brushed hair out of her wide eyes.

"The whole universe moves to one beat," Zig continued, placing his palm on his chest. "Even your heart and breath moves to the same beat. In fact, it never stops beating, unless your body is dead, course. It just gets out of rhythm sometimes and makes everything go crazy inside. That's when the drummer spirits come—to put the right beat back into you."

She could just imagine the gossip at school tomorrow. Kwami looked down the street for the drummers. Daniel could hardly contain his excitement. He put the inhaler in his pocket.

"I have a drum at home. Think that could work for me?"

"Zig, it's getting really late and cold out. We better go." Sheri steered him to the middle of the sidewalk.

"But I didn't even get to trick-or-treat!" he protested.

"Can't he stay a little longer?" Daniel and Kwami pleaded.

"Sorry, guys, we have to go. Thanks again for all your help, really. Nice meeting you!"

"Same here...get home safely," Gina said with uncertainty. Clara stared after them. The mothers waved but their brows were crumpled. There would be talk at school. Zig lagged behind a bit until Sheri yanked him by his sleeve.

"C'mon, Z!"

His two friends ambled into the street.

"See you tomorrow!" Daniel yelled.

"Bye, Zig!" Kwami yelled even louder.

"Bye, Daniel! Bye, Kwami!" Zig's voice was as crisp as the night, the cough and hoarseness gone. A breeze blew the feathered strips on his headdress straight up in the air, like a peacock fanning his plumes. He lumbered at her side.

"Why couldn't we stay?"

"It was time to go. Besides, you were spooking everybody out."

"No I wasn't. You're the one spooked out. You're always spooked out."

"I live with you; I'm the last person to be surprised at anything." Sheri got stuck behind a bunch of loafing teenagers.

"Then you shouldn't be afraid of everything I say and do, but you are."

"I'm not afraid, Zig. I'm just concerned."

"About what?"

"About what other people will think."

"Why should you care what other people think?"

"Because you're different, Zig. It's good to be different, and sometimes it's not so good."

"Like when?"

"Like just now, when you tried to explain your…curing yourself."

"Well, I'm still not wheezing, am I?" He breathed in and out deeply to show her.

"Yeah, but they won't understand it, babe, even if you explain it to them. So why bother?"

"You don't understand it either, Mom. You don't want to understand."

"It's not that I don't want to understand you, Zig. There are other issues at hand."

"What issues?"

"Like what's going on with you at school. You don't listen, you talk out of turn, and you're badgering Ms. Herman in class."

"What's 'badgering'?"

"It means beating up on her with words." She looked down at him. He was shivering.

"Mom, I'm just asking questions, that's all. Isn't that what school is for?"

"Yes, but you're going way overboard. And you're bringing a point of view to school that others don't appreciate. You've got to keep your bright ideas to yourself."

Zig stomped on a half-eaten Snickers bar.

"You mean what happened in the playground."

"Exactly. I also spoke to Bruce, and he played the tape for me."

"What tape?"

"The singing? Remember? When he recorded you singing an Indian chant? You never told me he taped you. You barely said anything about your interview with Bruce."

"I don't remember..."

"Oh, you don't remember? Well, those kinds of things—bragging about spirits and stuff—send up red flags at school. I don't want you singled out as a ringleader that needs to be watched. So just cool it from now on, okay?"

It was cold and there wasn't a vacant cab in sight on Flatbush Avenue so they took the subway. Zig didn't speak for a long while. *Was she too hard on him? Did he really believe she didn't want to know?* Truth is, she was afraid of the mysterious things he talked about, afraid to place meaning on it, yet she so wanted to know more, to make sense of it all. Maybe that was the problem—it didn't have to make sense for it to be true. But what if the school labeled his ways as 'attention deficient'? She saw a PBS show about bright kids who were written off as ADHD because they couldn't behave. To make it through school you have to conform to the norm, that's just the way it is. And what about the drummers? First, they appeared out of nowhere, then Zig's asthma attack disappeared. They came because he 'called' them? Sheri was not good at illogical; to her, all things had to be consistent with reason. Everything could be explained—except her son.

He flicked his thumbs in the seat next to her, his mind somewhere else. She started to put her windbreaker on him but knew he would object loudly. Inside her jacket pocket she found a Hershey's Kiss. She took it out and nudged him.

"Trick or treat?"

A smile crept over his face. He unwrapped the chocolate and popped it in his mouth. Finally, he broke his silence.

"Do you have the tape of me singing?"

"Who wants to know?"

"Me! I want to hear it."

"It didn't even sound like you." She found another chocolate.

"Who'd it sound like?"

"Like a craggy old man with a bad back."

They peeked at each other and laughed. Silence again. One stop on the train felt like four. He looked tired; the coughing and wheezing had worn him out. She didn't mention the rest of the conversation she had with Bruce, about the Guaymí Indians he'd lived with in Costa Rica, and the similarities between their chant and Zig's. Would she ever?

The neighborhood merriment had hushed considerably when they got home. The wicker basket of candy she had left outside her apartment door for trick-or-treaters was now bare. She pictured children sorting their goodies on the floor in apartments above and below hers, costumes trashed for the fruits of their labor. Zig came home empty-handed with a costume ravaged by the elements. Half the feathers had blown off his headdress, and many of the cloth fringes were gone, too. He tossed the headdress on his desk; his vest landed on the beanbag chair.

"What do you want for dinner, sweetie?" Sheri limped to the kitchen on aching feet. She opened the fridge, grazed the shelves.

"Z?"

Zig had dropped on his bed and fallen asleep.

This wasn't like him. Fear gnawed at her again. She pulled off the rest of his clothes and wrestled him into his pajamas. Then she got out the nebulizer and two vials of medicine—Albuterol and the steroid Pulmicort. She poured the contents of the vials into the cup attached to the face mask, elevated his head with pillows, and put the mask over his nose and mouth. She wasn't taking any chances. Drummers worked for him; drugs worked for her. After she turned on the machine, she dialed Dr. Breen and left a message. He usually called within the hour; she'd have to be ready for his questioning. The frothy vapor coiled around Zig's nose and open mouth while he slept. She sunk into the chair by his bed, her appetite gone. To her, these drugs were both a miracle and a curse; a nightmare of dependency ensued and she had to be careful when she weaned him off of them; it was so easy for him to have a relapse. Dr. Breen said he might outgrow his asthma as he got older, but to her it seemed to be getting worse. Now he wanted Zig on a steroid inhaler every day. What choices did she have? He missed too many days of school last year, and she would have to keep him home tomorrow just to be sure his symptoms didn't return. Besides, maybe when he went back in on Wednesday the rumors about him would have died down. She stared at the rapid rise and fall of his little chest. Zig slept deeply, even with the hard mask over his face, the loud drone of the nebulizer, and his mother's watchful eyes.

IN THE MORNING SHERI MADE Zig's favorite breakfast: french fries and a cheese omelet with jalapeño peppers. Usually just the scent would awaken him. She went into his room and saw that he had barely moved from the position he was in last night.

"Time to wake up, sweetie!" She took the covers from under his chin. His neck was hot and sweaty. She felt his forehead. Did he have a fever? He winced and moaned at the touch of her cool hand.

"Breakfast is ready. How're you feeling?" She opened his night table drawer, rummaged through Game Boy gear and a tangled mass of knickknacks to find the electronic thermometer. She put it in the corner of his mouth. Seconds later it beeped—102.5°F. Good thing he was staying home.

"No school for you today, Z. You've got a fever." She pulled the covers off to listen to his chest. Just a slight crinkle echoed on the exhale. He laid there listless, his eyes dull. No reaction to the thought of staying home. He was sick all right.

"Hmm, you weren't dressed right for the weather yesterday. It got cold so quickly." She undid some buttons on his pajama shirt. "Stay here. I'll bring your breakfast."

It was all her fault. Leatrice would have had made sure he dressed properly. She recalled how tentative Leatrice sounded on the phone Sunday night when she called to double-check about taking the day off. What was Sheri thinking, letting him run around in the street with that skimpy costume? Riddled with guilt, Sheri made a smiley face on a plate with his french fries, put it on a tray, and brought it to his bedside. He was sitting up, looking out the window.

"You must be hungry since you didn't have dinner last night. Eat a little before you take a Tylenol." He brightened a bit at his favorite breakfast, but after a few bites, he complained about a stomachache. Sheri grabbed his garbage pail just as he heaved, narrowly avoiding his throwing up on the bed. She got him to the bathroom to rinse his mouth.

"Sorry, sweetie. I guess that wasn't the best thing to eat with a fever." She toweled off his face. How stupid of her. Anyone with a fever would vomit up fried food and cheese.

"Feel better now?"

"I'm ccccccold." He shook in his bare feet on the tiled floor. She got him back to bed in a flash and wrapped him up in blankets. *Get the Tylenol in him, bring the fever down.* He managed to swallow the pill. Sheri held her breath, hoping he wouldn't bring it back up.

Twenty minutes passed and the color returned to Zig's cheeks. She brought him some weak tea and toast with jelly.

"What time is it?" He nibbled on the crust of the bread.

"Ten o'clock." Good, he wasn't shaking anymore.

"They're either in writing workshop or history."

"Hmm. I remember doing the same thing when I stayed home sick—guessing what everyone was doing in school. I was pretty lonesome."

"Really? I'm not."

"Well, you've never been home sick for a whole month."

"A month! Wow, that's a long time. What happened to you?"

Sheri shrugged. "I had a bad cold that wouldn't go away. The doctors weren't sure why. I couldn't get out of bed, so I watched TV all day and drew tons of pictures."

"Really? Can I see them?"

"Oh no sweetie—that was thirty-something years ago. Every day I gave pictures to my mom and dad as a gift; it was all I could do to keep busy. But when I got better I found out they threw them all away."

"What! Didn't they even keep one?"

"Nope. I found them in a bag behind the kitchen door. I started to cry and asked my mom why she didn't want them. She said my dad signed me up for an art class at the Met after school, so soon they'd get all new pictures from me. I figured what I had drawn wasn't very good."

Zig looked hurt. He took her hand in his sticky palms.

"Your mom was a meanie!"

"Actually I think Mom liked my pictures. Dad didn't. But he didn't like much of anything."

"Hmph! They weren't your real parents anyway."

"They were the only ones I had, Z. They did the best they could."

He twisted a ring on her finger. "Do you have any pictures from the art class?"

"I never took the class."

"Why not?"

Sheri brushed crumbs off his blanket. "I told them I didn't want to, and I never drew any pictures for them again."

"But now you draw at work…or used to."

"A little. Advertising is not like fine art. Creative directors don't do much drawing."

He looked disappointed. "What were they like? Your pictures?"

"Back then? Oh, they were all over the place—lots of squiggly lines and circles, stick-figure people and trees and animals…"

The telephone rang. She got up to take the handset from his desk. It was easier to park her journal, BlackBerry, and the cordless phone in his room since she would be spending most of the day in there.

"Hello?"

"Hi, it's Judy Jacobs. Sheri?"

Judy was a top headhunter and a longtime ally, the woman who found Sheri her first job in the business.

"Hey, Judy! You got my message?"

"I couldn't believe it! What happened at Aeon?"

"It's a horror story." Sheri eyed Zig. He eavesdropped on her frequently these days; the living room would give her more privacy. His Game Boy kept him busy while she updated Judy on her exit from Aeon.

"You just can't make this stuff up, Sheri. It was time to move on."

"So what's it like out there now?" Sheri opened the living room blinds, revealing vivid red and gold foliage in the botanic gardens.

"Not great. It might pick up after the holidays, but things are usually slow now through the new year. What were you making?"

"One seventy-five."

"After thirteen years! Marcus got his money's worth."

"Creative directors never get paid enough. It's killer work."

"And those jobs are hard to come by these days. I'm just telling you what I'm seeing. Far and few between. There are some senior art director positions, but you're way overqualified. Could you stand anyone telling you what to do?"

Sheri glanced at Zig's bedroom door. "My ten year old's already working on that. Actually, I'm more interested in freelance."

"Honestly, budgets are pathetic these days. Blame it on oil prices, Katrina, the war in Iraq. Everybody's tightening their belts. I've got some clients who are changing careers over it. Did you get a decent severance?"

"Six months, but JetSet was a huge loss. I doubt Aeon will stay afloat."

"You're lucky to get six months. Marcus's track record is shoddy. I'm still trying to collect my fee for a writer I placed there a year ago."

She felt a twinge of concern. "So it's not looking good, huh?"

"Send me your TV reel. I'll see what I can do. Do you have our new address?"

"You moved? Hold on a sec, let me grab my notebook."

She pressed the hold button on the phone and ran into Zig's room. Her snakeskin journal was missing from his desk. *Where'd it go?* Zig, with his head dangling over the side of his bed, was paging through it.

"Honey, I need my notebook."

"Mom, are these your drawings?" Flushed and excited, he opened to a page covered with her ink doodles.

"I have someone on hold! I need my book—"

"These are Indian symbols! The kind awas use for special ceremonies!" He held it away from her. "There're on almost every page!" Zig flipped through the notebook as if he had just discovered buried treasure.

"Hand it to me right now or you're gonna be in *major* trouble!"

He tore a page out just as she snatched the book from him. Sheri apologized to Judy for the long hold, got her new address, and hung up. She shook the handset at him.

"That was an important call, Zig. From now on, when I ask you for something—"

"You never told me about your drawings!" He had taken off his pajama shirt and was walking around bare-chested.

"Have you lost your mind? Put your shirt back on! Where're your slippers?"

"These symbols are found on ulu sticks, sometimes on drums," he said, studying the page he ripped out.

"Get your shirt on right now!"

"Listen to me!" he screamed at the top of his lungs. Sheri froze. He held up the piece of paper, his eyes wild.

"Who were you drawing these for?"

"I don't know what you're talking about, Zig. That's just… nothing."

He kicked some DVDs over on the floor. She tried to calm him down.

"I'm sorry, Zig. I've got a lot on my mind…too much. What were you trying to tell me?"

He ran into his room and slammed the door.

She let him be. They both needed some time and space. She cleaned up the kitchen. Made a couple of sandwiches for lunch. Checked her e-mail. But spinning in her head were all the things Zig said that flat out confounded her. It started to dredge up the nightmares she used to have. She was around his age when she fell sick, and every night the same dream came to her. She was standing in a shallow river. Brightly colored birds circled overhead. The birds flew lower and lower; feathers dropped as they merged into one enormous bird; its wide wings cast a shadow over the sun where she stood. She remembered being frozen with fear, staring up into the eye of the looming mystical creature. When it opened its mouth to speak she screamed in terror. Someone else was there, an old man, watching her. She would awaken in a cold sweat. Her parents didn't know what to do. It got so she was afraid to sleep at night for fear she'd have the nightmare again. They finally resorted to giving her prescription sleeping pills. For months black, dreamless sleep swallowed her until the vision faded. She had buried the childhood memory until recently, when the vivid dreams began to fill her nights again.

Zig was overdue for a treatment. Like clockwork, it had to be every three hours to ward off any worsening of his condition. She checked his medicine supply—there was enough to last a few weeks. What would it cost when her insurance switched to COBRA? The African drummers and their pulsating beat lit her mind. *Did he really heal himself? How could he?* She went into the bathroom to rinse out the nebulizer cup and face mask. The comforting advice of Dr. Breen echoed in her ears: *keep him on the medication through the winter unless you want to move into the emergency room.* For a pediatrician he had the worst bedside manner, and he intimidated Zig. Finding a new doctor was another task on her bottomless To Do list. Nausea and light-headedness plagued Zig whenever he took the steroids, at which point Dr. Breen would blithely remind her that it was a small price to pay to be able to breathe. Then there were a ton of other scary precautions that gave her pause. She pulled out the leaflet from inside the box of Pulmicort and read it again. *If you have switched from an oral corticosteroid (such as prednisone tablets) to this medicine within the past 12 months, your body may not produce enough natural steroids. Seek immediate attention if you experience any of the following signs: unusual weakness, sudden weight loss, vomiting, fainting, or severe dizziness...*

He was still in his room with the door shut. She knocked on the door.

"Come on out, sweetie. It's time for your treatment."

"Go away."

"Honey, you're an hour late and you really need to take this stuff." She tried the doorknob. It was locked. "Open the door, Zig."

"You don't care about me. You think I'm stupid."

She pressed her head against his door. "You know that's not true. I love you more than love itself." Guilt poured over her. "I'm sorry for not listening, Zig. Please open the door. I'll tell you the rest of my Indian story..."

He was quiet. She could hear him thinking.

He opened the door.

1899

Panama City, Panama

Last night I dreamt about you.

Louise filled the kettle with water and lit the stove. Then she fixed a tray of food for Maud: a bowl of Rosa's soup, freshly baked bread, a generous slice of papaya. She poured boiling water into a cup for Benjamin's tea. She didn't remember carrying the tray or the walk to Maud's bedroom. Her sister's familiar giggle trickled down the hall. When Louise reached the door Benjamin was standing at Maud's side, massaging her cheeks and temples. On the windowsill was a small mound of crushed leaves on a piece of paper. The paper rustled under a slight draft.

"This will release the pressure in your passages," Benjamin explained. "How do you feel now?"

"Much better! A moment ago my nose was completely stuffed!" Maud's eyebrows shot up at Louise. "Why didn't you bandage his hand? It's dreadful!"

Indeed, Louise had forgotten all about his hand. Blood caked in the slit and glistened bright red with his movements.

"It is nothing to be concerned about." Benjamin concentrated his attention on Maud.

"Well, I…between you and Benjamin I wasn't sure who needed attention most." Louise lowered the tray on her sister's lap. A gale shook the window, making the herbs inch to the sill's edge.

"I brought your favorite, Maud—Rosa's soup, bread, a slice of papaya, and hot *tea*."

Benjamin looked at the window. The herbs twittered, about to fall. Both he and Louise lunged to catch the drifting paper. Benjamin rescued it; a smattering of the herbs floated to the floor. Maud gripped her sliding dinner tray.

"My! I've never seen you move so fast, Louise." Maud said, with a look of amazement. "That must be some very fine tea."

Rain hammered the rooftop and Maud ate heartily, chattering away with stories of childhood injuries and past perilous storms. Louise sat on the edge of the bed, half listening to her idle conversation. Why wasn't he in a hurry, as she was? Louise crossed and uncrossed her ankles. Would he steal a glance at her? No, not in front of Maud. She barely joined the conversation; the memory of his kiss swept over her minute by minute. The teacup remained on the tray, waiting to be drunk. Would she ever stop talking? Maud's empty bowl and plate reminded her that neither she nor Benjamin had eaten since breakfast.

"Have your tea before it gets cold, Maud." Louise pushed the cup into her sister's hand and hastily removed the tray. "Watching you eat has made me hungry. I'll warm some soup for you too, Benjamin."

She left the room brimming with emotions. Everything around her took on a strange cast. The ceiling medallions disappeared into nothingness. Shadows on the wall stretched like a long black cat. The arched windows framed the storm as if it were an abstract painting. She touched the blurred glass. The idyllic scenes she often drew from this very window were now quite foreboding. A dish shifted on the tray and ended her musing. She went into the kitchen, finding spoons and ladling soup while her thoughts were wrapped in Benjamin's arms. Maybe she should not have left him alone with Maud—she might flirt with him indefinitely. *He fancies me—ask him!* If Maud knew how they had kissed. What if she didn't drink the tea? What if she spilled it on the bed? Louise looked at the empty void of the staircase. Suddenly a blaze of lightning flashed in the room. Cracks of thunder boomed, a patriarchal giant shouting at her from angry clouds. She hugged herself. It was just a storm—one of many she had weathered. But this storm swelled within her, throwing her into a sea of uncertainty. She carefully lifted her mother's delicate blue-and-white china from the closet. Her fingers traced the two birds gleaming on the intricate pattern. *It's called Willow…*Mother's hushed voice spoke to her. *There is a story. The birds were once young lovers who were forbidden to be together. They ran away but were found by the maiden's wealthy father. The father thrust a sword through her lover's neck. The daughter burned herself to death in mourning. Touched by their love, the gods immortalized them as two doves, eternally flying as one in the sky.* Louise placed the bowls on the table and felt Benjamin's palm on hers again. She put napkins under the silver spoons, imagining his breath on her neck. He was everywhere, numbing her thoughts until she forgot who and where she was.

Last night I dreamt about you…

"Louise."

Benjamin stood before her. She arose, awkwardly, from her chair at the table.

"How is Maud?"

"She's asleep."

The flame weakened in the oil lamp. He slid his hands, warm and strong, along her cheeks and pulled her mouth to his. The smell of herbs, the salty taste of his lips, his fingers on the back of her neck, sent her whirling. He kissed her hard and deep and she thought about the first time she saw him at the riverside in Guabito, how he had stared at her, openly, unabashedly, like no man ever had.

A chair toppled behind them. The lamp went out. In the purple darkness she felt him lift her damp dress, press his knee between her legs. His coarse trousers scratched her thighs. How many nights had she imagined this scene, words she would whisper, where she would touch him. But now she was only shaking, all of her, shaking. They heard a sudden cry. Could it be Maud?! They quickly stopped and listened. A sad wind moaned through a rusty shutter. He took her hand and placed it on his groin. She felt his growth, long, like the rest of him, and intuitively she closed her fist and squeezed. He pulled back. Had she ruined everything? His breath was heavy, his face a black void in the dark. He grabbed her waist and they tumbled onto the old narrow settee. Right there in the parlor, on the faded gold damask, where Mother had read her stories, where she once played hide and seek with Maud, where Rosa sang her lullabies when she couldn't sleep. Clumsily she fought the buttons on her bodice. Benjamin stripped off his trousers. He fumbled for her with one hand and himself with the other. Then the potent sweet odor of wild lilies overwhelmed her. Giant, white, hypnotic, vulgar. Blooming in the eye of the storm. She opened herself to him but did not wince. Finally, torn from the girl she wanted so desperately to cast aside. There was another flash of lightning. In that instant she saw him hunched over her, lips parted, holding her bent knee. He looks at her, his eyes wet.

2006

Brooklyn, New York

BY THURSDAY SHE HAD HAD ENOUGH of Zig's temperamental outbursts and was glad when he went back to school. The meds succeeded in curbing his asthma but not his attitude. Keeping to his dosages while juggling meals, dirty dishes, and laundry was insane, harkening back to those dark, sleep-deprived early days of his infancy. The heat hissed and the apartment was hot and she needed to get the humidifier out of storage in the basement. November ushered in another layer of clothes to put on, making the morning routine more chaotic. To top it off, Leatrice called to say she'd taken a new job as a nurse's aide at a rehabilitation center. Relieved of her conscience, Sheri felt happy for Leatrice yet sorry for herself. Zig barely noticed his babysitter's absence with his mother at home every day. How would she manage without any help? Disorganization gave her total brain fog; at the office her pencils had been centered neatly at the top of her desk, stapler and tape dispenser on the left, markers and drawing pad on the right. One item out of place would throw her into a fit. Crouched on the floor, she dug his right glove out from under the couch. His scarf was stuffed in his backpack. Hat…where the heck was his hat?

Zig gobbled up a bowl of cornflakes while she searched the apartment, swearing under her breath. Between mulling over her sordid state and finding his math workbook, she barely got him to school on time. After dropping Zig at the school gate she hurried down the block. She had just enough time for coffee before heading to someplace in Tribeca. Starbucks was already packed with the Laptop Nation—folks who rush in to grab their spot and set up office for the entire day. The sight of so many jobless types frantically e-mailing the world made her anxious. There was a Greek coffee shop around the corner, one of a dying breed, the kind with red vinyl–covered stools and Formica faux marble counters. She went in, sat at the counter, ordered coffee and a buttered bagel. She unfolded the flyer the school psychologist had given her. Today a man named Teka-mthi would be the last speaker in the Voices of the Elders series. She was tense. For some reason she kept picturing a seedy tarot card reader. She had Zig's tape in her bag. Should she go at all?

A woman who looked familiar entered the restaurant. Petite, with short-cropped hair. Of course. It was the viking's mother. Daniel was the son's name…Darn, what was hers? Why was it easy to remember a kid's name and not the mother's? She caught Sheri's eye and immediately came over.

"Hey, Sheri! How are you? How's Zig?" She had a slight British or Australian accent that Sheri had not noticed at the parade.

"Oh hi! Zig's just fine, thanks. I'm the one still recovering from Halloween." Sheri was of no mind to rehash anything that happened over the past couple of days. Her hope of having a cup of coffee in peace vanished. She pinched off a piece of bagel and popped it in her mouth.

"The kids are still buzzing about Zig and those drummers. Daniel and Kwami convinced everyone Zig made them magically appear and disappear!" Daniel's mother slipped onto the stool next to Sheri. "Black coffee, please," she said to the harried waitress. "The whole school must know by now. And just between me and you, Gina was totally spooked. The mother chuckled. "But to Daniel, Zig is like his own personal Harry Potter!"

"That's so funny. Zig couldn't get into those Harry Potter books." So the whole school knew. Sheri tried to dissolve the doughy lump in her mouth with a gulp of coffee.

"Oh, but they're fantastic! I read the first two. Daniel got totally hooked on the magic and wizardry."

"Zig would like everyone to think he's some kind of wizard. Things happen that are just such a coincidence."

"Well, actually I couldn't help but recall last summer when we saw a huge drumming ceremony at the Shinnecock pow-wow out on Long Island. It was an awesome experience, particularly for Daniel." The waitress came back and plunked down a cup of coffee in front of her. "At the end of the ceremony, the lead drummer told everyone how drums call out spirits to aid people—he called it the Sacred Language of Spirit."

"Really?" Sheri took another sip of coffee. "If I took Zig to a powwow he'd never want to come back to Brooklyn." She spit out the piece of bagel in a napkin.

"When Zig mentioned the drummer spirits I thought maybe you guys were at that powwow, too." Daniel's mom looked at her with bright, porcelain blue eyes. She was fishing for something, some reason behind what happened on Halloween night. Sheri pretended she got a text message. Maybe it would be a good idea to go hear the native elder.

"Actually, I've got to run or I'll be late for a meeting." She shoved a couple of dollars under her saucer for the tab. Nice talking to you—tell me your name again?"

"Clara."

"Clara! I'm so bad with names."

"Maybe the guys can get together for a play date sometime." Clara reached for her wallet, as if she might pay and walk out with Sheri.

"That'd be great—I'll call you!" Sheri backed out the door in a hurry. Why was she so paranoid? Any mother would be curious; Clara seemed honest enough. She just wanted to share a story, offer her take on a child as unusual as Zig. Powwow drummers and their Sacred Language of Spirit—that sounded kind of intriguing. But Zig like Harry Potter? How ridiculous.

She faced a row of identical three-story buildings near Franklin Street, none of which had any signage. Was this the right address? Sheri checked the building number on the flyer. A young man in suede moccasin boots hurried past her and opened one of the painted front doors. Behind the door was a long, floor-to-ceiling burgundy velvet curtain; a hint of burning sage puffed from its folds out into the street. In front of the curtain was a sea of shoes—a jumble of skinny heels, running sneakers, thick clogs—awaiting the return of their owners. The man removed his boots. Muffled voices came from beyond the velvet wall. This must be the place. Sheri hated being late. She reluctantly took off her shoes and piled them with the others, even though the door was unlocked and there were homeless bottle collectors lingering at the corner. Just then a woman with a doll-like face came up to her. She whispered a welcome and handed Sheri another flyer. The narrow, sunlit room had no furniture. Twenty or more people of various ethnicities dotted the floor, sitting cross-legged on small flat cushions. The ages ranged from early twenties to beyond retirement. She tiptoed between bodies and made her way to the back of the room, where a few people sat on folding chairs. Everyone's focus was on an old man at the head of the room. Dressed in ordinary jeans and a plaid flannel shirt, he wore only one native article— a breastplate made of bone and leather. Stiff, snowy white hair brushed his shoulders. The man was in the middle of a discussion, his tone calm yet firm. He looked directly at Sheri like an old friend, and in that brief glance he stripped away her doubts.

"We live a life of material longings and mediocrity, trying to find ourselves in things only to end up losing ourselves in them. The lies of the mind have only one purpose: to distract you from the truth of who you are. We are *spiritual* beings having a *human* experience. That is the truth. One day, maybe today, maybe this moment, you will move attention away from destructive thoughts. Then you will sense a deep awareness. You will sense the One within who is watching with you, through you. Just behind your thoughts is the One who observes all, knows all, sees all through you. Will we ever be happy, you ask? Happiness is here"—he pointed to the middle of his chest—"always here. True love and joy pours forth from the depths of our soul, yet we cannot feel it unless we connect with the Creator within."

The atmosphere was dense with thought. Sheri, too, pondered these words, feeling strangely at ease in this place. A hand went up.

"How can someone not identify with thought and things and still make a meaningful contribution to the world?" The man leaned forward, and she saw it was the guy in the boots who had passed her on the sidewalk.

Without hesitation the elder replied, "If what you want comes from your heart you must honor it, for whatever comes from the heart comes from the Creator. How can you hear the loving voice of your heart?" He paused to take in the audience with dark, steady eyes. "Be willing to stop relying on your thoughts as reality—thoughts of your past failures and successes, thoughts of your future goals. None of that exists. To discover what is real is to discover what is unchanging. That will lead you to make the right choices. All children can do this. Learn from them. Ultimately, it will be the young ones who will lead us from the long wintertime into the new springtime."

Sheri looked down at her fingers; the strap of her bag was wound tightly around them. She thought about Zig and his game of real pretend. He said he was once an Indian—his lives changed, but he didn't. What was unchanging? Who was Zig? Who was she? This man's claims sounded profound, but she couldn't grasp the meaning. She unwound her fingers and blurted out, "What is unchanging?"

Heads turned to see who posed the question. From their facial expressions Sheri could tell her question was in the minds of many.

"Anything that comes and goes is not real. What you are feeling in your mind and body—headache, hunger, anger, for example—that is just passing through you. Only what stays is real. It has always been here. That is the ultimate reality—awakening to what is always present regardless of your mental state. Turn your attention inward, to the Creator in you. Ask what is preventing you from knowing who you are? The answer will be this: what is true is always at peace and that is what you really are. Peace and love, that is unchanging."

Grace radiated to the corners of the room. Sheri stared at the still, humble old man. Peace. She was not at peace. A minute passed in silence. Lost in her thoughts, the buzz of more questions being asked brushed softly against her ears. *What is preventing you from knowing who you are?* She stayed awhile longer, then quietly stood up to leave. No one seemed to notice except the young man.

SHE HAD FORGOTTEN HER GLOVES, and her knuckles were turning a raw red already. It was too early in November to be this cold. Leaves settled into narrow brown strips and hugged the gutter; last week's burnished trees were now as plain as street poles, and the bare city streets looked like a vast asphalt stage. Mammoth emotions arose—lonely, disfigured sensations that bulged despite her pressing them down inside, the loss that had no home: *Who am I?*

They never talked about it. They believed if they raised her as if she were their own birth daughter everything would be fine. She wanted so much to talk about her adoption; her mother did not. Despite her parents' silence she remained loyal. But the void was always present; this craving that woke her up in the middle of the night would not let her be. She would do anything to fill that void, the greatest of which was giving birth to Zig. Even that euphoric feeling passed and the emptiness returned. Not knowing her ancestry, her real family, who she was. It was frightening how deep it ran. The only thing that took away her depression was her art. Drawing, painting, was once her sole outlet—it had the power to sweep away her sadness. *What was unchanging...*

She walked briskly back to Excelsior. Mrs. Johnston, with the phone tucked between her ear and shoulder, gestured to her to go into Jackie's office. Sheri was a little early for the meeting to review Zig's evaluation. As she approached the headmistress's office she overheard Jackie and Bruce inside talking.

"We differ on that point, Bruce. He's classic ADHD."

"Jackie, I'm not saying otherwise. My feeling is he could do just as well by seeing a therapist twice a—"

"Not in light of those recent rumors—"

Sheri knocked on the door.

"Come in!" Jackie's voice rang like the bell for the next class. Sheri entered the room, apparently unannounced.

"Sheri! Were you waiting long? Margaret didn't tell me you were here." Jackie glared at her phone.

"No, not at all," Sheri replied, feeling cautious.

"You've met Bruce Schumer."

"Yes, Hi Bruce."

"Hi, Sheri." Bruce, bearded and bohemian, looked out of place seated in the stately blue velvet armchair. He stood up tentatively to shake Sheri's hand, stretching his large clumsy frame.

"I'll take your coat. Would you like some coffee? Tea?" Jackie offered.

"I'm fine, thanks."

She hung up Sheri's coat in a corner closet. Sheri noticed the sofa she sat in last time was now under a window across the room. There was a matching blue velvet chair in its place next to Bruce's. She sat down in it. He smiled at her briefly, preoccupied, fingering papers on his lap. Jackie strode back and picked up a thin document on her desk.

"As you know, Sheri, Bruce conducted a psychological evaluation of Zig shortly after our meeting last week. We reviewed the report internally, going over the details of what happened, and what we can do to prevent accidents like this from happening in the future." Jackie glanced periodically from the document to Sheri.

"Academically, Zig is an excellent student. He is well liked by his peers. But there's another side to him that troubles us."

Bruce sat forward to explain.

"When I met with Zig we completed a BASC—a Behavioral Assessment System for Children. It's a series of questions that focus on both his strengths *and* weaknesses. In this way, positive features don't go unnoticed while potential problem areas are being explored."

"Ellie as well as the art and gym teachers also filled out Teacher Rating Scales." Jackie separated a few pages from her document.

"Teacher Rating Scales help us understand his behavior from the point of view of those who have the most interactions with Zig. They offer a well-rounded picture of him," Bruce remarked, shifting in his seat.

"What if I don't agree with his teachers' perceptions?" Sheri tried not to show her mounting agitation. "I know my son better than anyone."

Bruce, apparently used to this inquiry, hastily added, "That's where the PRS, or Parent Rating Scales, comes in." He sifted out a two-page form from the bundle on his lap. "After you complete this you can compare your observations to that of his teachers. Keep in mind that differences between teachers, parents, and psychologists' reports are common. That doesn't mean the evaluation is inaccurate"—Bruce pushed up his smeared glasses—"it just reflects real differences in Zig's behavior in various settings and around a variety of adults."

"It's important for us to take into consideration everyone's analysis of Zig," Jackie said, turning over a page. "After reading the teachers' reports and talking to each of them, we found Zig to be emotional and moody across the board. I'll quote from the report: 'He has a short attention span and tends to wander around the classroom. He constantly talks out of turn, won't take direction, and can be combative at times.'" Jackie looked expectantly at Sheri. Puzzled, Sheri turned to Bruce, who appeared to be deep in thought.

"An active imagination is a wonderful attribute. Zig has plenty in that area. But it can work for or against him—"

"The playground incident last week was a prime example of it working *against* him," Jackie added dryly, finishing Bruce's statement. Her emphatic "against" rubbed Sheri the wrong way. She observed Zig's interrogators. This was counter to what she discussed with Bruce just several days ago. She kept her mouth shut; flying into a rage would be something she would later regret. Bruce quickly summed up his analysis.

"All we're saying, Sheri, is we need to step up our efforts to help Zig."

"What are you recommending?" Sheri looked directly at Bruce.

"Zig would benefit from seeing a therapist twice a month." He twisted again in his chair. "In addition, a low-dose prescription drug like Ritalin would greatly help him to—"

"You're diagnosing him as ADHD?" Sheri blurted out; she could hardly believe what she was hearing. Bruce held up a hand as if to keep her at bay.

"Only a doctor can diagnose that, but it's possible he has a *mild* case of ADHD. His symptoms stem from more impulsive behavior than—"

"It was an accident! He didn't cause Francesca to faint. You yourself said that! The other boys didn't have a bad reaction." Sheri dug her nails into the antique armrest, her shrill voice odd in the genteel room. Jackie gave Bruce a cautious look before she spoke.

"Sheri, the PTA is demanding some explanation and rightly so. Every parent deserves to know that his or her child is safe and that what happened in the playground was an isolated incident. But there are clearly other issues at hand here. It's for Zig's own good and the good of the school."

"So you want to medicate him? Exactly how will that help? By suppressing his 'active imagination' so you can tell the PTA he's safe to be around?"

Bruce shook his head emphatically.

"It's not like that at all. I've seen great success with Ritalin, even in very low dosages. It's quite safe and has minimal side effects."

"Can't you find a less invasive way of handling him?" Sheri was exasperated.

"Methylphenidate is not newfangled or dangerous, as touted in the media. It's been in use for a very long time," Jackie said in a controlled, almost condescending voice. "I can understand your apprehension, Sheri, but I assure you, once you read the report, you'll see it's the best course for Zig."

"I'm not saying it's forever. We'd just like to see some improvement in his behavior." Bruce handed the papers he had on his lap to Sheri. "Here's a copy of the evaluation. I included a list of Web sites you can go to for information on ADHD, and some recommendations for a psychiatrist. You'll need a prescription for the proper medication and dosage." He looked sympathetic yet resolved. "Please feel free to call me with any questions. My extension is on the top of the page."

He'd completely flip-flopped on her. Bruce's face had a dog-beaten, spineless cast under Jackie's glower. This was not about Zig—no one gave a damn about him. The school's reputation was at stake. They didn't have the patience or desire to deal with a child who had a gifted imagination, even one with straight As. Zig didn't conform to Jackie's standards of excellence in character, so she had to find ways to shrink his head and shove him into Excelsior's mold. What was she to do?

Somehow she left Jackie's office without exploding. She told herself she needed to calm down, not rock the boat. The school year had just started. If she refused to comply with their recommendation they might ask Zig to leave. Could she realistically find another school now? Was it worth the risk? She clenched her teeth. Cold as the morning was, she needed to walk, needed the fresh air. On Montague Street she veered toward the Promenade. Except for the scattered pigeons she cut a lone figure on the brick-paved walkway. In the summer months the place was teeming with strollers and tourists; she would often wander there with Zig after dinner at their favorite Japanese restaurant, feeling the warm breezes off the East River, ice cream dripping from their cones down their wrists. She sat on the end of a bench, still clutching Excelsior's evaluation under her arm. One of the forms—the Parent Rating Scales—slipped out onto the ground. She snatched it up before it blew away and read some of the headings: Hyperactivity. Aggression. Conduct Problems. Anxiety. Depression. Somatization—what was that? She put the form on the bottom of her pile of papers and instead flipped through the teacher evaluations. All three teachers rated him within the same high range in most categories. She paged through to a chart that showed an overview of Zig's scores in all behavior areas. For each of these areas there was a shaded part on the chart with an asterisk next to it: *the shaded areas indicate problems your child is experiencing that are unusual and may require treatment.* Most of his behavior scores were in the shaded spots. She stuffed the report in her bag and leaned back on the bench, gazing out at the river. It always appeared cleaner and bluer in the fall, but just below the surface there was surely more garbage than fish. Across the river the South Street Seaport had the appeal of a ghost-town amusement park. Blocks of square buildings, pressed together like a Lego building set, lined the water's edge. And then there was the massive hole, the chunk cut out of the sky where the World Trade Center towers once stood. At that moment she felt akin to the void, plucked from the order of the universe. A tugboat cruised by, hauling a load of metal junk. Could that be more of the endless debris from 9/11? The city was like the scarab of Egyptian mythology; buildings were constantly being torn down and built up, an endless cycle of urban death and rebirth. She felt rooted to this ever-changing landscape. Her career, her son, and her life were falling apart. Could she restore them to their former state? What was worth salvaging?

A flock of pigeons perched on the iron railing to her right. Some meandered over to her, purling, heads bobbing, angling for the tiniest crumb to fall. In the bleached white sunlight they appeared soft and beautiful, not the germ-ridden "flying rats" they were called on the street. She took out the report again and read it through, her fingers warmed by the sun. Many of the claims were not unreasonable or untrue. Zig had occasional outbursts at home and at school. He was also very calm and focused at times; his behavior did not lean heavily one way or another. What would the prescription do to him? He took enough meds for his asthma, and now she was being forced to add yet another one to his list? She stood up from the bench and made her way to the train station. No. Absolutely not. She would talk some sense into Zig, scare him, make him promise to straighten up. Or else.

THAT EVENING AFTER HIS HOMEWORK was done and all the dinner dishes were cleared away, Zig took his shower and got into bed. Sheri watched him from her usual spot at the end of the bed. He had his Game Boy DS on, playing the latest brainless game that occupied his downtime. Why did she give in to the lure of electronic toys? What happened to the days when he played quietly with blocks and puzzles, his little face brightening at the right spot to place each piece? The puzzles were still there, in shoeboxes under his bed, collecting dust. She couldn't bring herself to throw them out.

"Ready to tell me the rest of Tima's story?" he asked. His eyes flashed, his thumbs moved like lightning over the plastic arrow controls, navigating squat, mustached cartoon men who tumbled off cliffs. She had been feeding him bits and pieces about Tima and her Indian adventures every night since last Sunday. They both looked forward to hearing it, especially since Sheri never knew where the story was going until she started to imagine it. All of a sudden a movie screen lit up and whole scenes came to life for her. It was refreshing to completely lose herself in a fantasy for his sake, to watch his enthusiasm grow to the point where he would sprinkle in glittery details to garnish the story. She was reminded of what the native elder said earlier, how children can teach you to live in the moment. But first she had some business to clear up.

"In a moment, Zig. I had a meeting with Jackie and Bruce this morning at school."

"Oh. They talk about me?" He didn't budge from his game.

"Of course."

"Am I in trouble again?"

"No, they just went over a report Bruce wrote about you."

"He wrote a report about me?" He turned away from the screen and the numbing arcade music for a second.

"Uh-huh—to help find out what's going on with you at school."

"Do they want to kick me out?"

"No way! You're one of their top students! Your grades make them look good. It's your attitude we have to work on."

"Attitude! I don't have any frigging attitude!"

"You're giving the teachers a hard time, Zig, wandering around the classroom…talking out of turn…"

"Mom, you don't understand. It's so boring there. They talk about the same stuff every day."

"Like what?"

"Like we're still going over the Haudenosaunees' longhouse, and we have to make a diorama of it, and Ms. Herman made crybaby Caleb my partner."

"Look, sometimes school's a drag, but I need you to be more aware of how you come off to your teachers. The things you do and say are disrespectful and disruptive to the class. It's getting so that—"

"I am not disruptive! I'm just trying to keep myself busy until lunchtime."

"This is very important, Zig. I want you to promise me you'll behave and keep your mouth closed even if you think Ms. Herman is wrong about something." She massaged her temples. "Write it down or ask me to speak to her. Just don't interrupt anymore. And don't walk around in class like you're the mayor. Do you hear me?"

"Yes, Mom."

"Good, I'm counting on you, Zig." Her warning had better sink in. The "game lost" theme chimed on his DS. Zig scowled, shut down the gadget, and threw it aside.

"Now, where were we in the story?" She buttoned the top of his pajama shirt. "Oh yes! Tima was mad at her grandfather for not letting her go to a birthing ceremony so she ran into the rain forest alone. She was too proud to mark her path since she knew the forest better than anyone. But she took a wrong turn and lost her way. Some of the animals in the forest sensed her fear and one of them, a coral snake, bit her on the ankle. She tried to get away but her leg grew very heavy. She had to rest and soon she got very sleepy. In a dream she saw very unusual, fantastic things, like fairies and rocks that could sing, and the ground moved like it was rolling under her. Then she felt something lift her off the ground."

"Grandfather found her! He picked her up and carried her to the river!" Zig unbuttoned the button on his shirt.

"Yes! Her grandfather saw the snakebite and tried desperately to help save her. He took her down to the river—"

"The *sacred Rain River*." Zig added.

"Right…the *sacred Rain River*—"

"And all the time she kept pointing up at the sky at the strange bird circling her, until feathers started floating down."

Zig fluffed his sheets up in the air, turning them into billows that fell gently over his lithe body. His comment jarred her. Shadowy images from her childhood dream began to swell in her mind, like ominous storm clouds. She had never told him about the nightmares she used to have. Zig kept talking, his sheets sailing in the air.

"Grandfather heard what the bird was saying and wanted her to wash her foot in the river, right?"

Confusion washed over her. There was a memory of doing… seeing… being… She started to feel nauseated. Sheri stood and the queasiness eased. Zig was kneeling in bed; his sheets fell to the floor. He nudged her.

"Tima saw something in the water." He took her hand and squeezed it. Her heart started to pound. She felt hot. Her memory strove to grasp it, the image that was just out of reach. Zig stared up at Sheri, waiting. She had a vision; a girl at a river, a man behind her, a short, wiry, brown man. The girl put her foot in the river, long dark hair fell in her face. She peered into the rushing water, the current strong, steady, the sun's rays streamed through the ripples, forming a honeycomb pattern, a matrix, then flashes of silver…then an image in the moving water, something not of the water. A girl bending into the river, looking beyond the water… The vision started to fade.

"She did…see…"

"Something in the water." Zig shook her hand. "What did you see?"

At once the room came back to her. Zig was kneeling in bed, eyes wide, hanging on her every word. All at once she understood. This was no story. She grabbed Zig by the shoulders.

"What did *'I'* see?" Sheri searched his face.

"I…I meant Tima."

"You know what she saw in the water. *You know who she is!*"

Zig shrugged and sank back into bed, feigning a careless attitude.

"I don't know. You tell me."

"How did you know about the bird, about the dream? Tell me, Zig!" She snatched him again and shook him repeatedly; he tried to pull away. *"What is this about?"* she yelled.

"You tell me, Mom!" he yelled back. "It's your story!"

A sense of fear gripped her. *"I have no story! It was taken from me!"* she screamed.

"No it wasn't. No one can ever take your story. You can't lose something that you are." He blinked back tears. "You just don't remember."

Sheri threw her arms around her son, flooding his neck with tears. "Who am I, Zig? Please tell me."

"You have to finish the story, Mom. You promised." He pried himself away from her and grabbed his pillow, pressing it hard over his head and ears. Frantic, Sheri tried to wrestle it from him.

"Tell me!"

A second wave of nausea hit her. She ran to the bathroom and spilled her stomach into the toilet. Flushed and feverish, she splashed water on her face, hands trembling. When she lifted her head from the sink, the face reflected in the medicine cabinet mirror was not her own.

The river water moved across the glass, swallowing Sheri's reflection, drowning her ignorance in its current. Only then was the image clear. Silver flickered and swirled into a daguerreotype of an elder native woman. The yellow moon shone in her eyes. A constellation of beaded light encircled her head; sparkling shells hung from her neck. The woman's smile stretched across the universe. Sheri stared until dizziness made her shut her eyes. She opened them to see her cold, wet face in the mirror. All was the same again.

1899

Panama City, Panama

AT DAWN THE STRONG GALES had run their course. Trees lay battered and broken. Lost curtains, undergarments, shoes, pottery, and roof shingles were scattered on the grounds. The garden furniture had vanished; only the table remained intact. Louise stood naked and transfixed at the garden window, awakened by a cock's crow. Slowly the fog cleared from her mind and she faced the spoils of the previous evening. Benjamin slept unclothed on the settee, which was moved three feet from its place near the end table. His smooth tan chest gently rose and fell; his long legs hung off the end of the cushions. The sight of him nude in the sitting room both enthralled and terrified her. Was Maud still asleep? And Rosa...she might walk in at any minute! What about Father? Could he be far away? The untouched soup, bread, and papaya were on the table, stiff and stale in the elegant china. Panic-stricken, she dashed to the powder room clutching yesterday's soiled dress. A few of mother's old gowns were still in the closet. Louise threw on a blue and white one and fumbled to fasten the scores of buttons at her waist, recalling how only hours ago she had unbuttoned her dress for him. A glimpse in the mirror brought a rude awakening: her hair was in an alarming state! But beneath the disarray a euphoric reflection shone back at her, a face that glowed.

Now decent, Louise went about in a frenzy to hide the vestiges of the night. She ran back and forth, from table to china cabinet, kitchen sink to pantry, her anxiety heightened by the slightest sounds. Rosa would thoroughly examine the house and Maud's condition upon her arrival. Louise glanced at the top of the stairs and listened for any stirring. Benjamin woke with a start, as if he sensed her dilemma. His sleepy gaze caught her off guard; the tureen she held slipped from her hand and crashed to the floor, the cold, thick soup splattering everywhere. Louise held her breath—had the noise awakened her sister, too? Except for the tick of the pendulum in the hall clock, all was silent. Benjamin clothed himself in haste. She knelt to gather the broken pieces of the precious bowl; the last time it was used was years ago, on Father's birthday. Mother had worn a ruffled blue and white dress that seemed to float about the room. Louise shook splinters from her hem before realizing she was wearing the very same dress. On that night, even though it was Father's birthday, Mother was the center of attention—beautiful and sensual, her dark eyes sparkling. One of Father's colleagues had too much wine and had tried to fondle her on the terrace. She remembered seeing Mother casually brush the man's hand away. Louise looked down at the dress—it fit her perfectly.

"What are you smiling at?" Benjamin whispered. He was helping her toss the broken porcelain into an old flour sack and gave her a long, curious look.

"I was just remembering this dress—it was my mother's. She wore it at my father's birthday party years ago," Louise whispered back.

"She must have been very beautiful. Like you." Benjamin beamed at her; she had never felt so alive and desirable.

They hid the sack in the back of the pantry, wiped up the spill and moved the settee back to its proper place. Though they worked quickly in silence their eyes spoke volumes whenever they met. Shortly after they restored the room to its former state Maud came scurrying downstairs.

"Is the storm over? Where's Rosa?"

Maud blushed when she saw Benjamin come out of the kitchen drying his hands on a towel. "I didn't know you were awake!" She crossed her arms over her chest and looked at Louise.

"The storm is gone, Maud. I dropped a bowl and Benjamin was kind enough to help me clean up the spill," Louise said, hoping to ease the awkwardness. A key turned in the lock on the front door. Maud dashed for the door; Louise followed tentatively, checking her reflection in the foyer mirror. Rosa bustled in. She dropped her pocketbook on the floor and ran to Maud.

"Oh, my little niña!" Her face was red and winded. "How I worried about you last night! God forgive me! Let me look at you."

Rosa took Maud by the hands and stood back to study her from head to toe. She prodded under her chin for swollen glands. She pressed her ear to Maud's back to listen for any tight sounds.

"Your chest is quiet, but your face is so drawn. Have you eaten?"

Maud yawned and shook her head. Rosa finally glanced at Louise.

"I was about to look for tea cakes." Louise rubbed her knuckles. Rosa spotted Benjamin behind her, who was picking up leaves that had blown into the alcove.

"Aye! What happened to your head?" Rosa let go of Maud's hand and walked over to him. Maud gushed with minute details of his heroic rescue of the garden table and the resulting accident. Rosa hummed and nodded, paying more attention to Maud's zeal than to the story. Louise observed Rosa's tightly folded arms, her firmly grounded feet. Though Rosa had a similar rural upbringing, it was obvious she considered herself a class above Benjamin, having been employed by a prominent family for almost twenty years. Benjamin, on the other hand, showed little interest in class and race. Rosa would be shocked to know that Benjamin's father was a missionary, that he was raised in a fine home in San Jose, that he was more educated than she was. At the conclusion of Maud's story Benjamin stooped down for Rosa to examine his wound. Louise felt a twinge as she yanked off the bandage.

"You will need a doctor for this." She poked at the scab with a meaty finger.

"I can take care of it myself, Señora. Louise was kind enough to clean the wound for me."

"A wonder since it got so dark! Louise took forever to light the oil lamps," Maud reported eagerly, shifting her weight from foot to foot. Rosa raised an eyebrow and tilted her head at Louise. Color rose to Louise's cheeks.

"It's half past nine and we are without breakfast! I'll brew some café."

Louise rushed away, but not before she heard Benjamin offering to survey the damage done to the property. Maud put her arms around Rosa, leaning her blond head on the solid woman's shoulder. Benjamin discussed Maud's health and how she had improved greatly over the past week. Louise tinkered in the kitchen, stalling, relieved that Benjamin had distracted their housekeeper. She worried about Rosa. *Did she sense a change in Louise? Could she tell that something happened last night?* Louise rejoined them in time to hear Rosa's charge.

"Now that Maud is well enough you can go back home to your grandfather. A coach comes on Friday."

"So soon, Rosa?" cried Maud.

Louise could not believe her ears. "But we're not sure how the storm has affected Maud—you even said she looked drawn! Shouldn't he stay as a precaution for another few weeks?" The note of desperation in Louise's voice made Rosa all the more firm.

"Those were your father's orders. The coach comes at dawn on Friday."

To her astonishment, Benjamin thanked Rosa, saying his grandfather would be very happy to have him come home. "I'll pack my belongings and be ready to leave."

"But that is just four days away! What if she falls ill again?" Louise blurted out.

"Actually, I feel fine! The best in ages!" Maud answered cheerfully with a touch of spite.

Benjamin grinned at Maud, his posture relaxed and easy.

"Yes, you're strong enough now. Grandfather will be pleased."

The kettle screamed. Louise went to the stove, her eyes brimming over. How could he leave her now? Rosa entered the kitchen to start breakfast. Louise quickly wiped her face with the back of her hand.

"That dress is very nice on you Louise." Rosa's wide back was turned.

Louise touched the flouncing skirt. "It's one of Mother's old gowns…"

"I know," Rosa replied.

AFTER A SOLEMN BREAKFAST Rosa immersed herself in housecleaning. Maud lolled on the settee where Louise and Benjamin had spent the night, flipping through a picture book on rare orchids. Where was Benjamin? Her heart ached. She went up to her bedroom to be alone with her sorrow. The room now had a mundane quality about it. Her bed, unslept in for just one night, felt cold and lonely; the rose-patterned coverlet seemed juvenile. She sat on the edge of the bed but soon became restless. She threw open the window shutters, hoping to see Benjamin in the garden. Some of the broken branches, fronds, and debris from the storm had been cleared, but he was not there. Could he be packing his bags already? She opened her door and went down the hall to the bathroom. She picked the bottle of iodine and gauze off the shelf in the medicine cabinet again. In four days he would leave her, perhaps forever. Louise closed the cabinet and continued on to the guest bedroom. Before she knocked the door opened. Benjamin stood there, undressed to his waist. Quick as lightning, he slipped his arm around her and pulled her to him, closing the door without making a sound. He kissed her eagerly, his lips, his smell, transporting her back to last night. The pain of his near departure disappeared. She wanted nothing more than to allow the weakness in her knees, in her hips. Suddenly she heard Maud's and Rosa's footsteps near his door. Louise gasped.

"They won't come in here," he whispered, his breath warm on her neck. "Those two will be inseparable for most of the day."

Their laughter faded past Benjamin's door into Maud's room. She could hear Maud's muffled babble and Rosa knocking around, straightening the room, picking up clothes. Benjamin and Louise clung to one another, listening to every move on the other side of the wall, the threat of discovery heightening their desire. Benjamin pulled back.

"Go now—they won't hear you. Promise me you'll come again tonight, after midnight. I'll undo the lock on the balcony door."

Louise felt drunk; her lips pleasantly chafed.

"I promise."

He opened the door as silently as he had closed it. Louise passed undetected, as through a looking glass, from lover back into her common place as daughter and sister.

2006

Brooklyn, New York

CHAPERONING A FIFTH-GRADE SCHOOL TRIP is not for the faint-hearted. With one other mother and the teacher, Sheri helped corral seventeen wired kids into the Borough Hall subway station, steering them on the narrow sidewalk away from dull-eyed city workers. Crossing the hectic two-way intersection at Adams Street, she made herself a human roadblock in case a kid straggled behind when the light changed. The National Museum of the American Indian was at Bowling Green in Lower Manhattan, just a few stops on the No. 4 train. She stood in the middle of the subway car so she could get a good look at Zig's classmates. Each kid had such quirky expressions, but what she noticed most was their teeth. New front teeth too large for their mouths, so big their lips never fully closed over them. Some with braces, some stuck with food, some with wide gaps waiting for adult teeth to sprout, black holes that punctuated their giggles with little flying bits of spit. They laughed too loud and belched and scratched their butts. She found it amusing that they were not at all self-conscious, not as much as they would be next year when puberty would steal the elfin sweetness from their faces.

The children were giddy, happy to be out of the classroom, eager for a diversion, even if they had to write a report about it for homework. Zig was holding court with a group of boys and a girl or two. Every so often he glanced at Sheri, mindful of the showdown they had two weeks ago. Since then he seemed to be on his best behavior; at least she didn't get any more calls from school. She made no motion to take him to a therapist or get the prescribed drugs. As long as he listened to her he'd be okay. She watched the dynamics between Zig and some of his classmates. He was quite popular. They tended to follow him around and repeat the things he said. Although Zig did not seem arrogant, it was clear to her how teachers might be annoyed at his reputation. Kids who are saucy and smart give teachers a hard time. They said he was disrespectful. He said they were bubbleheads who couldn't teach him anything he didn't already know. Zig's questioning, steady brown eyes gave him an air of maturity compared to his gawky counterparts. Herding the crew off at the Bowling Green station, Sheri did a headcount before they left the platform. She was relieved when the museum door closed behind her and the kids were in a contained environment. Everyone craned their neck to take in the stately lobby. She had passed this building many times on her way to someplace else and never noticed the imposing neoclassical sculptures of Indians and soldiers that guarded the entrance. The entrance led to a great hall, ornately festooned with marble columns and gold, rose, and green mosaics. To her right and left were curved staircases, rich Victorian-era details, bronze railings, and more marble. She read that there were several ceremonial areas within the building, and she wondered what kind of rituals took place on those polished stone floors a century ago.

The kids chattered, jostled each other, swung their bag lunches. Ellie got their attention by ringing a small brass bell.

"Okay 5-B, our guide is ready to take us on the exhibit. Food and drinks are *not* allowed in the museum, so as you enter please place your lunch bag in the *blue* bin until lunchtime. Place your coat in the *red* bin!" She spoke so loud corded veins popped out of her skinny neck. *What was with the bell?* Ellie then turned to Sheri and the other mother, dropping her voice a few decibels.

"There has to be one chaperone per ten students—Janis, would you mind going with the first nine and Sheri, you cover the other eight? That should work out just fine."

"No problem." Sheri sized up her group, which included Zig and his posse.

"Just FYI, the guides are prickly about chaperones and children staying with their group. The museum will shut down the tour if anyone acts up or strays from the rules." Ellie tried not to look directly at Sheri, but she got her drift.

There was no talking during the tour unless you raised your hand. Zig's followers dispersed and formed one straight line down the hall. The guide, called a "cultural interpreter," introduced herself as Mary and led them to their first exhibit. She was a sturdy young woman with a single long braid trailing down her back. At the entrance to the exhibit she turned to address the class.

"Welcome to the National Museum of the American Indian. *Who stole the TeePee?* is the title of the exhibit you're about to see. Anyone have any idea what this title means?"

A few hands went up, including Zig's. The guide picked him.

"It's about how white men took everything our native ancestors ever had."

Sheri's eye twitched. She remembered that night at home, how Zig knew her childhood nightmare, the image of the old woman in the mirror. She couldn't stop thinking about it. *What else did he know?* Since then neither one of them brought up the story again. The thought of it made her uneasy.

"Well, that's one way of explaining it," the guide replied, smiling at Zig. "Anyone else?"

The class followed the guide through a vast collection of photography, fine art, pottery, sculpture, and crafts that depicted various stages of change among the Indian Nations. The pieces were fascinating, the history depressing. Sheri was drawn to a late-nineteenth-century photo of two native men, perhaps brothers. One was dressed in traditional Indian attire—a long tunic and a feathered headdress—while the other wore typical American cowboy boots, hat, and a vest. A holster with a gun and a bullet holder was slung low around his hips. Standing straight and proud, the brother dressed in native clothes radiated an inner peace. The other brother was bent to reach his gun, basking in its newfound power. A smirk curled his lips. Was this an actual portrait? Or were they dressed up and posed for the shot? She looked down and read the caption. *Photographer Unknown.*

"Native Americans used art as a way to cope with change on the reservations. Take a look at this painting—can you tell what the artist was trying to say here?"

The class crowded around a large colorful mural. Janis stood post behind her group. Sheri stepped over to her group and counted out seven children. One child was missing—Zig.

While everyone was engrossed in the mural, Sheri's eyes darted wildly about the room. Zig wasn't anywhere in sight. *How could he do this to her?* Perhaps he was still in the other exhibit hall, reading the artist notes on the wall. She tapped Janis on the shoulder.

"I think Zig is still in the other room. Would you mind covering my kids for a few minutes while I grab him?" she whispered.

"Not at all—go right ahead," Janis whispered back.

Sheri slipped out and started retracing her steps, her mind racing faster than her feet could carry her. An elderly couple was admiring a beaded vest in the previous exhibit. He wasn't there. Panic set in. *Which way should she turn? Did he sneak into the museum shop? What if he was abducted?* Faces of missing kids on milk cartons flashed across her mind. She shook it off. Zig was too clever to be lured by a stranger. He had to be here somewhere. She ran past the great hall into the equally enormous rotunda, past glass cases filled with gold and silver amulets, masks, vessels, jewelry—no Zig. She dashed through a photo gallery; tribal men and women in larger-than-life prints watched as she almost tripped in the dim spot lighting. She made a left now, going practically full circle on the second floor, looking in corners and around columns for a glimpse of Zig's red and white rugby shirt. In the museum shop were two saleswomen—one folding a star quilt, the other writing on a pad at the register.

"May I help you with something?" the cashier asked.

Sheri hesitated. If she said her son was missing it would cause a stir. She turned away. The few people walking around did not notice her anxiety. After bursting into the men's bathroom, causing a security guard at a urinal to swear and fumble, she found herself at the information desk. The receptionist showed a bit of concern.

"Are you all right, Miss?" She paused from stacking her brochures.

"Actually, I'm trying to find my ten-year-old son…He wandered off somewhere on this floor."

"Did you check the reference library? I saw a boy walk in there a little while ago." She pointed to an opening behind the desk with heavy carved doors. In her chaos Sheri thought the area was for museum staff. She rushed over and looked inside. To her left she saw the blue jean–clad rears of a man and a boy standing side by side, poring over a large volume of some sort on a desk. Was that Zig? She couldn't see his shirt. Was he wearing jeans today? She crept closer to them to get a better look.

The two were talking quietly. They spoke in another language, Spanish maybe. A word or two sounded familiar—yes, it was Spanish. The boy turned his head and she saw her son's face.

"Zig!"

At once Zig straightened up and turned around. The school tour sticker was missing from his shirt. He held a crumpled piece of paper in one hand. Sheri recognized the man, too—he was at the lecture, the one in the moccasin boots. He had a chopped ponytail and a small gold hoop earring in each ear.

"Mami!" Zig exclaimed. He turned to the man and spoke hurriedly, excitedly, but what he said she had no idea. It was not in English. He waved the piece of paper in the air like a white flag. It was the page he had ripped from her journal, filled with her squiggly ink doodles. She was stunned. Was he speaking Spanish?

The thirty-something man extended his hand to Sheri. He spoke to her in Spanish. Sheri stared at his open hand before placing hers in it. She looked at Zig.

"No hablo español."

The man's face went blank.

"I'm sorry...I..." The man glanced at Zig. Zig didn't flinch.

"What's going on here?" she demanded.

The young man volunteered an answer. "I'm Miguel Murillo, the education curator for the museum. Your son came in to ask some questions about the drawings on this piece of paper." (Zig held the page in front of his face, as if to hide behind it.) "He wanted to know what tribe they came from and what the symbols meant."

The awkwardness passed. The man took the paper from Zig and moved closer to Sheri.

"Show my mom what we found about the drawings!" Zig said.

"Sí, it's right here." A weighty encyclopedia was open on the desk. But the clock overhead gave Sheri a jolt. How long had she been gone?

"Zig, we have to go right now." Her eyes darted at the door.

"It'll only take a second!" Zig pulled her over to the book before she could protest further. On the page were several drawings that were strikingly familiar—the feathery dashes and partial circles, the inverted stick figures, the spindly trees. The heading at the top of the page read: *Ulu Healing Cane and Setee Diagrams. Nrvai.* All the drawings seemed identical to the doodles she drew as a child and in college; the ones she still drew absentmindedly when she was on the phone or in meetings, in doctor offices, brainstorming for creative ideas... The nausea and dizziness started again. Was this some sort of trick? Wasn't she on a school trip? Somewhere children and adults were waiting. She heard Miguel explain the drawings—sacred symbols shamans used in healing ceremonies...vary slightly from tribe to tribe...Central American region... particular to indigenous groups in Costa Rica.

He read aloud from the text: "Ulu symbols are perhaps one of the most original and unacculturated graphic art forms remaining in the Central American region, and is a highly concentrated cultural artifact. Whereas many other indigenous art forms in the region are undergoing rapid acculturation, the ulu, by its very nature as a healing instrument, has a higher purpose. Though the ethnographic details may not be long remembered by anyone but the specialist, the sense in which we are linked with nature, psychic, somatic and environmental, may remain."

Sheri watched Miguel take the book away to make copies, dazed by what she had just heard and seen.

Zig whispered triumphantly, "Told you so!"

Too much was happening at once. The school. The symbols. The Spanish. Her voice cracked when she spoke.

"What were you saying to that man?"

"What?"

"I heard you talking just before I came in here...You were speaking Spanish!"

Zig paused. "I was?"

"Yes!"

He shrugged. "So?"

Sheri looked at her son, bewildered. "How did you? It sounded like fluent Spanish!"

"I dunno. It didn't feel any different."

Miguel came back and gave the copies to Sheri. His long arms dangled at his side, as if they were itching to be used.

"We met somewhere before." He stared at her, searched her face. "Voices of the Elders. You were there—you asked a question."

She smiled. "So did you."

"What's Voices of the Elders?" Zig asked.

"Tell you later, Zig. We better go."

"I wish you had more time." He eyed Sheri. For a second she almost blushed. He was kind of young, and it had been a while since she paid attention to a man's roving gaze.

"We'll come back tomorrow!" Zig suggested.

"Thanks for the copies," she said hurriedly, hoping Ellie and his class would not see them leave the library.

Miguel dug in a leather satchel that was slung over a chair. "Take my card, please."

He quickly scribbled his cell number on the back of the card. "I'm here everyday except Mondays. I'd like to help you with your research." He locked eyes with her. A peculiar feeling came over her and she looked away. She walked out, Zig grinning alongside her. When no one was in sight she snatched him aside.

"Are you crazy? You think you can do whatever the heck you want? Disappear whenever you feel like it?"

He stared back at his mother's black expression. "I needed to know where—"

"Everyone is waiting for you!"

He looked at the journal page Miguel had given back to him. "These drawings are special."

Her cell started vibrating in her bag. *Shit.* She had no idea where his class was. What if the tour guide found out and the kids had to leave the building? She fumbled to answer her phone but it had stopped buzzing. There were two messages—both from Ellie:

"Sheri, it's Ellie…We're waiting for you at the third gallery. Janis said you went to find Zig. I hope everything's okay. Please call me."

She sounded annoyed. Sheri pressed delete. The second message played; Ellie's voice was now completely agitated.

"It's Ellie again. We have to cut the tour short and leave the museum. If it's warm enough we'll eat lunch in the park out in front of the building. Please give a call as soon as you get this message." She pressed delete again, dropped the phone in her bag.

"Come on Zig, let's go."

OUTSIDE THE MUSEUM in the gloomy daylight Zig's classmates were perched on the edge of wood benches in the park, quietly eating their lunch. She waited for the looks she was bound to get and the dialogue she was about to have. Ellie sat with a sandwich on her lap, talking to Janis, who listened with patchy interest. Ellie stood up abruptly when she saw Sheri and Zig enter the park.

"Ellie, I am so sorry." She didn't waste a moment apologizing. "I got your messages shortly after I found Zig."

"What happened? We were worried about you, Zig." The sharp wind blew her thin straw hair in every direction. She looked cold and anything but concerned.

"He had a question for the reference librarian that couldn't wait." Sheri took a knit hat out of his coat pocket and pulled it on his head. Zig just stood there, eyes downcast.

"We missed a lot of the exhibit and were asked to leave because you didn't stay with your group, Zig," Ellie said in a controlled, peeved tone. Sheri nudged Zig.

"Sorrrry," he said reluctantly. She hoped he would look sheepish, but he obviously didn't care.

"I'm terribly sorry, Ellie. Is there anything I can do? Will they let us finish the tour?"

"No, unfortunately. We'll have to try again another day." Ellie threw the rest of her sandwich in a garbage can with an air of disgust. She walked over to the children.

"Okay, 5-B—line up!"

Zig ran to his posse, only now they all shunned him. With sidelong glances they watched him, the way kids do when one of the clan is in big trouble, not wanting to be party to it. No one said a word to him. He stood at the very end of the line, his hands in his pockets. Sheri felt horrible. She was sure this would have repercussions at school. Yet she was calmer this time; she didn't stress over what the results of his brazenness would be. Her thoughts instead turned to the scene in the museum library, the relief of finding her son safe, the wonder of him speaking Spanish to the handsome curator, the amazing likeness of her doodles to the Nrvai shaman drawings. She unzipped her bag and touched the folded copies from the reference book, as if the pages were alive.

After they got off the subway Sheri walked behind her group of children back to Excelsior. Zig was still ostracized and hung back a bit, separated from everyone except his core followers—Daniel and Kwami. They skipped beside the incorrigible class troublemaker, drawn to the element of danger and freedom he represented. He was the best bad boy they ever knew. Sheri walked close enough to catch snippets of their conversation.

"Guess what?" Daniel said to Zig. "We don't have any homework since we didn't finish the tour!"

"Ms. Dodson will probably throw me out of the school, so I

won't have to do it anyway."

Sheri was alarmed by his remark. *Did he do all this on purpose, to try to get expelled?*

"I bet she won't!" Daniel protested.

"She might. She's mean and ugly," Kwami added, emphasizing the "ugly."

"I don't care. I hate this school anyway," Zig admitted.

"You weren't even gone so long. That woman kept talking and talking." Kwami rolled his eyes and his head in a circle.

"And you missed the scary sculpture," Daniel added.

"Yeah! A bunch of naked dead bodies kneeling on the ground like this." Kwami collapsed on his knees in the middle of the sidewalk and crossed his hands behind his back.

"With rope tied around their wrists and the rope went up to the ceiling," Zig said, kicking a paper cup to Daniel.

"Hey—how'd you know?" Daniel kicked the cup back. Zig did not answer. The boys were quiet for a few moments. Zig took off his hat; cowlick curls popped out.

"Since there's no homework we can all have a play date!" Daniel said.

Kwami looked disappointed. "Shucks…I have piano after school."

"Mom, can Daniel come over for a play date? Please?"

She stared into his pleading eyes. Any other mother would severely punish their child for the downright craziness Zig put her through, but Sheri was still staggered by what he had discovered. Something propelled Zig to break the rules, drove him to single-handedly investigate her drawings. He seldom asked for play dates, and she knew he was feeling rejected.

"I'll check with Daniel's mom."

Zig glowed at her.

DANIEL CAME HOME WITH ZIG, and the boys spent the afternoon cloistered in his room. Sheri put some frozen chicken nuggets and bite-size pizzas in the toaster oven, listening to the muffled sounds of them comparing cell phone features and rap music ringtones. While they played she went into her bedroom and left the door slightly ajar. She spread the photocopies Miguel had given her out on her bed. Again her pulse raced at the sight of the photos and illustrations. Several of them looked almost exactly like her doodles. The text next to the illustrations was entirely in Spanish. At the bottom of the page were Miguel's handwritten notes for Web sites with more information. Sporadic sword fighting and melodramatic warrior role play carried on in the next room. She quickly booted up her laptop and went online. The first Web site showed the same page she had from the museum—in both Spanish and English. She clicked on English and began to read:

Inverted figures, as seen here in a drawing done on paper by a Nrvai awa, or shaman, represent serious imbalance in the health of the patient. Illness is considered to have a somatic, social and ecological character in the local belief structure.

Sheri scrolled through the page until her eye caught a paragraph on the philosophy of illness:

Good or bad health results not from the presence of or absence of pathogens alone but from the proper or improper balance of the individual. Health is harmony, a coherent state of equilibrium between the physical and spiritual components of the individual. Sickness is disruption, imbalance, and the manifestation of malevolent forces in the flesh. In general, physical ailments that can be treated with herbal remedies are considered less serious than the troubles that arise when the spiritual harmony of the individual is disturbed. In such cases, it is the source of the disorder, not its particular manifestation, that must be challenged.

ACROSS FROM HER BED was a walk-in closet. She switched on the closet light and opened the accordion doors. On the floor in a corner under the hem of an evening gown was an old cardboard box taped shut. The tape was yellow and stiff; the glue had worn off and the flap was loose. She slid the box out into the middle of the room and sat down on the floor, chipping the tape off like old paint. Inside was a mishmash collection of memorabilia. Her high school prom corsage, summer camp emblems and stickers, a long flannel bag containing her recorder, old perfume bottles, a spiral notebook with eighth-grade poems, her elementary, middle, and high school yearbooks. She chose the middle school yearbook. Inside one of the pages was a faded piece of construction paper folded into quarters. The paper had once been badly crumpled and smoothed out. She removed the paper and unfolded it carefully; sections had torn apart in the creases from age. The page opened to a drawing she made long ago at home, sick in bed, one she saved from the trash when her mother wasn't looking. The crayon colors were dull and patchy, but the pencil lines were still clear. She remembered spending so much time drawing the upside-down figures, the domes with crisscrossed lines, the tree symbols and arcs of flame. A single stroke divided groups of drawings; only some of the figures were colored. She got up from the floor and lay the torn pieces of paper next to the ulu drawings from the library. They were one and the same.

THE BOYS CHUGGED DOWN the snacks she had made, and soon Daniel's babysitter came to pick him up. Afternoon turned into evening; Sheri and Zig passed it mostly in silence—Sheri studying Zig, contemplating everything that had occurred, and Zig anticipating the consequences of his actions. At dinner they both picked at their cold mashed potatoes.

"Are you still mad at me?" Zig asked.

"I don't know what to feel." Sheri took a sip of water and longed for wine.

"I was right about the symbols, wasn't I?"

"Well, it was a pretty amazing coincidence."

Zig looked at her defensively. "There's no such thing as 'coincidence.'"

They both fell silent again.

"I'm baffled about a lot of things, Zig. First you disappear, then I find you with a piece of my journal, speaking Spanish to that museum guy—"

"Miguel likes you. He said your drawings were fascinating."

"Never mind that. The whole class missed out on the tour. Ellie was quite upset."

"Who cares?" he mumbled under his breath.

"*I care!* And so should you. That was a selfish thing to do, and your classmates had to suffer because of it."

"They were glad to get out of the homework."

Sheri thumped her fist on the table, rattling the dinner dishes. "You listen to me. The school wants to medicate you because you keep getting out of line. I thought you were responsible enough to behave. Now I know you're not. I don't want to give you that stuff unless I have to. Ms. Dodson will probably ask if you're taking the Ritalin. I can't afford to put you in another school, Zig. It's almost the holidays and the public schools around here are awful and—"

"Mom, when I was an Indian I used to chew all kinds of roots and herbs...I bet they were more powerful than...what's it called? Ridden?"

"*Ritalin.*"

"Oh. I thought you said *ridden,* for like, 'getting rid of somebody.' Psssh. That's nothing. I think Kwami takes it. And if Kwami can take it, I can take it."

How'd she end up with such a swaggering, smart-mouthed kid? Ridden. She started to laugh. He joined in too, but it was a cautious laughter, as if they were whistling in the dark. Sheri hugged him tight.

"I don't want you to take any more medicine than you need to. In fact, you need a neb treatment tonight." She looked at the clock on the stove. "It's almost ten already? Hurry up and get to bed!"

AFTER ZIG FELL ASLEEP she spent the night Googling and devouring all she could find about the Nrvai Indians. From travel sites to scholarly papers, she scoured Web sites and images of these indigenous men, women, and children. The Nrvai settlements were near the Panamanian border, along Costa Rica's Caribbean coast. It all made sense. Guabito was the small border town in Panama where she was adopted. Someone must have brought her from Costa Rica to that orphanage in Panama, the place that had a fire and closed down shortly after she was adopted. Each picture she found was like peering into a faded mirror. There were glimpses of features that favored Zig: the slight body frame, chiseled cheeks, but in particular the eyes—not only the shape of the eyes but the expressiveness of them; the sparkling clarity, keen and penetrating, that could cut right through you. He had her eyes.

Her mind spun with revelations. *Could it be true? Was this a link to her past, her true identity?* It was starting to creep up inside her again, the unresolved years of grief that terrified her. She grabbed her carbon pencils and drawing pad, the only things that could save her when darkness fell on her mind. Sheri drew long into the night through crashing waves of tears, her paper stained with teardrops and smudges of black.

THE SOFT MORNING LIGHT BUTTERED the living room walls and followed the curves of Sheri's body as she lay curled like a baby on the sofa. She awoke with a start, but her memory was soon restored. She picked up her drawings, put them in a duffel bag along with Zig's audio tape, and set them at the apartment door.

At 9:30 A.M. she walked into the research library at the National Museum of the American Indian, where Miguel was unlocking a glass cabinet filled with old books. They saw each other at the same time. He came right over, staring, studying her face.

"Sheri! I was hoping you'd come back."

He was more mature and striking than she remembered.

"Hi, Miguel. I'm sure you heard what happened with the Excelsior school tour."

He rolled his eyes. "Rules are ridiculous here. Zig asked questions those tour guides never could've answered."

"That's sort of why I'm here. With all the information you gave me I…I hardly slept last night. Maybe you can help me."

She reached into her bag and pulled out a handful of drawings.

Hours passed like minutes in the library. Miguel piled reference books, articles, microfilm, notes, and monographs on the table—every text available on the Nrvai settlements in Central America. He took great interest in the similarities between her art and the shamanic drawings. Wheeling a cart with audio equipment into his tiny cubicle, he played Zig's tape over and over again. Several of the words sung were matched to the Nrvai language. Miguel's honesty and openness moved her to let her guard down. She told him about her upbringing, her adoption, the silence surrounding her origins, the little information she had found, and how she started drawing as far back as she could remember. Every day for five days Sheri came to the library while Zig was at school, and like a jigsaw puzzle with a thousand bit pieces she tried to fit the borders of her origins together. A gaping hole in the middle remained.

On the fifth day her research hit a wall. Miguel suggested she take a break, and they went outside for a walk. Just behind the museum was Battery Park. She thought she knew all the parks in the city, but as she strolled along the barren, winding paths that led to the Hudson River, she realized she had never been there before. The famous World Trade Center sphere that had survived September 11 was displayed, not unlike a scene from *Planet of the Apes,* in the entrance to the park, an eternal flame nearby keeping vigil. Triple-decker Statue of Liberty ferries were docked at the shore as frosty visitors filed on. The steely river was turbulent, the wind bracing. Her body ached from storing up information; the muscles in her back and shoulders refused to relax, and it hurt her eyes to blink. Miguel walked beside her with an athletic gait. She couldn't conceal her disappointment, and he didn't ignore it.

"You said the orphanage was in Panama, but the symbols are clearly from the Nrvai," he said, reflecting on her work.

"It doesn't matter. The orphanage burned down long ago. I'll never find an original birth certificate." She hugged herself. The cold crept through her hat and froze her ears.

"The Nrvai have a strong oral tradition. Stories about the village shaman and his travels are passed down from generation to generation. If you're a descendant there must be someone still living who might know what happened to your family."

He was serious. Sheri shook her head.

"I doubt it, Miguel. With so many people and villages and stories, it would be impossible to find the right leads, and then there's the language barrier—"

"I can take you there. I know Costa Rica quite well. I was born there."

Sheri stopped walking. She looked at him in surprise. He never mentioned where he was from.

"I was raised here in New York, but when my parents retired they moved back home to San Jose. I go every year for the holidays. I could show you and Zig around the country. Now's the best time. It's the dry season, and the Talamanca Mountains are so beautiful. Come with me—get firsthand answers to your questions."

His smiling face was radiant against the stark November sky. Her first instinct was to decline. She hardly knew him. And what would Zig think?

"That's a very tempting offer, Miguel. I'll have to think it over," she finally replied, "but it might not turn up anything."

"You'll have access to much more information and artifacts in Costa Rica. What have you got to lose?"

Everything I ever believed about myself, everything I'm used to feeling, she thought. He looked sincere. It was possible to go, she had time. She could find the money. Nothing was holding her back.

Sheri tried not to show it, but she was excited. Miguel was knowledgeable about many things so far, and she could hardly believe he was from the very place she needed to explore. Most important, Zig liked him. So did she.

That night Sheri told Zig about their travel plans.

He jumped around the apartment like a cartoon character, totally elated. They hauled their summer clothes out of storage in the basement. She brought home glossy brochures and a Costa Rica pocket travel guide. Zig planned their itinerary, minute by minute, from Christmas Day to New Year's Day. In a little over a month Sheri would discover the forgotten place where she was born.

1899

Panama City, Panama

FOR THREE NIGHTS LOUISE CREPT along the stone balcony outside her bedroom to meet Benjamin in his. They explored each
other's bodies in secret, eagerly and without a sound, but with
a passion that left her physically and emotionally spent. Days
were wasted as she thought of little else but midnight and Benjamin. He intoxicated her. Often she would become dazed at
the slightest memory of his touch. No one cared to notice the
change in her, and she was glad. Maud's tutor came daily, as
did the piano instructor. Since Maud had gained her health
back Benjamin took less care of her in his last days. He spent
time outdoors, helping to repair the damage done to the garden
and staying within sight of Rosa, who kept one eye on him and
the other on her chores. She slept every night in the parlor guest
room; Charles had not yet returned from his business trip due
to the flooded roads. Bursting with a need for expression, Louise immersed herself in art. She sat on her balcony at daybreak
with a chipped wooden box of pastels at her side, comforted
by its familiar oily scent. She chose a poppy red and began
a different portrayal; her early sketches of Benjamin evolved

into abstract renderings of passion and desire. The morning sun caressed her fingers as she drew, her hand gliding over the cottony paper, blotting out the reality in the back of her mind: in two days he would leave her. Now Maud was rushing over, an impish grin spread across her face. *Must she pester me?* Louise put down her pastel. She was in no mood for gossip or small talk.

"I have a grand idea, Louise! Since Benjamin is leaving Friday morning and we've been in this dreary house for so long, let's plan a picnic for him!"

Maud loved picnics and would clamor for them as often as her health would allow. The thought was appealing. Louise pictured herself with Benjamin under the lush forest canopy, the way she did when they first met.

"Show him a bit of the countryside. It's the least we could do. He's done so much for us," Louise replied guardedly. "What did Rosa say?"

"Well, I didn't mention it to her yet. I thought we might ask together." Maud searched her sister's eyes for agreement.

"Travel should be tolerable now, and it is a lovely ride—"

"Let's go to El Valle! To our waterfall! It's close enough and so beautiful. Rosa can pack sandwiches. We'll take the carriage early tomorrow." Obviously Maud had already planned the whole outing. Louise put away her crayons. Thinking about the forest trail lifted her spirits. The verdant valley floor rose to breathtaking views of the cloud forest. What would it be like with him, watching white billows drift through the moss-draped trees? And all the birds—the symphony of blue and yellow, red and green macaws that streak across the vale! They might even spot a golden-headed quetzal! Suddenly Charles's image popped into her head.

"What if Father arrives while we're gone?"

Maud tossed her pale head. "Papi won't mind—we'll only be gone half a day. Besides, the roads from Balboa are not likely to clear soon. Rosa said there's still a lot of work to be done."

Maud and Louise went looking for Rosa. They found her elbow deep in a washing tub, scrubbing laundry. Maud was expert at asking for things; applying her sweet lilting voice, however grating and phony to Louise, usually got her whatever she wanted. So she wasn't surprised when Rosa approved of the outing and agreed to chaperone them to the waterfall in the morning. It would be Louise's last full day with Benjamin.

THE NEXT MORNING THEY ALL ATE a hearty breakfast and set out for the countryside. Louise had met in secret with Benjamin the night before, and though they sat apart in the carriage, she was aroused by the nearness of him. She kept her eyes on her hands in her lap. He looked out the window at the passing landscape, careful not to let their eyes meet. At last they pulled into the valley region and got out of the coach. Benjamin and Louise linked arms with Maud, and the three strolled briskly in the direction of the mountain trail, trampling over the thick green groundcover. Rosa struggled to keep up with them.

"Maud, do not rush! You will strain yourself!"

Maud ignored Rosa's fretful orders. Heading upwards they climbed the mountain trail to the grasslands and on to the cloud forest. The varying air temperatures, vegetation, and views were exhilarating. When they had gotten a good distance from the carriage, Rosa insisted Maud stop at a boulder to rest.

"Slow down, you two!" Rosa warned while Maud fussed loudly. Happy to be alone for a few moments, Louise led Benjamin to her favorite place. When they became shrouded in a mist and Maud and Rosa were out of sight, Benjamin grabbed her hand.

"Look. *Bajareque!*"

Beyond the mist, as if by magic, a rainbow of pink, yellow, and green swept the sky.

"My, how beautiful!" Louise exclaimed. She threw her arms around his neck. They stole urgent kisses, the cool foggy air seeping into her nose and mouth.

"Louise! Where are you?" Rosa's voice filtered through the fog. Louise pressed her lips to Benjamin's ear.

"You must see these trees with their enormous square trunks!" She took a step forward. No sooner had she done so than she heard a loud crack.

"Aye!"

Something hit her ankle. She looked down to witness a red snake writhing away. Benjamin saw it too and quickly smashed its head with a stick. In the next moment he picked Louise up and carried her back, in long strides, to where Maud was resting.

"It's just a little snakebite…I'll be fine!" She had been bitten before—why did he look so worried? As he trudged with her down an incline her ankle began to get numb and hot. Maud and Rosa emerged from the haze. Rosa snatched Maud's arm when she saw Benjamin approaching. An alarmist by nature, she gaped at the two of them with frightened eyes.

"What happened? Did you fall?"

Louise shook her head. "A snake bit me."

Rosa covered her mouth. "Father Mother God!" she cried. Maud reacted to the housekeeper's shock.

"Don't worry, Benjamin knows all about snakebites—don't you, Benjamin?" Maud rushed to his side, her voice had an uncertain edge. "She'll be fine, won't she?"

Benjamin said nothing. Rosa and Maud followed close behind him as he angled toward the boulder and placed Louise on it. When he hiked up her dress Louise was stunned to see her ankle had swollen to twice its size. With swift motions he yanked off her shoe and stocking and tied the stocking tightly around her calf. He pulled out the pocketknife he often used to whittle sticks. Though confused, Louise tried to reassure everyone.

"It can't be serious! The dozen times I've traveled that path I've never once seen a snake." Louise winced; Benjamin nicked her ankle just above the tiny tooth marks. Dark blood flowed over her heel. Maud drew back in horror, burying her face in Rosa's shoulder. Louise watched Benjamin squeeze blood from her ankle before placing his lips on the incision. He sucked the blood and venom into his mouth and spat it out on the ground, repeating the action five or six times without a word, her blood staining his teeth as he drew long draughts from her flesh. At the sight of him cradling her foot, his lips pressed against her skin, she felt no pain or sense of emergency. Nothing could endanger her more than her wanting him. Gradually some feeling came back to her foot.

"Can you move your toes?"

Her toes were stiff but she wiggled them slightly. Benjamin snatched her up in his arms again.

"We must get back before the fever sets in." He wiped his mouth on his sleeve and carried her to the carriage. Louise was not worried. She felt safe in his arms.

Maud and Rosa ran ahead to alert the driver. Rosa reproached herself, invoking all sorts of patron saints and angels. Louise looked up at the heavens. *What could Saint Patrick, Saints Luke and Francis, Ruth, Rita, and Christopher do for her now? If she called on them, would they stop Benjamin from leaving her? Could they keep her heart from breaking?* Louise rarely got sick, but in many ways it was the same as falling in love. She felt helpless, weak, and vulnerable, open to infections and even death. Laying her head in the crook of his neck, she surrendered.

"*Te amo,*" she whispered in his ear.

2006

Brooklyn, New York

A TONE FROM HER LAPTOP signaled a reminder. Sheri put a bagel in the toaster and went to check her Outlook calendar. Jackie's e-mail from school had slipped her mind. In the subject line were three words: "Can we meet?" She clicked to open it again.

Sheri,

Are you available to talk tomorrow morning in my office after dropoff? I'd appreciate it.

Thanks,

Jackie

Why didn't she say she was busy? Then again, delaying the inevitable might not be the best thing for Zig. Almost a week had passed since he'd made a mess of things at the museum. With suitcases flung open and half packed on the living room floor, all other issues took a backseat to the details of their travel. Zig was so wound up about the trip he could barely settle down to do his homework, and she could only image what he was like at school. She showered and got dressed before he stirred. Happily, their morning routine was getting easier. At dropoff she saw Jackie greeting parents in the lobby. When she spotted Sheri she immediately came over, not once glancing at Zig.

"Good morning, Sheri. Would you mind waiting in my office? I'll be just a minute." The headmistress glided across the lobby around the elbows of parents and children. Sheri kissed Zig on the cheek and hugged him tight.

"Go on up to class, sweetie. See you at three."

She made her way to Jackie's office and sat in the same blue velvet chair. She felt like a juvenile delinquent, being summoned to the principal's office more in the past few weeks than in all twelve years she spent in school. Today the empty room reminded her of a highly decorated mausoleum. Jackie barreled in shortly after Sheri sat down, closing the door behind her.

"Sorry—I had to catch the Collins twins' mother before she left for work." Jackie smiled briefly at Sheri and scanned her desk for messages. Having found nothing of importance, she sat down; long lines formed in her forehead.

"I heard from Ellie what happened at the museum. Zig disappeared?"

"Yes and no." For a second she thought about lying, making up some story about him getting lost on his way back from the bathroom, but thought better of it. "He got overly excited about some family research and lost track of time in the library."

"The museum shut down the tour! Ellie said they had to leave less than an hour after they got there." Jackie leaned on her desk. "Were you aware of the rules regarding students straying from the group?"

"I had a serious talk with him."

"How's he doing on his medication?" Jackie cut to the chase.

"Actually, I haven't had time to get a prescription."

"Oh! He didn't see a psychiatrist yet?"

"I've been really busy and haven't chosen one."

"Sheri, I'll be frank with you. Zig has to get help if he is to stay at Excelsior. He's causing more trouble than our staff can handle."

"I understand your position, Jackie, but he was just—"

"I'm sure he had his reasons for leaving the group—all the more reason for you to follow through on our recommendations. Do you still have Bruce's list of doctors in the area?"

"Yes, I was about to—"

Jackie loudly ripped a sheet of paper off a notepad on her desk.

"Here's one more. Dr. Pollock is excellent and he's right here in Brooklyn Heights." She wrote the phone number from memory. "I can fax him the evaluation today. His office will call you to set up an appointment. They are very prompt."

Jackie stood up and walked briskly around her desk, pointing the piece of paper at Sheri. "Give his office a call after one P.M. if you don't hear from them. Zig can get started on the medication as soon as he meets with Dr. Pollock. I assure you, it will make your life and his much easier. You'll be very happy with the results." Sheri took the paper and Jackie ushered her to the door with barely a moment to react. There was no stalling this time.

Dr. Pollock was swift, just as Jackie predicted. Zig had an appointment the very next day after school, and now she was on her way to pick up his prescription from the pharmacy. She tried to clear her head, tried to tell herself it was okay. Maybe this was what he needed to get by in school, to "fit in." He was in the world but not of it—that was the problem.

Many things troubled her. The bird dream, her drawings, the Nrvai Indians—how Zig knew so much and she so little. Finally, it was clear to her what her son had been trying to get at for years, peeling away the thin layers of her life to reveal something deeper, something she had stopped yearning to know long ago—who she really was. There was that moment, it was unmistakable, the vision she saw in the mirror—who could that woman be? *Was it her mother? Grandmother? A messenger?* In a second there was hope, a glimmer of truth in her life. She couldn't think her old thoughts anymore; intellectual certainty fell away like fine sand through her fingers. She felt emotionally naked. She was the one who'd needed changing, not Zig. But because of his curious behavior, he had to alter his ways, to be detached, out of touch with himself. To be more like her.

Rain poured on her miserably; gusts of wind almost blew the prescription bag from her hand. She couldn't help feeling like she had let Zig down, betrayed him. Had she been a more sensitive mother, had she paid closer attention to his wild ideas she might have found a way to save him from the school's bureaucracy. She kept walking until she found herself in front of Excelsior. She took the stairs up to his classroom, suddenly out of breath, shaking out her umbrella on the way. Through the glass-paned door she saw him sitting at the far end of the room, staring up at the ceiling, tilting his chair and head back a bit too far, while the other kids were packing up their desks. When he saw her he jumped up, grabbed his coat and backpack, and bolted out of the classroom. Ellie glowered at him.

"Hi, Mom! What's in the bag?" His whole disposition brightened. She looked at the bag as if it had just magically appeared and pushed it into her jacket pocket.

"We'll talk outside, Z. Let's get out of here."

She took him to the Court Street theaters in hopes of catching the latest Pixar movie, but the show was sold out. Instead, they saw *It's a Wonderful Life* at BAM's Rose Cinemas. She had seen it countless times. Growing up, she almost always watched it alone; it would inevitably be aired on the night of some client's holiday party that her parents left her at home to attend. At first she thought the vintage black-and-white movie might be too old-fashioned for Zig, not pack enough action, but once it started he became absorbed in the story. Afterward they went to their favorite Japanese restaurant on Montague Street, the one she had been going to since he was a baby. The owner,

Shirley, a warm and gracious woman, made a point of coming over to greet them, fussing over how much Zig had grown. He smiled proudly. He was in great spirits; the movie and dinner made Thursday feel like a Saturday. All the stores were pushing Christmas. Tinselly street decorations hung across Flatbush Avenue; evergreen garlands with mini lights glowed in windows; wreaths with red velvet ribbons swung over store entrances. On the way home Zig commented that if it were snowing it would almost look like Bedford Falls, the fictitious town where the movie was set.

"What was your favorite part, Mom?"

"That's hard, there are so many great scenes. When George tries to kill himself and the angel Clarence rescues him."

"To show him what the world would be like if he hadn't been born. I like that part, too."

"It means everything you do, no matter how small, affects the lives of people you love." She squeezed his gloveless little hand, which was surprisingly warm.

"Like your drawings and my finding where they came from at the museum." He skipped out in front of her, walking backwards, his breath forming small puffs in the cold air.

"Those were drawn by a shaman, Z. They're similar but not easy to understand." They waited at a corner for the light to change. "I spent my whole life trying not to think about who I am or where I'm from…or if I even have a real family."

"Nobody said you have to understand it. Just believe and wait."

"For what?"

"For the rest of the story!"

He skipped in front of her again, changing the subject.

"So what's in the bag?"

Sheri tapped her pocket and heard pills rattle in the bottle. "It's the medicine the doctor prescribed."

"The one that Kwami takes?"

"Yeah, that one," she replied. "I just don't want to cause any more trouble, Zig."

"It's no big deal, Mom." He peered up at her, hat pulled low over his brow. His bright eyes still sparkled the way they did when he was a newborn. "I'll take it."

Their conversation took the chill off the night. Sheri went home feeling much happier than she had at the start of the day.

THEY BOTH WOKE UP LATE the next morning, forgetting it was Friday. Sheri rushed Zig through breakfast and ran out of the apartment when she remembered his medicine.

"I almost forgot to give you your *Ridden*!"

She unlocked the door and ran back in; the bottle was on the kitchen counter. She opened the childproof cap. Shook out two capsules. Filled a glass with water. Gave the glass and the pills to Zig. He downed them in one gulp and put the glass in the sink. They dashed out for the elevator again. At school the lobby was bare; they were ten minutes late. Zig kissed her good-bye and raced up the stairwell instead of waiting for the elevator. Sheri exhaled, glad the weekend was almost here. She pushed open Excelsior's front doors and decided to revisit that Greek diner for some real breakfast. The diner was bustling to-day; plates clacked and piled up on every table. To her dismay, there were clusters of expats from Starbucks, plugging away on their laptops. The waitress who had served her before ignored her. She chose a booth this time, slid into the narrow seat and buried her bag, coat, hat, and scarf in the space next to her. No sooner had she done so than her cell phone started ringing. The muffled chime filtered through layers of her clothing. She decided to let it ring; she'd check her messages after ordering. Finally it stopped. Fingers still stiff with cold, she took out her *New York Times* and opened to the business section to catch up on the bad news. Her phone started ringing again. She dragged her coat off her bag and dug for the phone. An exterior shot of Excelsior was displayed on the caller ID screen. *What now?*

"Hello?" she said, half expecting to hear Jackie's drawl. A high-strung voice replied.

"Hi—I hope I dialed the right number…This is Sandra, the school nurse at Excelsior. Is this Sheri?"

"Yes, it's Sheri. What's the matter?" She got up, pressing the phone hard to her ear.

"Everything is stable. Zig had a seizure in the classroom a few minutes ago."

"*What!* I just dropped him off! Where is he?" she shouted into the phone. Patrons paused with their mouths full of food.

"The ambulance is pulling up now—"

"I'm at the corner diner. I'll be right there." She snatched her belongings from the booth and ran with the bundle in her arms between traffic, against red lights. Half a block away she saw the blinking ambulance in front of the school; a crowd had gathered around the open doors of the vehicle. She shoved through the crowd to the EMS workers lifting a stretcher into the back. Jackie stood next to the school nurse with panic written on her face. She saw Sheri and called out to the workers.

"Here's the boy's mother!"

Everyone turned around. Breathless, Sheri rushed up to a female paramedic.

"How is he?" Her lips trembled.

"His pulse is steady, but he's still unconscious. LICH is the closest hospital."

Sheri's heart beat wildly as she climbed into the ambulance with the woman. The other paramedic, a man, shut the doors and got in front behind the wheel. Zig was pale and had an oxygen mask over his face. A bedsheet, tucked in on all sides, covered him up to his chest. She reached over to touch his forehead—he did not move. He felt cold and clammy. *Was he breathing?* She shook uncontrollably, lost her sense of what to do or think. She looked at the hard face on the woman across from her.

"How is he?"

The woman checked the oxygen monitor and his pulse.

"His breathing is a bit shallow. Has he ever had seizures like this before?"

"He's never had a seizure! I just dropped him off at school!" Sheri flailed her arms.

The paramedic gave Zig a thoughtful look.

"Did he do anything different this morning? Was he upset about something?"

"No!" Then she remembered the pills. "Yes! I started him on some new medication this morning."

"What was it?"

"A low dose of Ritalin."

"Hmm. I've never heard of a child having seizures from a stimulant, but there are always warnings on those packages. Are you sure it was the right dosage?"

Sheri tried to picture the label on the prescription. She never checked to make sure the dosage matched the written prescription.

"God…I'm not sure…"

"Double-check the dosage. I've seen a lot of serious emergency situations because of wrongly dispensed prescriptions. It's a major problem."

The ambulance took a sharp turn. Sheri grabbed the van hand railings as it sped through traffic, siren blaring. What was written on the bottle? She remembered trying to read Dr. Pollock's scrawl on the prescription note, wondering how anyone could read a doctor's handwriting. She thought she knew the dosage, but they had rushed out this morning—did she give him one too many pills? Sheri burst into choking, wrenching sobs. She couldn't remember. Zig lay motionless on the stretcher. *God help me.* She repeated the words in her mind, words she had never uttered until this moment. Shaking, she took his limp little hand in hers and kissed it, rubbing his fingers against her wet cheeks.

"Zig, sweetie, I'm so sorry!" she cried. "Please…please open your eyes…tell me everything's gonna be all right. Please tell me you're all right…"

1899

Panama City, Panama

THE CARRIAGE SPED AWAY from the Eden-like beauty of El Valle. With her foot on Rosa's lap and a jittery Maud squeezing her hand, Louise drifted in and out of delirium. Benjamin sat across from her, fanning her feverish cheeks with a torn banana leaf. Her eyes were fixed on him for the entire ride; even when closed she still saw his face. Far off she heard Maud tell the driver to go faster. Visions of Rosa peeping through a keyhole lit the corners of her mind. A door blew open and liquid moonlight drowned their naked bodies. Magenta, gold, and umber pastels smeared across Father's face. Searing heat trapped her inside Mother's china pattern. *It's called Willow.* Soaring lovers, indigo blue, sad, sorrowful, blue blood bleeding. A torn banana leaf. Hoofs barreling. Branches breaking. Wind howling. Black. Black.

Louise awoke to the sight of a plump hand above her head pouring a milky elixir from a bottle into a medicine cup. The brown and gray hairs in the man's nostrils puffed as he labored to discern the dosage marks on the bottle.

"Aha! Awakened precisely at the prescribed time. Do you know who I am, Miss Lindo?"

Louise blinked.

"Dr. Nassi?" She felt groggy; her tongue thick in her mouth.

"Correct! My dear, you are quite a lucky young lady. If it weren't for the Indian who extracted most of the venom from your ankle, your condition would have been quite serious. Yes, you would have been in a crisis. Your father has just arrived from Balboa. The main roads were treacherous—flooded all the way to the canal." He tipped a bit of the liquid back into the bottle. "Here, sit up and drink this down. It's not as distasteful as it looks." Louise found the strength to lift her head. She gagged on the medicine before swallowing it all, picturing her father's stern gaze. It seemed he had been gone for ages. Or was it she who had been gone?

"How long have I been in bed?"

"One day and one night."

"Where is my father now?"

"Your devoted father and sister were at your side just moments ago. I assume they are dining in the parlor. Your father looked worn and out of sorts. I recommended he eat immediately. Rosa is fetching supper for you."

"Where is Benjamin?"

"Who, my dear?"

"Benjamin! Don Pedro's grandson."

"Oh! You mean the young Indian. He must be halfway to his village by now."

Dr. Nassi wasn't the least bit aware of how his words impacted her. She sprang up on her elbows.

"He's gone!"

"Now, now, don't exert yourself!" He pitied her for a moment. "Your father returned and found your sister in fair health, and simply released him from employment. If you ask me, I'd say the Indian didn't do anything remarkably different for Maud than what was done in hospital. Should your father have followed my directives he would have achieved the same results for her, perhaps in less time. All that chanting and herbs and folly! Who knows how sanitary—"

"Dr. Nassi, I'm quite tired…Would you please excuse me?"

Louise collapsed on her pillow. The doctor shook his head.

"Of course, yes, recovery from a coral snake bite is slow and arduous. Such a lucky girl indeed. I'll have Rosa hold off on supper. Rest well, my dear, rest well."

The door closed behind him. Louise sobbed uncontrollably, reaching for her handkerchief in the night table to silence her anguish. A small object fell out of it onto the blanket: Benjamin's whistle! He must have stolen into her room and placed it there while she was asleep! The sight of it filled her with joy. She pictured him by her bed, opening the drawer, touching her handkerchief. Perhaps he even kissed her. How could she not have awakened! Louise held the smooth bone flute to her cheek and cried herself to sleep.

IN THE WEEKS THAT FOLLOWED the swelling completely dissipated. The scar from the snakebite and Benjamin's nick faded, as if it nothing ever happened. The guest bedroom was cleaned and the bedding changed. The calico sack of herbs and the drums were gone, replaced with a polished mahogany side table, a crocheted doily, and a vase of flowers. The room looked the way it once had—still and empty. All traces of him were erased. Maud was absorbed in talk of dances, a new wardrobe, and upcoming theater events. Father had gotten over the shock of his daughters' perilous adventure and immersed himself in telegrams and cablegrams and usual business at the canal. Rosa went about her chores. The house and its inhabitants were the same; Louise was not. No one saw how broken she was. She became pensive and withdrawn, spending days in her room sketching and writing in her journal. Every morning she retched until her whole body shook, as if she were trying to expel Benjamin from her insides. The sound of his voice, his touch, his smell haunted her like a never-ending melody. Months passed yet she still felt him deep in her being, and soon she realized a part of him indeed lived inside of her. She was with child.

By and by Louise became more robust, until Maud made a pointed comment one evening when dressing for a party. Maud, outfitted in the latest style of evening gown, hair coiffed, Mother's pearl necklace dangling from her fingers, burst into Louise's room.

"Louise! Why are you in your nightgown?" she cried, ogling her sister from head to toe. "The coach is outside waiting for us!"

"I changed my mind. I'm not going."

Maud stomped her slippered feet in frustration, sending wafts of her sugary sweet perfume around the room.

"What do you mean? This is the grandest dance of all! Every fashionable young man will be there. You must come!"

"No, go on without me. Tell Father I'm not well and want to rest." Louise began to turn down her bed, hoping to dismiss the subject altogether. But Maud did not hide her disappointment.

"You've been so boring, Louise! You never want to go anywhere or do anything!" She threw the necklace at Louise for her to fasten it around her neck. "You stay cooped up in here scribbling in your stupid journal and getting plumper every day." Maud scoffed, frowning in the dresser mirror. Louise approached her from behind with the string of pearls. Maud softened her tone, tried to bargain with her. "Oh, please come! I can tell Father you need a little more time to..." Maud turned around. "Goodness Louise! You *are* fat!"

Louise's protruding belly brushed up against the small of Maud's back. She quickly moved aside, but it was too late. Maud saw the roundness of her sister's stomach beneath her thin nightgown. She gaped at Louise, her callous remark turned into a cry of disbelief. Louise placed her palm firmly over Maud's mouth.

"Don't say anything—not one word. Or else I'll never forgive you, Maud. Ever."

Fear flashed across Maud's eyes. Louise released her hand from her quivering lips.

"Oh, Louise!" she whimpered.

Louise sat down on the window seat, hugging her ripe stomach. At more than six months pregnant she could no longer hide her condition.

"It's Benjamin, isn't it?"

Louise nodded. She covered her face with her hands.

"I…I knew there was something," Maud stammered. Louise looked up to see her poor sister in shock, trying to fathom it, jogging her memory for glimmers of how and when, for evidence of their romance.

"In a hundred dreams I never thought this would happen to me, but it has. I'm frightened, Maud." This admission to her little sister made her tremble. Maud started to cry.

"What are you going to do? When Papi finds out—"

"Father will not find out! He mustn't suspect anything!" Louise warned. "I plan to visit Aunt Ester in a few days, but instead the driver will take me to Guabito. There I'll hire a boat and guide to take me across the river to Benjamin's village."

"Not *alone*! I'll go with you."

"Shhh! Don't worry about me, just keep my secret. Now go tell Father I have a headache and am staying home tonight." Louise wiped Maud's tear-stained face. "Compose yourself! Father is waiting."

Maud obeyed, taking a last look at Louise. Louise kissed her sister and mustered a courageous smile. Maud left; her tiny voice ringing down the empty hall.

"Coming, Papi!"

Her light steps faded away. The carriage door opened and closed; there was silence before the horses started down the street. Flutters of life tumbled within her, a life that knew nothing of the torment she went through day and night. She felt in her pocket for Benjamin's whistle; its presence comforted her. Louise put it to her lips and blew a long, soft note. Soon she would be with him again.

2006

Brooklyn, New York

THE AMBULANCE CAREENED into the emergency entrance of Long Island College Hospital. Two EMS doctors ran to the back of the vehicle, flung open the doors, and carried out the stretcher. The paramedic Sheri rode with gave a quick report on Zig's condition before leaping back into the ambulance and disappearing down the road, putting distance between one emergency and the next. Sheri ran alongside the EMS team as they sped Zig into the emergency room. Nurses and doctors spun into a tumultuous carousel of masks and gloves and green hospital uniforms. All the while her eyes were fixed on her son. His unconscious state rendered his stubborn little face docile and rubbery. Though his head tossed to and fro with the yanking of the stretcher, his slumber was undisturbed.

The emergency waiting area was starkly lit, crammed with rows of plastic chairs occupied by mothers with screaming babies, broken-boned teenagers, and elders lost in their pain. She followed the stretcher with an uneasy awareness. The smell of disinfectant mingled with the odor of overcooked cafeteria food. She cupped her hand over her nose, tried not to breathe. A bucktoothed orderly grinned at her from across the hall.

Doctors made their demands out loud like gamblers, shuffling medical terms along with their shower cap–covered feet on the linoleum floors. *Postictal…full workup…CAT scan… EKG… neurologist screen… respirator…blood pressure… pulse… IV … unresponsive…oxygen…*

"What's happening to him?"

She found her voice just as they were transferring him from the stretcher to a bed, its pitch high and shrill. No one answered. Her knuckles were bleeding. Despite the pushing and shoving she had tried to hold on to the stretcher, even when her fingers got jammed between the metal railing and the mattress. Finally her hand fell away. Amidst the chaotic hospital scene her anchor of sanity was cut and Sheri was lost, drifting out to sea.

"What are you doing?"

Medical terms continued being hurled about. Doctors were swift with their tasks, working with great absorption. She tried to read badges and scrutinized the faces of all who crowded around her son, watching their reactions for positive or negative signs. Zig remained unresponsive, not troubled at all for being moved from classroom to hospital room, not sharing in her terror. An East Indian woman with the body of a teenager had her stethoscope pressed to Zig's chest. She gave Sheri a flat look before taking the black cord out of her ear.

"Are you the boy's mother?" she asked, shining a light under his eyelids, prying open his mouth as you would a fish to remove a hook.

"*Yes!* What's going on?" Sheri stepped up to the woman.

"Does he have any allergies? Penicillin?"

"No, he—"

"Is he on any medication?"

"Zig has asthma…He's on Albuterol and Pulmicort…Are you the—"

"Antibiotics?"

"No!" Sheri paused, then added, "He took a dose of Ritalin this morning for the first time."

No reaction. None of her answers seemed to faze the deadpan doctor. Zig's blood was extracted; tubes went down his throat.

"Somebody tell me what's going on with my son!"

Her scream was effective. For a moment all movement ceased. The little doctor turned to Sheri and held out a narrow hand.

"I'm Dr. Patel, head of emergency pediatrics. I'll be treating the patient."

Sheri searched for the years of training in the young woman's sad, glossy eyes. "His name is Zig," she said.

The doctor's blue gauze mask bunched under her chin. She tipped her head lightly toward the door.

"Let's go out in the hall for a moment…I can explain your son's condition."

THE GROWL OF BROOKLYN rush hour traffic began to seep through the hospital windows. Sheri's elbows pressed into the spongy vinyl armchair where she sat next to Zig's bed. She had not spoken or moved from that chair for hours. With trepidation she witnessed the tent set up around his head, the oxygen mask over his face, the several monitors switched on. An IV inserted into his wrist dripped watery liquid into his veins. Test results were inconclusive—no one had a definite prognosis as to what caused his seizure. Dr. Patel's report showed his airways were clear, his breathing normal albeit shallow, his pulse within range. He didn't have a fever. Earlier Dr. Breen, her pediatrician, had waltzed into the room with that "yet another inept mother to bail out of disaster" smirk on his moldy face. Sheri shut her eyes. Although he spoke at length to the hospital staff and Dr. Patel, in the end he offered no better forecast. It finally dawned on her that these doctors could not help Zig. Suddenly she was hurling fast through time and space, falling down a black hole. The sense of losing control, the world slipping away devoured her. The only one who could save her was the very one who could die. In that dark abyss memories surfaced; snapshots of moments alone with Zig: shivering in Prospect Park, red rubber boots crunching newly fallen snow, breaking tree branches and testing walking sticks, him talking about his past life, his Indian family.

You weren't always my mother.

She saw again his eyes blaze with the telling of the mystical bird in her dream; his anger at her parents when he learned they had thrown out her childhood drawings; his miraculous recovery when he breathed in the drummers' beat on Halloween…

A stretcher carrying a skeletal shape beneath thin sheets rolled past the doorway, breaking her reverie. She rubbed her numb shoulders. Zig's unconscious state was a mystery. Since he was born mysteries had become a part of her, and she had no choice but to accept them. The neurologist recommended a spinal tap. After the hospital team mulled over its pros and cons, jabbering about test outcomes, Sheri consented. They moved Zig to a private room, and the procedure was ordered for eight o'clock the next morning.

Alone in the room she kept vigil at his side, absorbed by his deep rhythmic breathing, his still, flat face. Computerized beeps and sliding mechanisms became a metronome, keeping time with the living. Hours passed in deep concentration brought Sheri to a curious new awareness of her surroundings. She moved closer to Zig's bed, lifted the edge of the plastic tent. He wasn't asleep. He was not unconscious due to drugs or even a blow to the head. His face glowed in the ugly fluorescent light, as if in some kind of trance, an altered state. Reaching carefully into the tent and around the tubes, she caressed his cheek. Where was he? What was he dreaming? The light flickered. Her eyes focused on her handbag dumped on a low metal cabinet that housed nurses' supplies. She let go of the oxygen tent, opened her bag, pulled out her journal. A business card marked a page; the handwritten cell phone number, scribbled in haste, stopped her. She turned over the card. *Miguel Murillo. Education Curator. National Museum of the American Indian.* Before pride and reason could change her mind she took out her phone and dialed the number.

"Miguel, it's Sheri."

"*Hey!* I was just thinking about you and Zig. Are you all set with the tickets?" Miguel's voice was like a newly lit fire—comforting, burning with enthusiasm. She let her shoulders drop.

"Something happened to Zig today..."

"What happened to him?" Immediately his tone changed.

Her throat tightened. She tried to steady her voice, but little tremors broke free.

"He had a seizure at school this morning. I'm at the hospital with him right now."

"My God! Is he okay?"

"The doctor's aren't sure. He's unconscious." She paused again, saltless tears slipped into the corners of her mouth. "I've been here for hours just staring at his face and...wondering. With everything I read about the Nrvai, their history, I wonder...if this is something else." She wanted to squeeze the pain from her words. "I'm so sorry to be telling you all this."

"No, it's okay. I'm honored that you thought of me. I remember how incredibly knowledgeable Zig was about the Nrvai."

Sheri stood up. The back of her head tingled.

"He knew the symbols were special, but he wasn't sure why. As soon as I showed him the book sparks flew. He started rattling off the makings of an awa—the sacred plants and stones, talking to spirits, going to sleep when you're awake—

and getting instructions. The symbols are instructions, the story…" Miguel's voice faltered. "You drew those symbols."

For a moment Sheri was silent. Blue-green shadows danced around Zig's head.

"I always have." Saying those words released a strange ardor into the air, as if a bird flew out of her mouth and spread its wings.

A garbled PA system announcement streamed through the phone.

"Sorry, I'm at the airport, leaving for a conference in Boston," Miguel said.

"Oh! You did say you'd be out of town. I shouldn't have called," Sheri said, embarassed.

"I'm glad you did…I'll be in the city on Sunday. Can I call you?"

"I'd like that very much," she said. Warmth spread over her.

His tone changed again. "There's one other thing I want to tell you."

"I'm listening." She pressed her ear to the phone.

"When a shaman works in the spirit world, only he knows when the work is done."

She was staring at Zig's tightly sealed eyes, his bottomless expression. "Thank you, Miguel."

The PA system blared again. He had to go. She promised to call again, to let him know how Zig was doing. She promised.

Moments later Sheri began to write down everything. Everything that had happened since she woke up that morning—every doctor, the medications, the ambulance ride, the procedures. Nothing was left out, not even how many times her cell rang before she answered it. What was missing were words. She wrote entirely in pictures. She drew fast, the images simple, primitive. The pen felt alive, the movements right. The act grounded her. Pages filled quickly; her hand glided, feverishly depicting every minute, emptying her thoughts into the notebook. A night nurse came by to check the IV drip and oxygen tank.

"Miss, there's another armchair right next door." The woman fiddled with the IV tubing. "You could rest your—"

The nurse stopped talking. Sheri didn't take her eyes off the page. She didn't feel the woman's stare or the cramp in her leg or the black scab forming on her scraped knuckles. No food or drink had passed Sheri's lips since breakfast. Suspended in time, she continued to draw. Just as the nurse left, Sheri glanced up. Her pen dropped and rolled underneath Zig's bed. She quickly retrieved it to resume her drawing, but there was a shift.

Suddenly cryptic symbols came quite rapidly. The graphic designs grew and grew; she couldn't turn the pages fast enough. Her hand flew out of control. Tree forms and animals, stick figures and spirals; arcs of flame, waves, curves, and vertebrae dashes rushed from her pen to the page. When the last sheet in her journal was filled she started to draw on the metal cabinet next to her. The ballpoint pen slipped on the smooth enamel surface. With her pen in the air like a hummingbird in flight, she sat forward in the chair, gazing at the ceiling. Floating before her eyes were stark hieroglyphics, symbols she could almost touch and hold. They swam around her head at a dizzying speed, swirling, colliding, and forming anew. Embedded in her mind's eye, these pictograms compelled her to record them.

Immediately she tossed the pen, turned her handbag upside down and shook it. Loose change flew about the floor alongside Advil packets, store receipts, tissues, ChapStick, keys, Tic Tacs, her cell phone, and wallet. Sifting through the debris with frantic hands, she spied her black Sharpie marker in a corner near the window. She snatched it up and bit off the plastic top. Directly across from Zig's bed was a bare wall that met with a window on one side. Sheri pushed the chair up to the wall, stood on it, and pressed the tip of the marker near the ceiling. Hundreds of signs then poured from her hand with remarkable skill and agility. Many of the images were unfamiliar, her fingers propelled by an unknown force. From left to right, up and down, her hand moved without rest.

She worked uninterrupted; no doctor or nurse passed in the hall, no one came in to stop her, to tell her that she had lost her mind. But at last she had lost her mind, lost the toxic thoughts that had bound her whole life with fear, lost her unknown story. In its place was something real, something unchanging. That was her birthright—the courage to believe in herself. The small room became a living canvas where she drew her picture of life, one encoded with a healing energy that originated before any hospital existed. Heat swept up her arm and spread over her body, consuming her with an inner fire. Perspiration flowed down her temples like baptismal waters, pooling in the hollows of her neck. She obeyed her hand's command until every inch of wall, from ceiling to floor, was covered with a vast mosaic of divine expression. All the while she sensed an awareness, as if someone were watching, waiting, alongside her. Something incomprehensible radiated from it, through her walls of flesh and bone, out into the dark night sky. Peace. The world fell away, and she experienced deep peace within herself.

Sheri stopped. Fingers hot and blistered, nails black with ink, she took an unsteady step back. Each character—every abstract, animal, and human form—sprung to life before her eyes. Trembling, the marker fell from her grasp. She collapsed in the chair, sobbing, until sleep silenced her tears.

A sound stirred her, a sound different from the drone of hospital machinery. The room was disorienting. Her eyelids were too heavy to lift so she looked with her ears. Someone was standing next to his bed. A doctor? Nurse? The person was of small stature and bent at the waist; he or she appeared to be examining Zig. The sound became more distinctive, more like a hum. She concentrated on it, and before long she heard a tune come through. A rough, uneven melody. Where had she heard this song before? The repetitive intonations drifted through the ether and settled like dust on her hair. She watched with detachment as the figure turned around to face her; an old man with brown leather skin filled her vision. A crown of feathers adorned his head. His expression was contorted; his parted lips moved ever so slightly to form the song. He grew closer, chanting louder and louder, imbuing the air with the brilliance of his voice. His wizened face was inches from Sheri's; sharp black eyes locked with hers as he breathed the song into her. In that instant she knew him as the old man in her dream, in her bedtime story, the one Zig called great-grandfather. She inhaled and her voice became one with the old man's. And as they sang together the song transformed her, the meaning came without words, without intellect, but with a power closer than the beat of her heart. The man began to recede. He drifted back to the dark place where Zig lay; his image melding into the body of her son. Yet the song filled her soul. In the background the tone of the heart monitor joined with the melody and did not interrupt it.

Zig opened his eyes.

1899

Panama City, Panama

AFTER A FITFUL NIGHT OF SLEEP Louise awoke to a sharp rap on her door. It was Father. The clock on her night table read five minutes to noon. There was another knock and the doorknob jangled. She'd taken to locking her door at night for fear of being walked in on.

"Louise! Are you all right? Open the door. I've brought your breakfast."

Hazy and light-headed, Louise climbed out of bed, pulled her robe around her, and hurried to open the door. Charles stood holding a large tray with several dishes. He eyed her and surveyed the room as he spoke.

"Maud said you weren't feeling well last night. It's nearly lunchtime—you must be hungry."

The smell of boiled eggs engulfed Louise, making her stomach heave. She ran to her washstand and retched violently. Alarmed, Charles put down the tray to help her when Louise grasped her stomach, revealing her pregnant condition to him. Charles took several steps back as if he might fall; his quizzical expression soon turned black. Louise steadied herself on the bedpost, awaiting her fate. His stare burned through her. There was a long deadly pause before he spoke.

"I'll put the tray out in the hall." He turned his back; Louise limped over to the window for air, her hand over her nose, the heaving less out of control. Father returned, closing the door behind him.

"Let me see you."

She had heard that contempt once before. Father and Mother were arguing late one night, the night of his birthday party. Their heated words woke her up; she remembered peeking through the balusters on the staircase. He accused Mother of something, what Louise wasn't sure, but he wore the same expression as he did now: dark, angry, disgusted. Louise moved away from the window. He rushed to her and parted her robe. Louise crossed her arms over her stomach.

"My God, Louise! What have you done?"

"Father, I'm in love."

"In love? With whom? The man who did this to you?"

"I love him and he loves me!"

"What man does this to the woman he loves and deserts her? I demand to know who he is!"

Louise said nothing, afraid of what the truth would make him do.

"Was it one of the naval officers? That lawyer's son at the commission? Answer me!"

He grabbed her shoulders and shook them in desperation. Terrified as she was, Louise remained silent. She could think only of her mother's quiet eyes, guilty not for something she had done, but for something she let happen to her. Charles paced the room like a maniac, pumping his fists and ruminating aloud. His tirade ended when he knocked her drawing pad off the dresser. The book lay open on the floor, exposing a detailed drawing of Benjamin's profile. Louise froze. Father saw the fear on her face. He picked up the book and slowly turned the pages. One by one he examined Louise's collection of portraits, with various angles, shadings, and subtleties, of Benjamin.

"The shaman's grandson? Benjamin?" he uttered, his face red and knotted. She didn't dare meet his glare. The room spun around her.

"Oh no…No!" He flung the book at her dresser; it careered across the surface, smashing bottles of perfume and a framed photograph of Mother. "I never should have left you girls alone with that Indian in the house! Damn conjurer! Where is Rosa?" He patted down his suit pockets with wild hands. Was he looking for his pistol? Would he dare go after Benjamin? He started for the door.

"Father, please! It's nobody's fault!"

"Is that why you wanted to go to your Aunt Esther? To hide the truth from me? Why, because she's like your mother? Because she will be more accepting of you and this…this *bastard*?"

"*Stop it!*" Louise screamed. He walked toward her, pointing a long, narrow finger like a dagger at her face.

"Love does not absolve you, Louise. Love does not pardon you from your duty to your family…your upbringing! I didn't get this far in life for you to throw it all away on *love* for some cunning trickster! No daughter of mine will *ever* wed an Indian, nor raise his child!"

She had heard enough. Louise tried to dodge him and run out of the room. He stood in her way and snatched her arm hard.

"You're not going to Aunt Esther. Rabbi Shonen will know where you should go. He will have a solution for your disgraceful act."

"*Let me go! That's not what I want!*"

"*You will do as I say!*" he roared, filling the corners of the room. I'll speak to him at once and make the necessary arrangements. Pack your trunk. Be ready to leave when I return."

Father stormed out of her bedroom. The hypocrite! He turned to his faith when it suited him, when his precious reputation was threatened by things beyond his control. She envisioned him in the vestibule of the stone temple, whispering to dry, unemotional Rabbi Shonen; pictured the sage's sparse beard and beady eyes. To them, her bleeding heart was like some sacrificial lamb; her pain and loss insignificant. Suddenly tradition mattered. Father would beg the rabbi's confidence and execute his plan with no time to spare. She had to act quickly. Louise put on her travel clothes and shoes. Inside her trunk was a small carpetbag; she took it out, opened it, and threw in her sketchbook, Benjamin's whistle, and a red velvet purse thick with her life's savings. Rosa must have gone to market. Maud was punching scales on the piano. When Louise hurried down the steps the notes ended sharply. Maud rushed to her side.

"I heard Papi yelling…"

"He found me out. I'm leaving, Maud." Louise moved through the parlor, snatching her hat off the rack by the door with Maud at her heels.

"You're leaving? Louise, please don't go. Papi will calm down, you'll see—"

"He never cared about me, and now he has a reason not to. My life is my own. I can't go on living here."

Maud began to cry. She latched on to Louise's sleeve.

"When will you come back?"

"Don't look for me, Maud."

Louise embraced her sister, blinking tears from her own eyes. She spied a carriage on the corner and, releasing Maud, darted across the street.

"Take me to the border at Guabito—*ahorita!*" she demanded to the coachman.

The carriage sped away, leaving behind all she had ever known for all she ever wanted.

LOUISE RODE BACK IN TIME to the mystical place she would soon call home; retracing her steps to the day she first met Benjamin. But it was a day unlike this day. Once-laden banana trees were now barren, the lush greenery now brown and limp with heat. Roads were pitted with gouges and dry hilly lumps of earth. The carriage rocked violently over a rough terrain, making her womb tighten and cramp. She caressed her stomach but still the cramps intensified, along with the thought of Father's pursuit. That he might reach her or Benjamin and what he might do terrified her. She ate quickly in roadside cafés, avoiding the stares of the local people. Exhaustion forced her to spend one sleepless night in a run-down tavern, during which the cramps returned. In the morning Louise changed to a hackney coach and pressed on. The trip was longer than she remembered. Her body seemed to be rebelling against her wishes. The dull pain in her stomach would not ease. Something was wrong. She tried to comfort herself knowing that every step brought her closer to her lover. But the aches became more constant and severe. At last relief came at the sight of the border crossing. It lifted her above her pain, and though hungry and thirsty, she was determined to cross the river. It was late afternoon; a dense gray mist glazed the water's surface. She needed a boatman and guide to take her to Benjamin's village. A canoe drifted into view as if floating on the haze; a man rowed toward her with slow, deliberate moves. The carriage driver hailed the boatman to shore. After a brief conversation Louise got in the canoe.

As the vessel pulled away the driver called out, "When should I come for you, Señorita?"

She was a distance from the shore when she answered, "Take the carriage back. I won't be returning."

The boatman was a native who spoke broken Spanish. A trace of tribal resemblance to Benjamin showed in the man's direct look and placid confidence. They rowed in silence for several minutes, listening to the language of the river. She had to know if he could take her to Don Pedro's village.

"*Señor, ¿me puede llevar a Don Pedro, el chamán, por favor?*"

A tattered, wide-brimmed straw hat framed the deep creases in his face. His arms were spotted with black scars. He casually observed Louise—her dress, her carpetbag, her swollen belly. He seemed to be composing his own story about her.

"*El camino es muy pendiente, Señora*" was his reply, a warning. Louise dismissed it. The path was not that steep.

"*He estado allí antes, y creo que puedo hacerlo, gracias.*" She had climbed this countryside with her ailing sister; she could do it again.

The boatman squinted at her thoughtfully.

"*Sí, Señora, entonces la llevaré.*" He agreed to take her.

The Talamanca embankment rose out of the fog. She glanced back at the river, seeing only an opaque gloom; the other side ceased to exist. The boatman helped her out of the canoe, and they began their passage. The moss-covered path she found so enchanting several months ago was now parched and menacing underfoot. Although it was steep and rocky, Louise went on. The trail was harder than before; her cramps started again and continued to build. She held her stomach—*just a little further, you're almost there.* The pressure was becoming too great. The baby was turning. It dawned on her that now, right here, her child might be born. But how could that be? It was all too soon. She was not ready. Where was Benjamin? She stopped to catch her breath by a stream. The boatman offered her some water from his gourd. Near faint, Louise drained the cup, grateful for the cool drink. Her fingers traced a long snake carved into its side. Just when she thought she could go no further the boatman pointed to the clearing ahead.

"*La aldea está bastante cerca de aquí, Señora!*"

The rustic peak of Don Pedro's dwelling stood out beyond the treetops. Excited, Louise jumped up from the log where she had been resting. A sharp pain in the abdomen astounded her. She pressed her palms under her belly to quell it, but the pain increased. The boatman came to her aid. She leaned on his arm and took short, heavy steps. Breathing became difficult. The thought of Benjamin's loving face gave her the strength to go on. Louise held that image until she collapsed on the ground. She heard the boatman yelling in his native tongue. Suddenly there was an earthquake in her womb. Light became dark; then the sound of footsteps running near, of someone calling her name. Benjamin! He cradled her head in his arms; again and again he called her name.

Louise! Mi amor Louise!

ON THE MATTED FLOOR in the awa's home Louise gave birth to a baby girl. Don Pedro safely delivered the child. He named her Tukitima, in honor of his mother, who had taught him the way of the shaman. Don Pedro worked the songs, incantations, and herbs into Louise, but at last he could not stop her bleeding. Benjamin stroked her hair, covered her face with kisses. Hours later Louise died in his arms. The soft midday air lifted Benjamin's laments over the treetops and mountains and pulled the sun down from the sky. Don Pedro, sensing Charles's looming arrival, feared for his grandson's life. He pleaded with Benjamin to leave, to save himself and his daughter. Benjamin would not let go of Louise. At dusk Don Pedro took up Louise's carpetbag, placed his great-granddaughter inside, and fled into the rain forest. Shortly afterward Charles appeared in the distance with two men. They followed the sound of tears falling, the sun tumbling in the sky, until Charles spotted Benjamin clutching his daughter. In an instant he pulled out his pistol and shot Benjamin dead from afar. The earth recorded Charles's footsteps as he ran to where the lovers lay. When he saw the river of blood and realized Louise had also died he drowned aloud in grief. The two hired men searched the area tirelessly for Don Pedro and the baby. They found no trace of them. With darkness steadily falling, Charles carried his daughter's body away, down the sleepless Talamanca hills, until night buried the day.

2006

Costa Rica

WHAT HAPPENED WAS NOT MEANT to be logical. Logic had no place now; it was broken and discarded at the bottom of a winding staircase. Logic had nothing to do with knowing, with trust. You either know or you trust. All this became clear in the weeks following Zig's recovery.

Miguel drove. The jeep rattled and bounced on a gouged clay road that led to the Talamanca Mountains. On one side a wall of green brushed the jeep with a soft, shirring sound. On the other a steep drop to emerald shadows edged with slithers of pearly coastlines.

She was an abandoned girl.

How strange this hope, this audacity to search for a family history. Beside her Zig twisted his narrow back to face the window and the moving green wall. He reached outside to let the pointy fronds tickle his fingers. It had been fifteen days since he left the hospital. He hadn't spoken a word.

After the hospital, after newspaper journalists and photographers hounded her about the wall drawings, after Zig's silence stretched from hours to days, she knew things would never be the same. Something had been trying to impart some knowledge to her from the moment Zig was born. The elastic blue cord that had dangled from her womb to his navel was never cut. It was an invisible bond that didn't exist with her adoptive mother and father. What they could give her was not enough to make her whole. But Zig, he could.

She let him be. Did not coax him to speak or make him go back to school. They continued their trip as planned, leaving her doubts and fears thousands of miles away. She looked at her hands. A black stain around her nails lingered from the ink marker. Tender blistered spots would not let her forget that night. How could she?

The mountains were as silent as Zig, silent as a memory. Memory bloomed like a moonflower in the stillness, petals uncurling the heady secret of a hidden reality. Here there was magic. In New York City cement and asphalt suffocated the ground. Here the earth breathed. The palms sighed; ancient trees creaked and groaned; ferns and mosses murmured. Deep inside she sensed a spark of something extraordinary, and she was filled with hope.

Zig suddenly whipped his body around. He lifted his chin, peered far left and right, like an overseer surveying his property. The blank, indifferent expression he'd worn for two weeks was replaced with a sharp awareness.

"Soon you'll come to a fork in the road. Take the right side."

The words came out of nowhere. Sheri wondered if she heard anything at all. Zig was staring straight ahead, his hands grasping his knees. Miguel did a double take.

"The map says to stay straight on this road, Zig, until we—"

"It'll take you up a steep hill that levels out at the top. Then we walk," Zig said, cutting him off.

Sheri and Miguel eyed one another. Zig blurted something strange out loud, startling both of them.

"Enjenui a medta! Beswanta a joeki. BESWANTA!"

Overjoyed to hear him speak at last Sheri didn't care if she understood him. But Miguel was not smiling.

"*¿Como, amigo?*" he said to Zig, confused.

Silence. Again.

Five minutes later they came to a fork in the road. Miguel slowed down. The road to the right was barely discernable; overgrowth and hanging vines obscured the steep path ahead. Miguel reached for the map spread on the dashboard. Zig snatched it out of his hand.

"*Tsaku pa!*" His hot words were foreign but their urgency was plain.

"I don't know what he's saying," Miguel whispered to Sheri. "That's not Spanish. It's something else, a different dialect."

Miguel rapidly shifted gears and accelerated the jeep.

"That's his language. He knows the way."

The jeep dug into the trail and whined its way up the hill. It leveled off at the top, just as Zig had said.

"*Batse!*" Zig commanded.

Miguel turned off the ignition. Zig opened the door, waved his arm for them to follow him. Sheri and Miguel hiked through the dense rain forest, fording several streams and finally a wide river, led on by Zig. On the other side of the river they came to a circular, cone-shaped thatched house. A small Indian woman with long quick fingers sat at the entryway, shelling peas.

"This must be a Nrvai meetinghouse," Miguel said, observing the large dwelling. "*Hola!*" he called to the woman.

She only stared back. She took the bowl of peas off her lap and placed it under her chair and stood up. Zig walked directly to her. He spoke with ease to the woman. She nodded her head, threw a cautious look over Zig's shoulder at Sheri and Miguel. The woman gazed thoughtfully at the ground, put her fingers to her lips. A hand flew up with an *"Ah!"* The woman pointed behind the house. Zig studied the direction and again waved for Sheri and Miguel to follow him.

The trek took them a short distance beyond the meeting-house to a series of small huts set back along a sparkling river. Spectacular views of the rising mountains and foothills, the scant, vaporous white clouds that weaved through the landscape took her breath away. Could this be true? The sun bathed her surroundings in a pure, clear light. Every stone, stick, and leaf gleamed.

She took dreamlike steps across an open field. The silvery sound of the river drew near. Her heart beat louder. Clusters of square wooden homes on stilts were a few yards away. The river ran in front of the houses. A girl, less than five years old, was splashing in the river. Another woman, much older than the first, sat on a low stool watching the girl. The woman rocked slightly. She clenched a thin pipe in her teeth. They approached her from the side, and when she turned her face Sheri froze. It was if she were struck by lightning. The lovely scenery collapsed around her. Her feet locked, her knees gave way.

WATER IN A BASIN. A music box of bangles jingles in her ears. A peculiar herbal smell, then a wet cloth presses over her eyes. Her eyelids slit open and light creeps in. The cloth lifts away. A hard old woman studies her. A woman with yellow for whites of her eyes. Coral, chalk, and stone-colored shells hang from her neck. It is the same woman as before, the woman in the mirror. Sheri meets her gaze with equal intensity. Miguel is at her side, Zig next to him, his face quiet.

"Sheri, this is Alma," Miguel says. "She has something to tell you."

Alma's speech is halting. Her hoarse voice cracks and snaps. She begins to rock and a scent of tobacco rolls off her body. Wrinkles carved in her forehead frown and tighten like lips, forming beliefs before she speaks. She draws a short, audible breath after every sentence. Miguel translates a beat behind her.

"When I was a little girl there was an awa who lived in the hills above the village. I was afraid of him. I was afraid because of the strange stories the elders told about him. One day my mother went to see him about a pain in her side. She took me with her. It was very far and soon I was tired and hungry. When we arrived we met a pretty young woman there. She gave me guavas to eat and played with me while my mother talked to the awa.

She looked very different, different from the people in our village. Tall. Pale. Long arms and legs. Around her face her hair floated like a brown and gold cloud. I was so curious. I asked where her mother and father were. She said with Sibo. The awa was her great-grandfather. I told her I was very afraid of him. She laughed and said he wasn't as scary as he looked. She said one day she too would become an awa. Right away I stepped back from her. She laughed harder and said, 'I'll tell you a story.

I was about your age when I ran away from the awa—my bis-abuelo. I was mad at him for not letting me go to see a birth in the village. I ran deep into the forest and thought, I'm on my own now, and then, POW! A snake bit me on my foot! Well, I was very lucky. My bisabuelo had followed me, and when he saw me lying on the ground he carried me to the sacred river. He pressed some corn seeds in my hand. When we got to the river he put my feet in. He told me to throw the seeds in the water, to tell him what I saw—'"

RIGHT THEN SHERI REMEMBERED. Not as a dream, but as a memory as real as the endless sky over her head, as real as the yellow moon in the old woman's eyes.

"White rocks. The seeds…*turned into white rocks.*"

She stared past the woman. Images of river water rushing, a pattern of glittering white rocks rose in her mind. Miguel translated Sheri's words. The old woman put her pipe in her mouth. She nodded slowly.

"If the seeds turn into white rocks, it's a sign the person has a choice—to become an awa. She said her bisabuelo picked out the white rocks from the river. He shined them and gave them to her to keep. He said now she was healed and he would teach her to use them to help other people." Almost breathless, the old woman leaned forward and whispered, *"Her name was Tukitima."*

Sheri looked at the spot where Zig had been sitting. He was not there. The old woman watched Sheri. She began to rock back and forth on her stool.

"Tukitima had a cloud of hair, just like you. And a space"—she tapped the chewed end of her pipe against her front teeth—*"like you."*

The old woman rocked faster, she drew on her pipe.

"Where is he?" Sheri quickly swung her legs over the edge of the hammock. A weighty palm came down her arm. Its sudden warmth and strength reminded Sheri of the homeless woman who grabbed her in the subway ten years ago.

"He knows where he is, Mami," the old woman said.

"It's getting dark!" Sheri cried.

"That is the time." A shrewd smile crept across her lined face. *"Sibo is his guide. Sibo knows every grain of sand, every blade of grass, everything you can see."*

A wave of calm washed over her. She pressed her bare feet into the wood plank floor; tiny roots seemed to stretch from her soles. It was true. She did have a story. A whole other world claimed her, opened its arms to her. An apricot sky soared beyond the thatched roof, silhouettes of forest trees danced in the soft breeze. Sheri walked out of the dwelling into the orange light. How long she stood there she didn't know, only that the light had changed to deep violet. A high, sweet note sang in the perfumed air like a lost bird. Zig emerged from the shadows of a bamboo grove. In one hand he held a tattered cloth bag, in the other a stiff, warped volume. A white whistle dangled from his lips.

Acknowledgments

Thanks to the People's Republic of Brooklyn for inspiring me to write this book. I am ever grateful to those who helped me along the way:

My agent, Regina Brooks, for her steadfast support. Nancy Peske and Lisa Shea for insightful editing. Catherine Texier for historical fiction guidance. Janet Goldstein and Elizabeth Marshall for sage publishing advice. Deirdre Fishel for story feedback. Elizabeth Kugler for proofreading. Laura Duffy for dramatic book cover design. A picture is worth 72,000 words.

I also wish to thank again the many friends, family, and colleagues who took the time to read parts or all of the manuscript, offer valuable comments, or help spread the word. My life, and this book, is richer because of you:

Amy Torres, Bisi Ideraabdullah, Brooklyn Society Writers, Dalia Hagiescu, Emma Farry, Folade Bell, Joan and Eddie Olbrich, Liat Justin, Margaret Vendryes, Margo Galpin, Maura Collins, Natasha Dure, Noel James, Regina O'Malley, Robin Harris, The Hermetic Society, Tricia Wang, Yvonne Presha. Thanks to all my wonderful writing teachers over the years.

Most of all my deepest gratitude and appreciation goes to my husband Carlyle and to my sons Hayward and Auguste, whose love formed the roots of this story. Thank you for encouraging my creative journey.